A Heart for Healing

To Sue

Joy in reading!

Ruth Thompson

RUTH THOMPSON

◆ FriesenPress

One Printers Way
Altona, MB R0G 0B0
Canada

www.friesenpress.com

Copyright © 2022 by Ruth Thompson
First Edition — 2022

All rights reserved.

No part of this publication may be reproduced in any form, or by any means, electronic or mechanical, including photocopying, recording, or any information browsing, storage, or retrieval system, without permission in writing from FriesenPress.

This is a work of fiction and all characters are entirely fictional; any resemblance to real people, living or dead, is coincidental.

Grateful acknowledgement is made to The Foundation for Inner Peace, Novato, California. www.acim.org for permission to reprint selected quotes from lessons in A Course in Miracles.

ISBN
978-1-03-912226-0 (Hardcover)
978-1-03-912225-3 (Paperback)
978-1-03-912227-7 (eBook)

1. FICTION, CONTEMPORARY WOMEN

Distributed to the trade by The Ingram Book Company

Chapter 1

Georgie rushes in the door from work just after six o'clock, dropping her keys with a clatter on the hall table. She strides to the kitchen to find a jar of peanut butter beside bread slices tumbling out of the plastic wrapper. Dinner will be late again, so she can't blame her two teens for snacking before dinner. She wishes she could be home earlier, but even though the clinic closes at five o'clock, there are often reports to prepare or file. Monday is always hectic, and today Dr. Randall called out a flurry of instructions that kept her at work for another hour.

What to serve that's quick? Will leftover pot roast do, or will her family complain? Sorting through the freezer, she spies a large frozen pizza, pulls it out, and turns on the oven. No one ever complains about pizza, but she wishes, once again, she had more time to prepare healthier meals. She gives her head a shake, regretful how often she resorts to processed or takeout food. To relieve some guilt, she grabs some lettuce, tomatoes, cucumber, and peppers from the crisper and reaches for the large salad bowl.

Georgie's work as the office manager at a busy medical clinic has some satisfying moments, but lately resentment rises in her throat about how hard she works and how little the doctor pays her. She always has work to do after Dr. Randall leaves for the day. *And I bet he doesn't rush home wondering what to prepare for dinner.* Some things just don't seem fair. That her job is not the career she envisioned for herself doesn't help either.

The oven timer dings in time with the bang of the front door. Georgie glances at the clock, realizing it's early for her husband, who seldom arrives home before seven o'clock. Such is the life of a business owner, or so Dwayne maintains. At least he doesn't complain about the meals Georgie serves. She smiles at her husband and gives him a peck on the cheek.

"Good timing, dear. The pizza is just coming out of the oven."

Dwayne slides on a stool at the kitchen island and inspects the large salad. "Mm, this looks good." He picks out a cherry tomato and pops it in his mouth, an odd expression between a smirk and a grimace crossing his face. Usually, Dwayne maintains a neutral demeanor, giving no clue as to his thoughts and feelings. Georgie's curiosity is piqued.

"What's up?" she asks as she lays out utensils and plates on the dining room table.

Dwayne rises and strolls to the dining room table, taking his usual seat at one end. "Georgina, there's something important we have to discuss. We'll talk about it after dinner."

To use her full name makes this an important "something." No one in her family calls her Georgina unless they are upset with her or have something meaningful to say. That Dwayne won't discuss this in front of their two teenagers is another red flag. She wants to press him for more details, but it is unlikely he will spill whatever this is before he is ready.

The pounding of teenage feet upstairs signal that Daphne and D.J. heard the oven timer, responding in a conditioned response like Pavlov's dog at the promise of sustenance. They bound down the stairs, saying, almost in unison, "Great! Pizza!" Sometimes teenagers are wonderfully predictable.

Georgie is on tenterhooks, hoping for clues from Dwayne about what he wants to discuss. She smiles absently when everyone laughs at Daphne's humorous anecdote from school. Dwayne and D.J. launch into a lengthy debate about whether the Cubs will get into the playoffs this year, but Georgie easily disengages from that conversation into her own musings. When was the last time her husband waited until after dinner to talk about something? Dinner has always been the time the Downies discuss family matters. No secrets in this house! That was it! Eight years ago, Dwayne took her aside to announce he was quitting his job to start his own accounting firm. That decision came with a sacrifice on Georgie's part, one she still bears today. She speculates what his "something" might be this time, and her thoughts cycle through the possibilities. Is there something going on with his business? Will the family need to cut back on extras? Or is it good news? After all, he doesn't seem upset. In a turmoil, she can't summon enough saliva to chew on the pizza. It tastes like cardboard, something she has often said in jest about frozen pizza. As her kids squabble over the last slice, she doesn't detect any displeasure with their "cardboard" meal.

Dwayne rises from the table, puts his plate in the dishwasher, and disappears into his study. This discussion must be significant for it to be behind closed doors. Georgie stacks the rest of the dishes in the dishwasher and joins Dwayne in his study. Closing the door softly behind her, she perches on the edge of the chair opposite his desk. He still has a mysterious expression on his face.

"Okay, what's so important?" she asks, resentful he made her wait.

A smile breaks over his face. "Well!" He places his hands definitively on his desk. "I've been over the company finances, and based on last quarter's earnings and our client prospects," he pauses, perhaps for dramatic effect, "we can now afford for you to leave your job and go back to school."

Georgie's mouth falls open, words failing her for a few seconds. "Dwayne! This is so unexpected. You were just telling me last week you were concerned about the bottom line."

"It all came together today. We just re-signed three big clients, and just last week I didn't know if we would land them. Another accounting firm was wooing them, but we pulled it off." Dwayne beams, his arms spread wide. "With these clients locked in for a few years, the finances are on solid ground. You can quit your job and go to medical school." His smile fades, his brown eyes narrow. "But I'm wondering why you aren't more excited. I expected you to jump for joy."

Georgie forces a smile. "Of course, I am. I am! It's just a surprise. You gave me no warning you were even thinking about this."

"I didn't want to build up your hopes until I was sure. So, now you can give notice at your job and make inquiries about medical school." With a distinct slap, he places both hands on the desk as if to say, there, problem solved.

Something occurs to Georgie that could change his decision. "The next admissions aren't likely until next September, so I might have to wait for a year to get into school. Are you sure I can quit my job now?"

"Look, Georgie. I know how stressed you've been at your job. You complain about it a lot. I would like you to take some time to prepare yourself for med school, and I can afford for you not to work now."

"That's wonderful, Dwayne!" Georgie goes around the desk and hugs her husband. After eighteen years of marriage, she knows what his expression means. He is incredibly proud to provide her with this news. Georgie knows his self-esteem took a hit through the years when he needed her earnings to prop up his business. When he started his company, his prediction was five years for the business to be flush and longer than that to be prosperous. It's been eight years. This is a big day for him.

Georgie smiles at her husband, pleased for him as much as anything. But his announcement does not give her much to celebrate, and she's not ready to tell him why. Not yet anyway.

Sun streams through her window, signaling the start of a glorious August day. Georgie lazes in bed, stretching out her slim, five-foot-nine-inch frame, in no hurry to get up. Lolling in bed at seven-thirty feels like a luxury. Her usual routine by now would have her showered, dressed, and rousting her teenagers out of bed to get ready for school, so she could be at work by eight o'clock. Today, Wednesday, is a day off she negotiated to give herself time to plan her next move into uncharted territory. Dwayne's announcement on Monday promises to change the course of her life, but not in the way she always imagined. There was a time when the opportunity to go to med school would have been the answer to her prayers. Now she cannot fathom where her life will go from here. Her one certainty was being fully prepared to give her two-week notice to Dr. Randall. Yesterday, when she gave her resignation, Dr. Randall lost his confident doctor's demeanor and pleaded with her to stay on for a month to help find her replacement. But she was proud of herself for sticking to the two weeks, promising to stay longer only if she couldn't hire her replacement.

Dwayne has already left for his office, which isn't surprising. That is his habit, a reflection of his favorite saying: "in a successful business, the owner arrives first and leaves last." But his early to work habit always leaves the morning parenting duties to Georgie. Soon, she will have to get out of bed to ride herd on Daphne and D.J., who might sleep in if she doesn't rouse them. Georgie sighs, rolls out of bed, and shuffles into the bathroom to take a shower. As the hot water streams over her head, she muses about her dream of being a doctor and how her father encouraged her in that direction. Some of her friends rebelled from such parental "encouragement," but she doesn't remember reacting that way. Her father's words echo in her ears: "Georgina, there are three generations of doctors in the Novak family. It's in your blood." Being a doctor always felt like her destiny, so from an early age, she told everyone she wanted to be a doctor, just like her father. Now, she isn't sure anymore. Too much has happened.

The water pressure through the shower drops, and the temperature cools, a sign one of her kids is running water in the other bathroom. It's a reminder she must get moving to make sure they have clothes to wear and school lunches prepared. She jumps out of the shower, towels quickly, and runs a comb through her light brown wavy hair. She keeps it short, so it is effectively wash-and-go. Peering in the bathroom mirror, she is grateful for a clear complexion and naturally long lashes framing her green eyes. Seldom does she feel the need to wear make-up—no time for such vanity, anyway. Quickly donning a T-shirt and capris, she goes down the hall, noticing the door to D.J.'s room is still closed. "Time to get up!" she calls out with a sharp rap, rap on the door. There's a groan and five seconds later, a thump. He's up! She descends the stairs to find Daphne standing at the kitchen counter slathering cream cheese on a bagel.

"Hey, Mom! Don't forget I've got a softball game today, our last one of the season. Can you come?"

There is hope in her middle child's voice, no doubt because Georgie's work schedule rarely allows her to attend her children's weekday games. Today she will not have to endure that guilt. "Of course. I have the day off. I wouldn't miss it!"

At fifteen, Daphne is already taller than her mother, a more athletic build but the same light brown, wavy hair that she desperately tries to straighten. This morning it's pulled back in a tight braid trailing down her back. She carries herself with a grown-up confidence, but Georgie knows that underneath, Daphne still has that middle-child angst about being ignored. Are her occasional acts of defiance misguided calls for attention? Georgie has waited up a few times after curfew, worrying about what Daphne was up to. Some of her friends are questionable, but so far, softball and soccer have kept her busy and out of serious trouble.

From above, the stomping of feet signal D.J.'s arrival, bounding down the stairs two at a time. Ever the energetic boy, Georgie can't recall when he walked up or down a set of stairs. He reaches into the fruit bowl, grabs a banana, and smirks at his sister.

"Hey! Daffy!" D.J. says.

Daphne scowls back at D.J. for using the hated nickname he coined as a three-year-old when he could not put the sounds "f" and "n" together. Instead of snapping at her brother, Daphne puts both hands on her hips and glares at Georgie, who understands what the look means. It's Daphne's unspoken accusation: "it's your fault for giving me this name!" More than once, she has threatened to use her middle name, but everyone agrees Grace doesn't suit her personality.

"Mom! Where is my new blue shirt?" D.J. asks, a younger version of Dwayne, dark-haired and tall, already eye to eye with Georgie.

Georgie stares at him, alarmed that, at his age, he expects her to know the location of specific items of his clothing. She's heard that it's easy to spoil the baby of the family, and she tried not to indulge him, but perhaps not successfully. And Dwayne's joy at having a son likely didn't help either.

"I need that shirt today for school pictures," he says through a mouthful of banana.

It's the first Georgie heard of school picture day, or maybe she was so wrapped up in her own school issues she forgot. She sighs, runs up to D.J.'s bedroom, and after a few minutes of rummaging, finds the shirt under some other rumpled clothes. Funny, she muses. He's never cared much about what he wears. Is he getting interested in girls? She can't recall what thirteen-year-old boys were like. Growing up with two sisters, she had limited experience with teenage boys.

On her return to the kitchen, she hands D.J. the shirt, notices the time and pulls out bread, ham, and cheese to make sandwiches for school lunches. The inviting aroma of coffee wafts through the air from the pot Dwayne made before he left but the elixir she needs to kick start her day will have to wait until her kids are off to school. "Dwayne Junior, you need to clean your room," she says over her shoulder, "or at least put your dirty clothes in the hamper! I'm tired of reminding you!"

"Yeah, yeah, I will, I will!" He pulls on the shirt, rifles through his backpack, pulls out a paper and thrusts it under Georgie's nose. "Mom, I need you to sign this consent form for football. Dad promised me I could try out."

Georgie puts a sandwich in a plastic container and wipes her hands on a towel. She grasps the consent form and frowns at the last-minute demand. It's not the first time D.J. has sprung something on her. "So, your father should sign this, not me."

"Well, I need it today, and Dad's already gone to work."

With a sigh and a shake of her head, Georgie scribbles her signature, recalling Dwayne being in favor of this. Georgie argued against it, citing D.J.'s young age and the risk of injury from such a violent sport, but she knew they would outvote her, two against one. Like most thirteen-year-old boys, D.J. believes he needs to play football to fit in at school. Dwayne seems delighted his son may have the athletic prowess for the sport he never had the chance to play in his youth. Perhaps his own unfulfilled dreams are part of the reason he supports D.J.'s aspirations. Georgie hands the consent form to her son and says a silent prayer that he won't become an injury statistic.

A last-minute flurry of grabbing books, backpacks, and lunches, and her teens are out the door just in time to catch the bus. Georgie pours herself a mug of coffee and flops on Dwayne's easy chair in the family room. Sometimes this routine feels like she's done a full day's work before eight o'clock in the morning. This week it is anything but routine because she is missing a body—Debbie, her oldest, whom Dwayne and Georgie delivered to college over the weekend. Now it seems odd that during the drive home, Dwayne said nothing to her about his big announcement. Perhaps he sensed how much leaving Debbie at college upset her.

It's only been three days, but Georgie is missing Debbie even more than she expected. But perhaps it makes sense. They share a special bond after Debbie's health challenges some years ago. The fallout from those times was Georgie's tendency to be overprotective of her oldest child and fearful she would never be in the position she is now—at college with a full academic scholarship. Pride swells inside as Georgie considers the obstacles Debbie had to overcome. She shakes her head in wonder at the serendipity. If not for Debbie's scholarship, it is doubtful the family could afford her return to medical school.

She lingers in the chair, enjoying her coffee, while at the front door, Shadow wags his feathery retriever tail, tongue hanging out. "Hm, I guess Dwayne didn't walk you this morning. Not now, boy!" The dog snorts, spins around, and thumps down on the floor, peering at Georgie with sad eyes.

Now alone with her thoughts, Georgie must face the nagging questions that surfaced with Dwayne's announcement. *Should I still go to med school? What if it's not for me? How can I make this decision?* Her mind in turmoil, she goes to the kitchen, pours a refill of coffee, and grabs her cell phone. Melanie. Maybe she can help! Her older sister by two years, Melanie, is the one Georgie calls if she needs anything. Not so for her oldest sister, Linnie, who typically finds something to criticize. Georgie is not sure why she and Linnie never got along. She had her suspicions, but it wasn't something anyone in the family talked about, least of all Linnie.

After seven rings, Melanie answers, "Whaa? Who's this calling so early?"

It's eight-thirty. Georgie often forgets her sister has artist's work hours, working late at night and sleeping late in the morning, but she isn't of a mind to apologize. This is important.

"It's Georgie. You'll never guess! Dwayne says we can afford medical school. Can you believe it?" She paces the kitchen floor, cell phone tight to her ear.

"Wow!" Melanie says. "But didn't you tell me a few years ago you weren't sure about being a doctor anymore? Didn't you ever talk to Dwayne about that?"

Georgie slides onto a stool at the kitchen island and braces herself with two sips of coffee. "I was going to tell him, but until we could afford med school tuition, there was no point in saying anything. Dwayne's company has had profitable periods, but the financial crisis hurt the business. Now he says his company is doing well, and I can quit work and go to med school. Mel, I don't know what to do!" She leans on her elbow, cradling her forehead with one hand. "If I tell Dwayne I've changed my mind about med school, he may lose respect for me. Of course, Dad will have a fit. He's been waiting for years for me to follow in his footsteps in medicine."

"Hm. There's just no way to please everyone," Melanie says with an edge to her voice. "Forgive the analogy, Georgie, but I've always thought Dad was grooming you like a prize calf for the fall fair. And you went along with it all. Of course, I'm the black sheep of the family. I can handle the role. But you! You care what Dad thinks—what everybody thinks of you. If you can't learn to care more about what *you* want, I don't know how you can make a decision you can live with."

Georgie takes a sharp inward breath, taken aback at her sister's bluntness.

"Georgie, learn to be more like me. Follow your passions and don't worry about what other people think. Our parents forbade me from leaving Terrance for New York City, but did that stop me? No! But you always accepted Dad's plans for you, and if you don't live up to his dreams now, you're in for a rough ride. I wouldn't want to be in your shoes!"

Georgie does not like the where this conversation is going—not what she expects from her one supportive sister. As children, they were allies against their older sister's tyrannies, but this sounds more like tough love.

"Okay, I've gloated too much, and I am sorry." Melanie's tone is now one of sisterly concern. "What can I do to help? Shall I distract Dad by creating a crisis?"

Georgie manages a weak laugh, admiring how her sister can inject humor into difficult situations. Her laugh sputters into a groan. "No need for that, Mel. Thanks for listening. It just helps me to unload this, but I'm not ready to say anything to Dad yet. Please keep this under your hat for now."

After the call ends, Georgie sits at the kitchen island, coffee in hand, stunned by Melanie's comments that challenged her long-held assumptions about her career goals. *I wanted to be a doctor, didn't I? And not just to please my father?*

Chapter 2

Georgie downs her second cup of coffee in three gulps and straightens up. *A walk will do me good!* "Let's go, Shadow!" The dog yips, springs to his feet, his tail wagging, and noses at his leash hanging by the door. While walking in the peaceful surroundings of the wooded path near her home, Georgie breathes in the pungent scent of trees and lush undergrowth and raises her face to the sun. She nods to a few dog walkers, likely retired folks, unknown to her because she never walks on a weekday morning. Shadow trots along without a care except for the hope of seeing a squirrel. Usually, time with her dog, and the woodsy sights and smells would lift her spirits, but today she can't ignore the question Melanie raised. *Was medicine my dream, or was it my father's?*

Georgie reflects on her childhood fascination with her family's history in medicine—how she pestered her father to tell the story again and again. George Novak always obliged, saying how she should "be proud" to come from a long line of doctors. He, his father, and his grandfather were all doctors. Her father would begin the family story by talking about his grandfather Novak, who came from Poland in 1912 with his family of five. As an immigrant, it was impressive how he was involved in setting standards for medical practice and rejecting the pseudo-medicine of traveling salesmen with miracle potions. The next generation, Georgie's grandfather, also became a doctor but struggled to support the family during the depression and war years. There had been no money for her father, the youngest of four, to go to medical school. His voice would ooze pride as he recounted how he worked evenings and weekends to pay his way through medical school. It had taken longer to get his medical degree, and he had not started practicing until he was in his thirties. He always ended the family history the same way: "Remember, Georgie, it takes determination and hard work to realize your dreams."

Throughout her childhood, Georgie got the message loud and clear. Her father expected at least one of his children to carry on the family tradition in medicine. If having no son disappointed her father, he never said so. However, Georgie often wondered at her name: Georgina. Perhaps her parents wanted a boy, and she was to be George Junior. To this day, she is not sure why her oldest sister, Linnie (short for Lavinia), did not pursue medicine. Did she lack interest or aptitude? Her parents were close-mouthed about why Linnie did not carry on the family legacy. She lasted only two years in college before marrying Brad, an older man already successful in business. Once, when Georgie asked Linnie about what happened at school, why she did not finish her degree, Linnie was offended by the question. That's Linnie! Whatever she was doing was the right thing to do. Melanie was never a candidate for medicine. From early on, she was adamant about being an artist. Georgie became her father's last hope, which accounts for his efforts to push her into medicine.

As she steps along the wooded path, she analyzes what her father said and did to ensure she became a doctor. Recollections flood in.

Georgie loved her tenth birthday present from her father—a doctor's kit. Her friends, Alison and Roberta, would play doctor with her for a while, but they preferred their Barbies. Georgie went along if her Barbie doll could pretend to be a doctor. When her friends tired of that game, she found a willing patient in Buttons, the family's spaniel, who endured her prodding and bandaging for the promise of a few dog treats.

Georgie recalls her twelfth birthday gift—a homemade trivia game with questions about illnesses and treatments. Her father had created the questions and answers and went to the expense of having the cards professionally printed. He would play with her for hours—just the two of them. Were Linnie and Melanie invited to play? She cannot recall, but it was only ever her and her father playing. In the beginning, he coached her on the answers, but he also allowed her to look up answers in a medical encyclopedia. He rewarded correct answers with a chocolate kiss or an outing for ice cream, a practice she now recognizes as the operant conditioning she learned about in college—rewarding rats with cheese for reaching the center of a maze.

On one school career day, when grade 7 students shadowed their parents at work, her father let Georgie be the receptionist in his office. Her distinct memory is how important she felt sitting at the desk and answering the phone using her best imitation of an adult voice: "Dr. Novak's office. How may I help you?" After that day, she developed an intense curiosity about her father's work. Countless times, she would press her ear to the wall between the family home and her father's office, trying to hear what he said to his patients. Her mother would shoo her away, but denying access only made her more interested.

As a teenager, Georgie turned to quizzing her father. "If someone comes to you with a headache and a rash, what would you do?" or "How do you know you have to send a patient to the hospital?" Her father patiently gave her detailed responses with medical terms Georgie rarely understood, but that wasn't the point. Her father thought she did, and she remembers feeling honored by his attention.

During high school, Georgie focused on doing well in school with minimal interest in boys or dating. It wasn't much of a sacrifice—she was shy around boys, despite having her share of admirers. Even though her high school science grades were average, there was no question about her college major. Georgie did as her father expected and registered at UIndy in science and pre-med.

As Georgie returns to her house, her big question remains: *Did I want to study medicine, or did I do it to please my father?*

She opens the front door to the insistent ring of her cell phone. It is Lisa, her best friend since they met in chemistry class during their college freshman year. A science wiz, Lisa, was the reason Georgie got through microbiology and biochemistry. After graduation, Lisa came to live in Terrance because it was her husband John's hometown. At first, Georgie maintained contact with Lisa because of proximity, but over the years, their friendship solidified. Lisa used her degree in chemistry and nutrition to formulate a greens supplement as an immune-boosting tonic, selecting and sourcing the ingredients, and contracting with a company in Indianapolis to produce the powder. Georgie admires her friend for building a successful business, supplying her supplement to health stores and naturopathic offices throughout the Midwest. And Lisa's greens supplement was one of the few things Debbie could keep down when she was ill.

"Hey Georgie, you told me you would be off work today. I want to hear about your school plans. Let's do brunch at Henrietta's."

"Great! I would love to talk to you about school. I'll meet you in ten minutes."

The café is only a five-minute drive away, ten minutes if there is traffic. Georgie enters to the welcome aroma of fresh baked bread and coffee, and the chatter of patrons, women who appear to be lunching after their golf games. Henrietta's is a favorite spot of many, but Georgie likes it because it's a family-owned business that caters to its customers. The matriarch, Henrietta, retired last year, and her grown children are running the place now. Georgie glances at the menu written stylishly on a chalkboard, an innovation of the next generation to allow regular menu changes. She nods her approval at the recent addition of organic and vegetarian items. There are two booths open and Georgie slides into one just as Lisa strides in the door, her signature blond ponytail bouncing and her face glowing. Four inches shorter than Georgie, Lisa has a commanding presence and confidence that makes her seem more imposing. Georgie has always thought of her friend as the epitome of the expression, "big things come in small packages."

Perusing the menu, they select their favorite wraps with a coffee. While waiting for their food orders, Georgie gets right into it. "Lisa, I've been pondering something all morning. I'm no longer sure whether medicine was my father's dream or mine. Have I fooled myself about this most of my life? It's really shaking me up." She grips her coffee mug and takes a sip as if the hot beverage might give her some answers.

Lisa gives a sideways glance. "When I first met you in college, you were ultra-focused on being a doctor. Now, you have decided medicine isn't your dream, so it's odd to me you're stressing over this. What difference does it make what you wanted when you were seventeen years old?"

Georgie considers this for a moment, recalling what Melanie said. "My sister says I care too much about what my father thinks. That got me thinking about all the things he did to point me toward medicine. He did a lot! Now I wonder. Did I go to medical school just to please him?" She pauses, taking another sip of coffee. "Lisa, here's the thing. If I was mistaken about medicine then, how can I be sure what I want to do now? And am I sure enough about it to break my father's heart?"

Lisa shakes her head. "Georgie! How can one person have so much angst? It's your life. You need to decide what's best for you now, not what your father wants or what you thought you wanted when you were young."

Georgie looks down into her coffee, not able to meet her friend's gaze. "It's still difficult to know what I want now."

Their wraps arrive. Lisa dives into hers, a veggie wrap with hummus, peppers and alfalfa sprouts, and takes several bites deep in thought. Her face brightens. "Say, when we were at college, didn't you tell me about having meningitis as a child and how it had something to do with wanting to be a doctor?"

While chewing a bite of her chicken Caesar wrap, Georgie searches her memory. "I'm amazed you remembered that. Yes, I was in the hospital for three weeks with bacterial meningitis. I was very ill to be there for so long. My parents told me later that I went on about a doctor in the hospital and how I wanted to be just like him. So yes, that experience definitely influenced me."

"Something the doctor did inspired you." Lisa takes two more bites of her wrap and cocks her head. "What about this? If you could recall what impressed you so much about that doctor, maybe it will help you with your decision now."

"Perhaps," Georgie says. "But I was just nine years old. I'm not sure what I remember that would help."

"Just take some time to think about it," Lisa replies. "I'm sure you'll figure it out." She downs the last of her coffee and glances at her cell phone. "Oops! I have a one o'clock appointment with an ingredient supplier in Indianapolis. Must go! Call me later."

Back at home, Georgie sits on her backyard deck, considering Lisa's suggestion. *What was so impressive about that doctor?* Memories of her bout of meningitis and being hospitalized are fuzzy. What comes to her are mostly emotions and sensations: terror when she woke up in a strange, narrow bed with machines all around her going beep, beep, beep; stabbing pain from needles in her arm; angry no one would take out the needles; fearful of the hovering masked faces and her parents' worried looks. Suddenly it comes to her. *I remember little about it, but I bet my mother will.* She calls her mother, asking if she can come over "to talk." Thankfully, Claire is at home today, unlike most days when she is at her women's club or a charity board meeting.

15

Georgie arrives at her parents' home, just a five-minute drive away. Her mother greets her at the door, elegantly dressed, her steel-gray hair coifed neatly, as if she has an important meeting to attend. Georgie can't recall a time her mother wasn't well turned out, knowing just how to drape her slim, petite frame to advantage. Beyond her hair and eye color, Georgie bears little resemblance to her mother, favoring the Novak side of the family—tall and athletic. They settle in the kitchen where her mother has tea ready. She hands Georgie a cup and stirs milk into her own cup.

"Okay, Georgie. What are you here to talk about?"

"Mom, I'm trying to piece together what happened when I had meningitis. I recall you telling me it was right after my illness that I started telling everyone I wanted to be a doctor. Do you have any idea what made me say that? Can you tell me what you remember?"

A pained expression flashes over her mother's face as if she is reliving that time. "Georgie, it was such an ordeal. Of course, I have vivid memories of it all. You were playing soccer one day and the next day screaming in pain and a fever of a hundred and two. Your father whisked you to the emerg right away. You were terrified, and I had trouble reassuring you. When the doctors did the lumbar puncture, you were beside yourself. I don't suppose you remember that."

"No, thankfully, I don't." Georgie has heard the psyche can block memories of traumatic events, which seems so in her case. "Mom, I'm interested in what happened while I was in the hospital. You always told me I was there for three weeks."

"Oh, yes. The infection had a good hold on you, and it took a while for the antibiotics to work. They had to try some different medications, I think. But your father would know more about it. You should talk to him about this."

"It's not the treatment that interests me. I vaguely remember a doctor who made a big impression on me, but I can't remember why."

"Hm. I recall something about that. When I returned to your room after stepping out to get a cup of tea, I heard someone talking to you, so I listened outside the door for a few minutes. Later, I told your father about it. Perhaps that's how I remember what the doctor said to you. He called you by your first name, introduced himself, and in a soothing voice said you had been very ill, but you were going to be better soon. You started crying about how the needles hurt and begging him to take them out. I almost entered the room then, but stopped when I heard his reply. He said: 'I know the needles hurt a little, but they are giving you important medicine to make you well again.' Then he asked if you could stand them for another day. It amazed me when you agreed and calmed right down."

"Was that the only time that doctor talked to me?"

"Oh, no, I expect he was there almost every day. When I would visit, you talked about him a lot—Dr. Hancock this and Dr. Hancock that. I found out later he was an intern, so not likely in charge of your care. I recall asking why you liked Dr. Hancock so much. You said, 'he talks to me like I'm a grown-up.'"

Georgie has a vague memory of a young man in a blue coat. That must have been Dr. Hancock.

Claire looks down, her brow furrowed. "I couldn't stay with you all the time because I had your sisters at home. I believe the doctor kept you from being scared when your father and I couldn't be there. When we took you home three weeks later, you were upset with Dr. Hancock, because he had promised you would be home in a few days. I explained he likely said that so you wouldn't be so scared and that seemed to satisfy you. Soon after, you started telling everyone you wanted to be a doctor."

"Thanks for filling me in, Mom."

Claire frowns and cocks her head. "You're welcome. I am curious why you are asking about this now, after thirty years."

Not wanting to alert her mother to the current anxiety about her career, Georgie waves her hand. "Oh, just curious about the reasons I wanted to be a doctor."

Claire raises her eyebrows. "Ah."

Georgie excuses herself so she can get to Daphne's game, as promised. While watching the game, she smiles and cheers on cue, but her attention is elsewhere. She considers her mother's version of events that confirmed she had a legitimate dream of becoming a doctor in part because of her meningitis experience. *I guess I can't blame my father for pushing me into medicine!* Still, she can't help but think she is missing something. Her day off settled nothing. She is no closer to knowing her next steps.

Chapter 3

Georgie puts the finishing touches on the advertisement for the office manager's position with only a week and a half until her last day. Attaching the advertisement to emails for newspaper want ads and an online job site, she hovers her hand over the "send" button. *Well, that's it. I'm committed to quitting this job now!* With all the finality of the decision, she clicks "send." Her cell phone rings, and the call display says Novak—most likely her mother. Her father would be with patients at this time of day. Curiosity gets the better of her and she accepts the call.

"Georgie, I was just going to leave you a message to call me before I forget. I know you're at work," Claire says.

"That's okay. I've got a few minutes." There is work to do, but in a way she is marking time in her job knowing some things could wait for the new office manager.

"I meant to ask you yesterday about Debbie," her mother says. "You were so focused on what happened years ago, and then you left so suddenly. How did it go when you delivered Debbie to college?"

"She was so excited to be there, but I got a little teary leaving her at the dorm. I expect after all Debbie's health issues, I will always be overprotective of her."

"Well, no use dwelling on it. She's healthy now. But she is only seventeen and away from home for the first time. Do you think she can manage on her own?"

"Yes, I do," Georgie replies. "Debbie is the sensible one of my three."

Claire asks for more details about Debbie's dorm, but Georgie has to beg off. "Let's talk about it later. I've got to get back to work." Instead, she stares out the window, musing about Debbie's two-year illness and how that experience changed her interest in becoming a doctor. The nurse interrupts her musings with demands to process a patient's referral to a specialist right away. Urgent requests from patients, the nurse and Dr. Randall fill the rest of her workday.

After dinner, Georgie starts some laundry, pours herself a goblet of wine, and retreats to her bedroom. Ensconced in her chair by the window, she sips her wine and stares into her backyard as the light fades. Her thoughts run back to how distressing Debbie's prolonged illness was. It all started after a family weekend away. On Monday, ten-year-old Debbie came down with what seemed like a virus; she recovered in a week, or so it seemed. At the end of the following week, she was sick again with the same symptoms, and this pattern of recurring illness persisted for months. Over the winter and into spring, Georgie dreaded getting up in the morning, wondering if Debbie would be okay. When entering her oldest daughter's room, her fears were too often realized finding Debbie curled up in a ball in bed, her forehead warm with a mild fever. The conversation would go like this:

"How are you doing this morning, baby?"

"Feel sick… just threw up… tummy hurts. Do I have to go to school?"

"No, dear, not if you are sick."

Georgie remembers the frustrating conversations with doctors who had few answers. When all the tests came back negative, the doctor returned to his original diagnosis—a virus. Georgie thought it made little sense, asking the doctor how a virus could linger so long and why no one else in the family was ill. Instead of explaining himself, he seemed offended, and as much as said, "I'm the doctor. I know best."

When Debbie's health improved throughout spring and summer, Georgie had to accept the doctor's conclusions. Then, in the fall, all the same symptoms returned. Back to the doctor they went. This time, he decided Debbie had a digestive problem and prescribed two medications, one to slow down stomach emptying and the other to reduce stomach acid. Debbie took the medicines for two weeks, but there was no difference in how she felt. She was still nauseous every day, and she could hardly get out of bed, much less go to school. Georgie stopped giving Debbie the prescription drugs, but had to justify it to Dwayne, saying, "it makes no sense that a ten-year-old would need such medications."

A year into Debbie's mysterious illness, the family doctor referred her to a specialist—a pediatric gastroenterologist at the university hospital in Indianapolis, an hour's drive away. Georgie had been pushing for this referral and looked forward to having some answers. At their first visit, the specialist ordered a battery of tests, including upper GI scopes, a barium swallow, and an ultrasound.

The follow up appointment with the specialist was memorable but in a good news/bad news way. All the test results were negative, and the specialist declared there was nothing physically wrong with Debbie, but ironically, that led to his bad news. Georgie remembers his exact words because of how upsetting they were. "I've seen this often with girls," he said. "Without a physical cause for symptoms like this, it is most likely an emotional issue. I want Debbie to talk to the counselor on staff." Georgie objected, saying Debbie had never had emotional problems before this illness. Were there any other tests or diagnoses to consider? But the doctor was insistent counseling was the best course of action. Georgie regretted her lack of medical knowledge to argue against the doctor's diagnosis. After all, he was a top specialist.

The first counseling session was the same day. Georgie recalls fuming in the waiting room after the counselor said she had to talk to Debbie alone. Most of the way home, Debbie was quiet, not responding to Georgie's inquiries. They were almost home when she blurted it out—her response was unforgettable. "Mom! That lady never asked me about my sick stomach. She wanted to know whether I worry about school, whether I like my family, and if someone has hurt me. What was she talking about? I don't want to talk to her again."

Georgie expressed her indignation to Dwayne, because it was apparent the doctor wrongly assessed Debbie's illness was all in her head, perhaps a result of emotional trauma, even child abuse. Georgie declared she would not be taking their daughter back to the specialist. Dwayne fought her on it, but she stood firm. She feared that continuing with the doctor's prescription for counseling might make Debbie believe she had emotional problems.

By giving up on the specialist, they had new challenges. Their family doctor wasn't of a mind to refer them to a different specialist—he had already referred Debbie to the top doctor in the area. He seemed disgruntled because Debbie stopped taking the medication he had prescribed and said he had no more recommendations. Essentially, they no longer had a doctor on Debbie's case. Along with Georgie's worries for her daughter's prognosis, there were awkward moments with her father, who kept asking about Debbie's progress. Georgie wasn't brave enough to tell her father the truth, evading his questions, or making it seem like they were waiting for a new specialist. Other times, she would say the doctors were waiting for more test results. She had to keep to short conversations with her father before he could press for details. Once Debbie recovered, Georgie could not tell her father it had nothing to do with the care of a medical doctor.

Now, years later, recalling those times evokes the same panic inside her. It wasn't just her worries about Debbie. Her two younger children suffered from her lack of attention, which might explain their sibling rivalries and acting out. She had to work full time throughout that time because the family needed her paycheck. Worry about Debbie would intrude on Georgie's focus at work, and, at home, there wasn't enough time to do anything well. The feeling she had in those times, of being overwhelmed, comes back now in waves.

Dr. Randall couldn't, or wouldn't, pay her for sick days, making childcare for Debbie another problem. Mrs. Pointer, Georgie's caregiver for before and after school, was not available to work all day, nor would she take care of sick kids. Her husband's health was fragile, and she didn't want to take something home to him. Georgie's mother stayed with Debbie for the first few weeks, but that was a temporary solution. Claire had obligations as the bookkeeper for her husband's medical practice and as the chairperson for two charities with daytime meetings. Georgie had to resort to an on-call care agency for the occasional days when Debbie was sick.

After a year of Debbie's recurring illness, Dwayne voiced his displeasure about the cost of the care agency, complaining it was taking almost all of Georgie's salary. He demanded Georgie make other arrangements, even though she explained that an on-call service was their only option. She couldn't hire a regular sitter because she never knew from day-to-day if Debbie would be sick.

Georgie recalls how angry she was with Dwayne for going on about money. Was that the day she polished off an entire bottle of wine? That's how she remembers it. When Debbie was sick the following day, Georgie had a hangover and called in sick, but that was also the day a solution presented itself. In the afternoon, while Debbie was sleeping, Georgie wandered into the backyard for a breath of fresh air and her neighbor, Norma Dodge, came out wagging her finger to Georgie to meet her over the fence. No one in the neighborhood called her Norma, perhaps because she could be a little intimidating. To everyone, she was Mrs. Dodge.

Mrs. Dodge demanded to know why all the strangers were coming to the house all the time. Georgie was aware of Mrs. Dodge's reputation as the self-appointed neighborhood watch with a tendency to gossip. To avoid nasty rumors from starting, Georgie explained that the "strangers" were occasional sitters from a care agency. That triggered more questions from Mrs. Dodge and Georgie shared more than she planned, perhaps out of despair, blathering on about Debbie's illness and the expense of the care agency.

To Georgie's surprise, Mrs. Dodge's demeanor changed from suspicious to sympathetic, and she offered to be an on-call babysitter. Georgie tried to object that it was too big an imposition. "Please call me Norma," Mrs. Dodge said, "and it's no trouble at all. I am grateful to your husband for all his help around the house since my Donald died." The irony of it struck Georgie—a childcare solution presented itself because Dwayne had been a good neighbor. She knew why she loved her husband that day.

Norma Dodge was a godsend, available on call Monday to Friday at a moment's notice to stay with Debbie if she was sick. The arrangement worked out well, except Georgie learned from Debbie that Mrs. Dodge watched TV most of the day, something about "needing her soaps." It turned out she didn't have cable TV at home. It wasn't an ideal care situation, but Georgie couldn't say anything because her neighbor wouldn't take any payment.

Georgie recalls having a lot of headaches during that time. The pain would develop in the morning and linger behind her eyes all day, making it difficult to concentrate on her work and be civil with the clinic staff and patients. More than once, her boss complained about her poor customer service. To this day, she has at least one headache every week.

Georgie glances at the goblet in her hand, realizing her daily consumption of wine started during Debbie's illness. A few glasses every day could numb her worries, but looking back, she must admit sometimes she had more than a few glasses. She still hasn't been able to break that habit.

Throughout Debbie's two-year illness, Georgie felt like a clumsy juggler constantly dropping balls. She had to navigate the medical system, manage work and a household, while caring for a sick child and feeling guilty about what she wasn't doing for her other two children. The overriding lessons were disturbing. The doctors mismanaged Debbie's illness and damaged Georgie's faith in the medical system.

She downs her glass of wine just as Dwayne enters their bedroom to retire for the night. He is asleep within minutes, but, for Georgie, sleep doesn't come easy. *Tomorrow I need to talk to Dwayne about my change of plans.*

Georgie paces from the kitchen to the family room and back, waiting for Dwayne to come home from work and rehearsing what she will say. When she tires of pacing, she plumps the couch cushions, her ears tuned to the sound of his car in the driveway. *What will I do if he doesn't go along with this?*

The thunk of a car door closing heralds Dwayne's arrival. Georgie goes into the kitchen, mixes his favorite drink, a dry martini, and places it on the table near his easy chair. Faint beeps and explosions suggest D.J. is playing video games in his room and the lack of noise from Daphne's room means she is likely texting with her friends. Other times Georgie would care what her teens are doing, but right now, she needs a private talk with her husband.

Dwayne dumps his briefcase in the hall, makes his way to the family room and flops down in his easy chair. "Whew! What a day! Friday can be so trying. Some clients wanted their reports done today, but I had to tell them that would not happen. Something smells good. What's for dinner?" He spies the drink on the side table. "Oh, good! Just what I need!" He settles back and takes a few sips of the martini.

Georgie marvels at how easily Dwayne can leave work behind once he is home. She wishes she could put her life into compartments that easily. Planting herself on the edge of the couch beside him, she clasps her hands together in her lap. "Your dinner is keeping warm in the oven—chicken alfredo. But can we talk first?"

Dwayne nods and takes another sip of his drink.

"Dear, we have to talk about my school plans." She takes a deep breath. "Do you recall how disappointed we were with the doctors' care for Debbie? How they misdiagnosed her illness?"

"Yes, of course. What's that got to do with your school plans?"

Georgie steels herself against Dwayne's disapproval and continues, unable to meet his gaze. "What happened to Debbie was not an isolated failure by doctors. I have seen several troubling incidents at the medical clinic that made me question how medical doctors operate. It's given me grave doubts to the point I don't believe medicine is for me anymore." She eyes him for his reaction.

Dwayne sets his mouth in a thin line. "Well, this is a piece of news!" He drains his martini glass, sets it down deliberately, and folds his arms. "You've been considering this for a while." His mood darkens, perhaps realizing Georgie had kept this from him. "So, what about these events at the medical clinic? You've never told me about them."

Georgie gets up and paces the room, wringing her hands. "A few years ago, a woman practically forced her way into Dr. Randall's office. I could hear her screaming and snippets of what she said: 'You should have warned me what could happen… he just lies in his bed and stares… he won't let me hug him… he just stopped talking.' Things were quiet for a while, and then the woman threatened to sue Dr. Randall. Later, I checked the boy's file. He was two years old and recently had two vaccinations—the MMR and DPT scheduled at that age. That was the only intervention in his file. This happened around the time of the controversy about vaccines and autism, and, by coincidence, the boy's symptoms screamed autism. But of course, there turned out to be no proof of a link between vaccines and autism. I concluded this was just a distraught parent wanting to blame someone for her son's health issues. And she never followed through on her threat to sue."

Dwayne nods. "I am familiar with clients wanting someone to blame for their financial woes. Not surprised it could happen to doctors too."

Georgie sits down facing her husband. "That was how I felt, too. I decided it was just an isolated incident, but over the next six months, Dr. Randall had five more young patients with health issues that parents connected to medical treatment or vaccination. I didn't want to question Dr. Randall's competency, but my doubts were growing."

Dwayne frowns and shakes his head. "Those are some serious accusations you're making. I don't suppose you told anyone else."

Georgie raises her right hand. "No, I'm sworn to confidentiality at the clinic, but since I'm leaving, it's okay to tell you. I now realize it wasn't Dr. Randall's lack of competence because he was following the accepted standards for medical practice. But that left me with only one explanation—the standards for medical practice are flawed. Given what happened with Debbie and those incidents, I can't in good conscience go into medical practice."

"Well, Georgie, medicine is, or was, your dream. It's practically the first thing you told me about yourself when we met in college. If you don't want to be a doctor, it's not a big deal for me, but I'm waiting for the other shoe to drop. You must have an alternative in mind, otherwise you wouldn't quit your job."

Dwayne understands me well. I won't be content keeping a tidy house and doing charitable work.

"Yes, I have an… alternative." Georgie almost chuckles at the word, but she must be serious for what she is about to say. "I want to study in an alternative health field. I've decided it is naturopathic medicine."

Dwayne stares at her, mouth hanging open. "I need another drink for this." He jumps out of his chair and goes to the kitchen. Georgie follows and watches him mix the vermouth and gin, then peer into the fridge. She reaches around him, pulls out a jar of olives and hands it to him.

"Dwayne, I can go to the Naturopathic College in Indianapolis—the commute is only an hour—and I expect they will give me credit for some courses from my time in medical school. I could graduate in less than four years."

He drops two olives into his drink, walks into the family room and sits down in his chair again, his face unreadable. "I'm not all that surprised you are disenchanted with medicine because of what you've seen at the medical clinic. And yes, Debbie's ordeal shook your confidence in doctors. But here's the thing. Naturopaths don't have the same respect as medical doctors." He sips his drink and fishes out an olive. "And people may not have insurance for naturopaths. Your patients might have to pay out of pocket, and that will limit your income potential. Did you consider this?"

"Hm. No, I haven't. What I have done is decide on the health care I want to practice. I would still be a health professional—a Doctor of Naturopathic Medicine. If you can afford to send me to medical school, does it matter what kind of doctor I become?"

"It could matter a lot." He throws his hands in the air. "I need to know you will earn enough to recoup the cost of tuition. You should take some time to research the earning potential for naturopaths before you make your final decision."

Georgie turns away and snorts in frustration, but Dwayne's concerns are not surprising. Ever the practical accountant, most of his decisions involve cost benefit analysis. She met him in her junior year of college. He was an accounting major, accustomed to seeing the world in terms of profit and loss, right and wrong answers. Georgie was struggling to maintain the grades needed for admission to medical school. While her confidence was hanging by a thread, Dwayne was so sure about everything. His assurance was the tonic she needed.

"And another thing!" Dwayne wags his finger at her. "Are you prepared for the pushback from your parents, specifically your father? And what about our friends? Many of them work in the medical field. How do you expect them to take this? Can you live with alienating your family and our friends?"

"I know Dad will give me a rough time about this decision. That worries me. But I didn't consider how friends would react. Do you really expect them to alienate us?"

Dwayne shrugs his shoulders and shakes his head. "Anything is possible. Please be sure about this." He picks up the evening newspaper, and makes his way to the dining room, signaling the end of the conversation.

Georgie goes back to the kitchen. After putting Dwayne's dinner on the table, she pours herself a tumbler of wine, and takes a big gulp. *That did not go well. Why does everything have to be so difficult?*

Chapter 4

Dwayne is out for his Saturday golf game and the kids are out with their friends, giving Georgie a free morning for the research Dwayne demanded. Her web search brings up websites for several naturopathic clinics, and she makes some discoveries that confirm her attraction to the field. She especially likes how naturopaths focus on finding the root causes of illness using a holistic approach that considers physical and emotional aspects of health. *This must be what they mean by the phrase "treating the whole person."* One website mentions the benefits of using natural remedies to support the body's innate healing, something she is eager to learn more about. The naturopaths she researches vary in the therapies they offer—nutrition, herbal medicine, homeopathy, acupuncture, and lifestyle counseling. When she delves into practitioners' bios, she discovers that, for many, this is their second career, coming from various fields, from business to social work. She won't feel strange about being a mature student and a latecomer to the profession.

After two hours of poring over the clinic websites, she still has no sense of how prosperous naturopaths are. The naturopathic association website lists a broad income range for naturopaths, and the lower level will not impress Dwayne. She can't call a clinic to ask how much practitioners earn. *Would I give out that information? Likely not.* She turns off her computer, disappointed she can't access information about earnings to satisfy Dwayne's concerns. Discouraged, she sits stewing. *Lisa! Maybe she can help.* She has consulted with a naturopath for years and should know some practitioners through her supplement business.

Lisa answers after five rings, out of breath. "Hey, you just caught me. I was outside in the garden. What's up?"

"I need your help. Do you have time to go out for lunch? My treat!"

They agree to meet at Henrietta's even though it will be busy. When Georgie arrives, the place is packed with families out for Saturday morning brunch. The faint aroma of pancakes and sausages lingers in the air. Lisa waves from a booth near the back, the last free table. She gets up to greet Georgie and gives her a bear hug.

I sure needed that!

The chalkboard menu lists the lunch special as a walnut veggie salad. They nod at each other and say in unison, "the special," knowing it is the best way to ensure a brief wait for their meal. Lisa starts by asking about Debbie's first weeks at college. She has experience with this—her only child, Kim, is one year older than Debbie and started college last year. Georgie shares her anxiety about Debbie being away from home at age seventeen and dealing with college antics. Lisa rolls her eyes. *What is she not sharing?* Georgie makes a mental note to call Debbie later to check on her.

Georgie waits until they have their salads to tell Lisa about her latest challenge to satisfy Dwayne's concerns. "Do you know anything about naturopaths' income level?"

"There is no simple answer to that question. It's my impression those who are effective with their patients make a good living. It's like any business. The better you serve your customers, the more successful you are."

"Fair enough. Do you know a successful naturopath I can talk to? It will help if I can give Dwayne an example of someone who is doing well. I'm sure it will help when I talk to my father, too. I need to make a solid case for Dwayne and my father to be okay with this."

"Georgie, I thought you already made this decision. It sounds like you might let Dwayne, or your father, talk you out of it."

"No, no. I just need Dwayne to know I've done my homework. And he's right. I should know what I'm getting into."

Lisa leans over the table, head in her hands. "I thought you were sure about your plans. Why all the doubt?"

"I don't have doubts, but I need to explain my decision to my family. Can you help me?"

Lisa shakes her head and heaves an enormous sigh. "Okay. I know a few well-respected naturopaths who are also good customers. I'm sure I can convince one of them to speak to you."

On Sunday after dinner, Georgie is finishing kitchen clean up when she has a call from Melanie.

"Hey! Congratulate me! I just sold two paintings."

"That's great news!" Georgie says, aware she is the only family member who will celebrate this success. Melanie's lifestyle is close to that of the stereotypical starving artist, but she has survived with no help or encouragement from their parents.

"What did Dad say when you told him your decision?" Melanie asks, moving on from her good news.

"I haven't told him yet. I'm doing research on income potential in naturopathic medicine to assure Dwayne I can make a living."

"Georgie! It sounds like you are waffling."

Georgie can hear the exasperation in her sister's voice. "Not at all! I'm just doing some market research."

"Hm." Melanie doesn't sound impressed. "When you were young, you had a single-minded focus on becoming a doctor. You should know, I was envious because you had our parents' full support, something I never had. You got to med school, but then you got married and never finished school. It was like you sabotaged your dream for the sake of Dwayne's. Now, I fear you will do it again."

Georgie winces as if her sister has slapped her face. "You make me out to be a feather drifting wherever the wind blows. And just so you know, I got married because I loved Dwayne, and well, you know, things happened that weren't in our plans, and we couldn't afford med school for a long time." *Why am I so defensive?*

"Please don't take offence. I'm just telling you how I see it. But here's something you should consider, and it might be the upside of your current situation. Maybe getting married was for the best. Maybe even then, deep down, you knew medicine wasn't for you, and it has taken you a while to accept it."

"Hm. That seems unlikely." Stinging from Melanie's comments about self-sabotage, Georgie makes an excuse to end the call. She sits staring at the phone, mulling over her sister's assessment. *Did I give up on my dream for what Dwayne wanted?* It didn't feel like it at the time.

Georgie has always thought it was fate meeting Dwayne because of how unlikely it was. She first saw him in the campus pub—the only time she was there in her years at college. Her roommate, Sally, had dragged her there one Saturday evening against her protests that she needed to study. Daily study was essential for her to keep up with the demands of the biology/pre-med program. But on that Saturday, Sally had insisted with the admonishment, "You need to get out and have some fun!" To put an end to Sally's badgering, Georgie had agreed to go, "but just for an hour." She thought campus pubs were nothing more than meat markets.

Alone with her glass of beer, loud music blaring and people shouting to be heard, Georgie amused herself by observing the campus pub culture. Some people were blatant about trying to meet someone, while others made it seem they were there just to play pool or throw darts. At least Sally was honest about her intentions; she was already dancing with someone. A few people were like Georgie, just sitting back and watching. She recalls the moment she saw a guy across the room leaning on the end of the bar, studying the scene just like her and looking as bored as she. He caught her eye because he was tall, dark-haired, and resembled her favorite actor, Tom Hanks, but with a more serious demeanor. Their eyes met, and it felt like they had a moment. Alarmed it might appear she was part of the meat-market scene, she finished her beer and headed for the exit. By coincidence, she and the Tom Hanks look-a-like almost ran into each other, both reaching for the door at the same time. They laughed, shyly introduced themselves and lingered talking outside the pub, soon learning they had something in common—both had friends drag them there. It turned out he also shared Georgie's opinion that pubs were meat markets. He invited her for a coffee, and they talked for hours. That was how it all started.

What did she find so appealing about Dwayne Downie? After eighteen years of marriage, has it changed? Georgie tries to put herself in her nineteen-year-old shoes. She recalls him as a dedicated student, sure about his goals, reliable, straightforward, and no game-playing—all qualities she admired. In some ways, it was a case of opposites attracting. His major was in business and accounting, and Georgie's focus was on becoming a doctor and saving lives. What they had in common was their value for working hard to achieve their goals.

For almost a year, Georgie didn't consider they were dating because their interactions were limited to sharing lunch on the campus quad and chats on the phone. They were both studying so hard there was no time for parties, concerts, or evenings at the pub. Friends would raise their eyebrows and give her knowing looks, but Georgie insisted she and Dwayne were "just friends." When she brought him home for Thanksgiving, her parents were curious, but she claimed she was just being considerate of her friend. For him, going home would have meant a gruelling nine-hour bus ride. When Dwayne joined her at Christmas, her father took her aside to warn her about getting involved, saying, "A serious relationship could interfere with your plans for medical school." Georgie assured him that would not happen, even though by now, the physical attraction between her and Dwayne had led them into each other's beds.

A week before final exams, just five months after assuring her father the relationship wasn't serious, Dwayne proposed. He was awkward about it, saying something about them making "a good team," but she remembers being pleased and did not hesitate to say yes. But there were logistical problems. By this time, she had her acceptance to medical school at Northwestern in Chicago, where her father wanted her to go. Dwayne had a junior accountant position in her hometown of Terrance, meaning they would be three hours apart.

To say George Novak was not pleased about their engagement would be an understatement. He put his foot down, insisting she and Dwayne wait a year to get married. Was this a stall tactic? Did he hope time and distance would cool things off? Waiting didn't seem to bother Dwayne. His practicality shone through. He said delaying the wedding would give him time to pass the CPA exam and entitle him to a bigger salary.

Georgie recalls having a twinge of disappointment that Dwayne was willing to wait to get married. He was not a romantic sort, but that had never been the tone of their relationship. They were friends first, lovers second. Now, thinking back, she views his practicality as a key insight into the man she married. His top priority is, and has always been, financial security—a welcome trait in a husband if not taken to the extreme. Once she learned more about his background, it made sense. It wasn't until their senior year he talked about his parents, who made a meager living operating a hardware store in a small town in northern Michigan. Georgie met his parents first at graduation, and since then, rarely. She suspected Dwayne was reluctant to visit his parents because their lack of ambition embarrassed him. More than once, Dwayne said, "I will not live hand-to-mouth like my parents."

Throughout her first year of med school at Northwestern, Georgie was planning to negotiate a transfer to medical school at UIndy, so she and Dwayne would be closer. But medical schools were not keen on accepting transfers. She grappled with two conflicting worries—not securing the transfer and, if she did, that her father would disapprove. He thought Northwestern was the best medical school in the area and he was paying the tuition. Georgie's biggest concern was keeping her grades up, and she continued to struggle, even though it seemed like she worked twice as hard as her classmates. She made it through the first year with acceptable grades, but still below her father's standards.

When she and Dwayne got married in June, it was not as joyous as she hoped. Her father was harboring disappointment over her grades, and she had yet to hear about her college transfer. Her parents kept asking how she and Dwayne could make a marriage work while living three hours apart. In response, Dwayne had been seeking a position in Chicago, but reluctantly so because he liked his job in Terrance. A week after the wedding, she rejoiced over her acceptance to UIndy med school. Her joy was complete when Dwayne offered to live in Indianapolis and commute to his job in Terrance, so she could focus on her studies.

Georgie felt like everything was falling into place until October, when she came down with a stomach flu that lingered. The previous winter, she was ill, rundown from overwork, and put this illness down to the same thing, but her mother insisted she consult a doctor. Georgie still recalls how stunned she was by the doctor's news; she was pregnant and due the end of April. While processing the news, she had mixed emotions—wanting to be excited about expecting her first child, but disappointed over the timing. Second year final exams were in May and there was no guarantee she could complete the term and take the finals. It was a tough decision, but she opted not to continue after Christmas. The only thing that kept her from despair was Dwayne's assurance that she could return to medical school someday.

Her father was livid—it was one of the few times Georgie could recall her father yelling at her. "You should know how to keep from getting pregnant! Didn't you use any birth control?" The irony was her father had forbidden her from taking birth control pills, claiming he had seen too many side effects in his patients. She and Dwayne had used some birth control, but a less reliable method.

The other upset for her father was the prospect of losing money on tuition—not refundable was the university's policy for dropouts. The school advised Georgie she could avoid losing the tuition fees, but only if she returned to the program the following January. She tried to convince her father this would be possible, that many women go back to school after having babies. Her father was not convinced and her mother backed him up, saying: "You don't know how much work children are. There is no way you can manage med school with a young child."

She recalls her father's attempt to put on a guilt trip, saying how terrible it was the family's legacy in medicine would die with him. One thing he said then seems prophetic now. He accused her of sabotaging her schooling and questioned whether she ever cared about becoming a doctor. Her father's criticism hurt her deeply, and it was a while before they spoke civilly to each other again. Over the years, her father seemed to love his grandchildren, but Georgie sensed his underlying resentment. He thought she had sacrificed her dreams for Dwayne and her children.

Years ago, her father accused her of sabotaging her career. Now Melanie is saying it too. *Are they right? Did I sabotage my dreams years ago? And am I about to do it again?*

On Monday at her lunch break, Georgie calls Rick Turner, the young pastor at her church, asking to see him in the evening. His predecessor, Pastor Borden, had provided emotional support during Debbie's prolonged illness, and this current situation seems almost as dire. At seven o'clock, she rings the bell at the church office door, not confident the young pastor has enough experience to be of help. Pastor Rick welcomes her into his office and offers her a seat in a cushy armchair. He has no clue of Georgie's current dilemma, so she takes twenty minutes to share her story—her childhood dream, how her dream changed, and concerns about upsetting her family.

Pastor Rick listens without comment and, when Georgie finishes, takes a minute to respond. "Georgie, I like how you are trying to be thorough in your decision. You're aware of how your actions affect others, and that shows empathy." He puts his hands in a prayer pose. "Now, you need to extend some empathy to yourself. I'd like you to consider where your heart is leading you. I believe you can come to terms with your choice if you accept that natural medicine is a calling for you—almost how I had my call into ministry. It applies to any helping profession. If you have a strong call, I believe God is speaking to you. You need to discern it is indeed God's voice telling you to be a naturopath." He pauses for a response.

Georgie stares at him like he is speaking a foreign language.

"Think of it this way," he says. "What is your overriding motivation? Do you have a positive reason for wanting to be a healer, or is this because you're upset the medical doctors didn't help Debbie?"

Hm. Tough questions!

"There is another possibility, and I don't know you well enough to suggest this. But is it possible you are doing this to defy your father?"

Georgie's eyes open wide, and she gazes out the window, mulling over everything he said. "I'm not sure I know the answers to your questions."

"You don't have to *know* the answers, but you can *discern* answers if you pray, reflect on these questions, and open your heart to God's plan for you. Then I'm sure you can make this decision and tell your family without fear."

"Thank you, Pastor Rick. You just reminded me I have not prayed about this decision. I've been trying to figure this out all on my own. Sometimes I forget how much prayer can help." Georgie sees a glimmer of hope for finding answers, but as she drives home, that hope fades. She has no clue what a strong call from God would feel like or sound like.

Chapter 5

Georgie acts on Pastor Rick's advice right away, even though she isn't sure what to say in her prayers. First, she asks God for wisdom and strength to follow through with her plan, but something about that prayer doesn't feel right. Next, she opts for a more open-ended prayer, asking God how best to help people improve their health, not presuming naturopathy is the only option. Pastor Rick also recommended reflection and Georgie already knows her best time for that is while walking the dog. On her Tuesday evening walk with Shadow, her thoughts dwell on how Debbie recovered from her illness and how that led her to consider naturopathy.

It was almost two years into Debbie's recurring bouts of illness when Georgie gave up on the medical specialist. Whenever she talked about Debbie's lack of progress, Dwayne would shrug his shoulders and tell her to trust the doctors. He did not seem to grasp how medical doctors had failed them, leaving her alone in her fears for Debbie's long-term health—that she might never get better.

Without Lisa, Georgie would not have considered seeking answers outside medical practice. When her friend first suggested a naturopath for Debbie, Georgie had doubts, not knowing what a naturopath could do that the medical specialists hadn't already tried. Until then, Lisa's belief in naturopathy had been one area in which they disagreed because of Georgie's career focus in medicine. But Lisa made a compelling case, explaining how thorough the naturopathic assessment would be, including tests medical doctors didn't have. By this time, Georgie was desperate and finally agreed to act on her friend's advice. What was there to lose? Still, it was a giant leap of faith.

Dwayne protested because their health insurance did not cover naturopaths, but Georgie somehow convinced her husband to take a chance on the expenditure. She likely cried on his shoulder at her wit's end, trying to work full time, manage the other kids, and care for Debbie, who wasn't getting better. Georgie had to remind Dwayne they were out of options. Still, it took a few days for him to accept the situation as desperate and agree to the naturopath.

Even with Dwayne's consent, Georgie had another concern. She couldn't tell her father she was taking Debbie to a naturopath. He had always referred to naturopaths the same way — "quacks selling false hope to the gullible." Until then, under her father's influence, Georgie had similar suspicions about naturopaths, but she also respected Lisa's opinion. And there was her desperation for answers.

Lisa had been right. The naturopath, Peter Young, was thorough. The first consultation took well over an hour in which he took a complete health history back to when Debbie was born. He conducted a test called live blood cell analysis revealing abnormalities in Debbie's white blood cells, a sign of weakened immune response. The naturopath identified Debbie's recurring low-grade fevers as confirmation her immune system could not mount a defense for whatever was challenging her. The next step, he said, was to determine the cause of the immune suppression.

Much like a detective, Dr. Young asked a lot of questions until he uncovered a significant clue. To his inquiry about what Debbie was doing just before she got sick, Georgie told him about the family spending the weekend at a resort hotel. The naturopath delved deeper, asking specifics about their weekend activities. Georgie remembered Debbie had spent hours in the hotel pool practicing her diving, a significant accomplishment for her. Daphne and D.J. didn't like putting their faces in the water and had been content to paddle at the shallow end.

Dr. Young determined Debbie's symptoms and their onset after her time in the pool pointed to a water-borne parasite. He assessed Debbie's apparent recovery in the summer was a pattern consistent with a parasitic infection—in the summer, when immune systems are more robust, parasites can have fewer ill-effects. To confirm his diagnosis, he recommended testing at a specialty lab in North Carolina. Georgie was skeptical, pointing out the family doctor had already tested Debbie for parasites. But Dr. Young advised local labs did not have comprehensive testing and often yielded a false negative result, ruling out parasites when they were present. The test at the North Carolina lab cost four hundred dollars, and without consulting Dwayne, Georgie put it on her credit card.

Georgie recalls her profound relief at the test results that confirmed an amoeba parasite. The diagnosis vindicated her decision to go with the naturopath and dispelled her lingering doubts about giving up on medical doctors. Many times during Debbie's two-year illness, Georgie questioned whether they were with the right doctor, and how long to stay with a doctor's recommendations before seeking answers elsewhere. With the speed of this diagnosis, she didn't have to endure such angst. Dr. Young prescribed an antiparasitic protocol of herbs and homeopathic remedies and, within a month, Debbie rallied and was back in school. Georgie's relief was complete when, a few months later, Debbie passed the seventh grade. She has never relapsed since and has maintained top grades in school ever since.

Over the years since, one question has haunted Georgie. *What if I hadn't taken Debbie to the naturopath?* She shudders. Is it the coolness of a late August evening or the thought of what might have happened? She has since read stories on the internet of unresolved parasitic infections leading to colitis or irritable bowel syndrome. Her daughter might have permanent health problems to this day, and her academic success might not be possible. By consulting with the naturopath, Georgie stood up to her husband's opposition and went on faith. *Will acting on faith help me now?*

On her return from her evening walk, Georgie makes herself a chamomile tea to soothe her nerves. Dwayne and Daphne are at D.J.'s first football game, which Georgie begged off, citing "too much to do." She had no time during regular work hours to go through the thirty applications for the office manager's position. But it only takes an hour to select five candidates and dash off emails to set up the interviews on Thursday.

Sitting in the family room, the house quiet, Georgie sips her tea and considers the question she has yet to answer: *Why did I want to be a doctor? Was it just my father's influence?* She goes back over her meningitis experience once again. Dr. Hancock, the intern who inspired her to be a doctor, was not in charge of treating her. All he did was talk to her and ease her fears. He had an excellent bedside manner, what she now recognizes as caring for a patient's emotional and psychological health. In her child's eyes, this was what a doctor did, but as an adult, she knows it's not a primary focus for medical doctors. It occurs to her the encounter with that intern could just as easily inspire the dream of being a counselor or psychologist, but, given her father's profession and influence, medicine was the only option she considered. It was like she had blinders on to other possibilities, such as naturopathy.

Georgie can't wait to tell Lisa and phones her. "I found it, Lisa, I found it!"

"What have you found?" Lisa asks, mirroring Georgie's excitement.

"My childhood dream was about caring for the person, not just treating the illness. Naturopathy is the best fit for me."

"I'm so glad you figured this out. Did you talk to my naturopath contact?"

"Yes, I had a great talk with Dr. Portiss on Sunday. I appreciated her willingness to reveal her yearly income, which is impressive. She also gave me more insights into how naturopathy works. I knew naturopaths look for root causes of illness, but she explained how she makes those assessments using health history, diet, lifestyle, and symptom patterns. And she talked about how she prepares treatment plans for each patient's individual situation. That is most impressive to me—how naturopaths personalize their treatments. It made me consider where the medical doctors went wrong with Debbie. They didn't ask enough questions to make a proper diagnosis and then compounded their error by giving her drugs to eliminate her symptoms. They addressed the symptoms, not the patient."

"It seems like you have a good handle on the naturopathic profession."

"There's something else that helped. Pastor Rick suggested I pray about whether I have a calling to practice natural medicine. From my prayers and everything Dr. Portiss said, I know naturopathy is a calling for me. I don't have the same call to practice medicine."

"Good! Now you can stick to your plan, even if your family opposes it."

From outside, car doors slam shut, and Georgie ends the call. Her family bursts in the door.

"Mom! We won!" D.J. says, bouncing towards her.

Dwayne is smiling ear to ear. "You should have seen D.J. He made four tackles."

"He did okay," says Daphne, as she heads upstairs.

Dwayne and D.J. grab a bag of chips and settle in the family room, still chattering about the football game. A few minutes later, Georgie hears the TV and what sounds like a baseball game, and she plops on a stool in the kitchen to wait for the game to end. She hears a loud, "No!" D.J. strides past and takes the stairs two at a time, saying over his shoulder. "That reliever just gave up a grand slam. No use watching anymore. Game's over!"

Georgie sees her opportunity and joins her husband, who has his arms folded, glaring at the TV with the sound muted. She knows that look—he's upset over the game. Georgie sits next to him on the couch. "Dwayne. I took your advice and researched naturopathy. This is the doctor I want to be."

"And you're sure you can make a living at it?" Dwayne keeps his eyes on the game.

"As sure as I can be, but it will be like when you started your business. It took a few years for it to be profitable. My career will be the same."

"Okay, if you're absolutely sure." He turns to her, his face stern. "I don't want to pay the tuition and find out you can't make a decent income."

"You needn't worry. I've waited seventeen years for this." Georgie doesn't tell him about being "called" to naturopathy and using prayer to help with her decision. He might take her decision less seriously if it isn't based on market research and income potential. However, her father is a person of faith. A faith-based decision may impress him.

Georgie has learned from experience the best way to approach her father about a delicate issue—talk to her mother first. She sees her opportunity when Dr. Randall closes the clinic on Wednesday afternoon for a family commitment. Her father also takes some Wednesday afternoons off, and she knows today is his service club lunch meeting. At twelve-thirty she arrives at her parents' house to the unmistakable aroma of cinnamon buns, her father's favorite.

"Sorry the buns are still in the oven," her mother says, "but I have tea ready for you." Once seated at the kitchen table with her mother, cup of tea in hand, Georgie lays out her plan.

Claire raises her eyebrows and her jaw drops. "Oh, my!" She stares at Georgie a full ten seconds. "Well, this is a surprise. Have you considered how difficult this will be for your father?"

"Of course, he won't like it. That's why I'm here, to break it to him gently, if that's possible."

The frown and the shake of her mother's head show she has no sage advice on how to handle George Novak, whose car can be heard pulling into the driveway. Georgie's mouth goes dry.

Her father is pleased to see her but expresses surprise at her mid-day visit. They settle in the living room, so he can sit in his favorite easy chair.

"I heard your great news! Dwayne told me you can afford medical school," says her father. "I expect you will go back to Indianapolis, but please keep an open mind. Northwestern is still the better school." He doesn't seem to notice Georgie's pained expression. "You will make the right choice, I'm sure, but if you need any help, just let me know."

Claire is hovering by the door to the kitchen and says, "I need to watch my buns so they don't burn." She escapes to the kitchen for reasons Georgie knows are suspect. Her mother has never burned buns, or anything else. This is about avoiding a confrontation, something her mother does well, especially when it is between her family members. Now Georgie is alone with her father.

"Dad, I need to talk to you about my choice for college." She takes a deep breath. "I have considered this carefully, and I've prayed on it, and… I am convinced medical school is not the right path for me."

Her father's eyebrows shoot up. Georgie plows on before she loses her nerve. "I feel called to practice in natural medicine. I want to be a naturopathic doctor."

"What did you say?"

"I want to be a… naturopath."

"Have you lost your mind?!"

"Please listen, Dad. You must understand I have valid reasons. Some of this has to do with what happened to Debbie. She was sick for two years before we found out she had a parasite. Dad, the doctors missed the diagnosis—even the specialist." Georgie pauses for emphasis. "It was a naturopath who found the parasite and successfully treated it. I didn't tell you because I was afraid of how you would react."

Her father glares at her, his color rising. "Georgina, you of all people should appreciate doctors will never be perfect, but are you seriously telling me that because of Debbie's ordeal, you are abandoning medicine? You know something about the scientific method. You don't make conclusions based on one case, even if it's your daughter's." His voice grows louder, and he jabs his finger for emphasis. "And how do you know for sure it was the naturopath's treatment that helped Debbie? Perhaps the doctors' treatments laid the groundwork. Or maybe Debbie was about to get better, anyway."

Her father's challenges are like a tidal wave hitting her. "Believe me, Dad, I thought of all this. I gave the medical doctors two years before I sought another opinion. And by the way, I stopped taking her to the specialist a while before seeing the naturopath. Dad. It was the naturopath who cured Debbie. He found the parasite and treated it."

Georgie detects no softening in her father's demeanor; it's time to make her ultimate argument—the best evidence for her case. "Dad, the medical doctors misdiagnosed Debbie's illness for two years. The biggest disappointment was the specialist at the university hospital. His tests showed Debbie was physically fine, and he wouldn't listen to my accounts of how ill she was. He thought Debbie's illness was all in her head and put her in counseling, and that shook Debbie's confidence as much as the illness did. She wondered if she actually had emotional problems."

Her father is out of his chair, pacing the room, his face thunderous. "Still, Debbie's experience is an isolated case. And how do you know she didn't get better on her own? Georgie, I am part of a profession that saves lives. How could you turn down the chance to be part of that? And for what? To take up a profession that peddles quack cures and false hope? I've seen it many times—patients come to me after a naturopath sells them a load of remedies, and they are still sick."

Georgie cringes as her father stands up, and hovers over her, hands on his hips.

"This is preposterous! This family will be a laughingstock when the community finds out the doctor's daughter is choosing quack medicine. I won't be able to show my face at the country club or the Rotary Club." He throws up his hands and snorts in derision. "You may not think it matters, but we build our lives on the respect from people in our community." He slumps back into his chair and turns away.

"Really, Dad? This isn't about you." Georgie struggles to keep her voice calm. "I don't expect you to understand right now, but I hope you will come to accept that this is my choice."

"Of course, it's not just about appearances. Think of all the medical diagnostic tests and treatments, and advances in surgeries that save lives. Are you telling me that doesn't matter?"

"Dad. Of course not, but there are other issues. People are losing respect for doctors because of their overreliance on prescriptions. It seems like the pharmaceuticals train today's doctors to hand out pills like candy before there is even a diagnosis. Maybe this has changed since you started practicing. Sure, we need some drugs, but many have side effects that cause more problems than the original illness."

Her father is nearly apoplectic. "Georgie, you are attacking my life's work! Do you truly believe I would knowingly hurt my patients? How could you think that of me? You cut me to the quick!"

Claire re-enters the room, placing a hand on her husband's shoulder. "Now, George. Please don't upset yourself. Remember your blood pressure."

Dismayed by the accusing looks on her parents' faces, Georgie says, "Please don't take this the wrong way, Dad. You may help most people, but not all. There is more to health care than medicine can offer. I want to be part of the movement toward complementary care—offer a natural alternative."

"Complementary care! Just fancy words for a bunch of hokum! But it all amounts to the same thing. You are rejecting my work and what I've taught you since you were a child. If you do this, don't bother talking to me about it. I won't be a party to your folly."

Georgie's heart sinks. Her father's reaction is as she feared. She is close to tears but keeps it together for one last plea.

"Dad, please! You must know, I've prayed and reflected on this decision. I feel called to natural medicine. Just because it's not accepted by everyone doesn't mean it's wrong. Think about it! Jesus didn't preach the gospel because everyone accepted his message. His own people opposed him, but that didn't stop him. He focused on his calling. Natural medicine is what I am called to do, with or without your blessing."

Her father jumps to his feet. "Your decision hardly compares to the work of Jesus." He punctuates each word with his finger, the blood vessels on his head pulsing.

Georgie has never seen him so angry. She winces, but then stares at him in defiance.

He throws his hands up and waves her away. "It seems I can't reason with you. I think it's time you left. Perhaps your mother will take your calls, but I won't be." He stalks out of the room into his office and slams the door.

Claire shakes her head, her brow lined with concern. "I think you should go now. He shouldn't get so upset. His blood pressure is too high."

Georgie has no choice but to leave. On the drive home, she fights back tears, the road swimming before her eyes. Her worst fears are realized. Her father will not accept her plan and, if he follows through with his threat, he might even cut her out of his life. By the time she arrives home, pain is throbbing behind her eyes, the onset of a real doozie if past headaches are any measure. She sits in the car in her driveway, her head on the steering wheel. *This is going to take all the determination I have.*

Chapter 6

Two big salads, a squash casserole, and a huge ham are on the dining room table, but it's the smell of fresh, baked rolls that permeates the room. As Claire sets the basket of rolls on the table, the four young people, Georgie's two and Linnie's Michelle and Ted, reach across the table to grab one. Claire tut tuts at their table manners, but her smile shows satisfaction that her grandchildren like her baking. She is the orchestrator of this family gathering, an annual tradition to celebrate George Novak's birthday. Everyone is there from Georgie and Linnie's families except for Debbie, who just left for school two weeks ago. Melanie sent regrets because of an art showing in New York, but Georgie suspects it to be a ruse. Melanie rarely attends family gatherings because of repeated, critical comments from their father about her lifestyle, of which he disapproves—unmarried and making a meager living as an artist. Given their altercation on Wednesday, Georgie expects her father will heap disapproval on her instead.

Georgie eyes her father as he carves the ham, watching for signs of his displeasure. It is subtle, but it is there. He did not acknowledge her when she arrived and hasn't looked at her since. Bowls of food pass from hand to hand and everyone digs in. The lunch conversation is about recent achievements in the family—accolades for D.J. in his first football game, Debbie's full ride scholarship, and Michelle's graduate fellowship in economics. Daphne appears miffed, likely because no one mentions her prowess in soccer. But Linnie dominates the conversation by sharing the minutia of her latest fundraiser to benefit the local Alzheimer's respite program, and how three other charities want her to organize their fundraisers. It strikes Georgie that her oldest sister has discovered her talent—planning benefits, galas, and donation campaigns. No one mentions Georgie's school plans, even though she suspects they all know about it.

The aromatic scent of apples and cinnamon fill the air as Claire serves the apple crumble pie, another of her husband's favorites. Georgie doubts she will enjoy the pie because she has figured out what is going on. Her father is pleasant to everyone else, but when she speaks, he turns away or glances down at his dinner plate. Has anyone else noticed him giving her the cold shoulder? She offers to clear away the dishes just to get away from her father's unspoken hostility.

Georgie returns from the kitchen and Linnie rises from her chair, stating for all to hear, "Georgie, we need to talk in private." She turns on her heel and strides into their mother's sitting room, leaving Georgie no choice but to follow. She closes the door and sits on her mother's settee opposite Linnie, who sits ramrod straight on a chair. A striking resemblance to their mother in face and body frame, Linnie's sullen, sour expression is not so inherited. Georgie has long believed her oldest sister was jealous of the extra attention their father gave her as a child. She recalls how Linnie took delight in Georgie's childhood misdeeds and tattled to their father, hoping to put her out of favor. Linnie's glare and folded arms say it all. Georgie prepares for something nasty.

"So, what is this all about, Georgina? Mom told me you're not going to medical school and, worse than that, you plan to study some quack medicine. Oh, I did some research. There are three states in the country where it's not even legal!" Grim-faced, Linnie seems ready for a reply. As Georgie opens her mouth, Linnie breaks in, "You know Dad is livid. He thinks you are going to disgrace the family."

Georgie squirms in her seat, but then straightens up. *I'm not a child anymore. I won't let Linnie intimidate me.* "Linnie, this is not about the family name. I have spent years coming to this decision, and it's not been an easy one." She explains how she lost faith in medical practice after Debbie's ordeal and the incidents in Dr. Randall's office. Because she rarely confides in her oldest sister, much of this is new information. "Linnie, I can't in all conscience finish med school and go into medical practice. It's just not for me."

"But you are judging the entire system based on a few doctors," Linnie says, mimicking their father's objections. "You know that's not fair, and I always took you for a reasonable person. Are you sure this isn't an early midlife crisis? Is everything okay with you and Dwayne?"

Georgie has had enough. She stands up, rising to her full height, and sticks out her jaw. "I am sorry you feel this way, but nothing you can say will change my mind. And if you believe I would make this decision lightly, maybe you don't know me at all!"

"You're right! If you do this, I don't know who you are. I just hope you don't give Dad a heart attack with all this craziness. Just keep that in mind." Linnie bolts from her chair and storms out of the room.

Georgie's hands are shaking, and she slumps down on the settee. It takes a few minutes to compose herself before rejoining the family gathering. She is eager to go home, but eating and running is a breach of etiquette that would incur her mother's wrath. She doesn't need more criticism right now.

By mid afternoon Georgie and her family can leave her parents' and she escapes to her bedroom to take stock of her situation. Carrying out her plan is going to be more difficult than she imagined. Her list of allies is thin. Her mother has taken a neutral position, so she doesn't have to choose a side. Melanie will be an ally, but she lives in New York City and is the self-acknowledged black sheep of the family. As much as Georgie loves her sister, that support won't count for much. It's a novel experience because her family has always been a source of support. Apart from Dwayne's financial backing, it looks like she is on her own. She then has a comforting thought. *I have a source of support: God.*

Georgie remembers a prayer to help in this situation from a lesson in A Course in Miracles. She bought the course manual because the title was intriguing, and, though she hasn't read it all, many course lessons and prayers have resonated. Pulling out the drawer of her bedside table, she finds a scrap of paper with a favorite prayer scribbled on it. *Your healing Voice protects all things today, and so I leave all things to you. I need be anxious over nothing. For Your Voice will tell me what to do and where to go; to whom to speak and what to say to them, what thoughts to think and what words to give the world. Father, Your Voice protects all things through me.* As she repeats the prayer a second time, her resolve grows. Naturopathy *is* her calling.

Georgie's last day at Dr. Randall's clinic was yesterday. With all her personal turmoil, she wasn't sure how she hired a new office manager so quickly. The new hire, a recent grad in medical office administration, had the skills but won out because she was available to start right away. Georgie spent all day Monday in orientation with the young woman who seemed to pick up things quickly, but would also have the manual for the office procedures Georgie created. The new hire knew she could call if she had questions.

With her office manager role in the rear-view mirror, and sure of her path forward, she has the confidence to learn about the naturopathic college in Indianapolis. Her kids just left for school and, with coffee in hand, she turns on her computer to check the college website. To her horror, she discovers something she had not noticed before—the school does not have accreditation from the naturopathic association. She clicks on the association website to find the closest accredited school. It's in Chicago, over three hours' drive away. *How foolish of me not to check schools before announcing my plans!* She based her expectation to find a naturopathic college nearby on the availability of medical schools, but today she discovers accredited naturopathic colleges are less common. There are only six in the entire country. Head in her hands, she leans over her computer, despair descending on her heart. Then she sets her mouth in a firm line. *There must be a way I can do this.* She completes the online application for the naturopathic college in Chicago and emails her transcripts from college and medical school.

Unable to sit still, she sets to cleaning out the fridge. At a time like this, a mindless activity is just what she needs. Two hours of scouring shelves and throwing out past dated food and her fridge is spotless. She closes the fridge door with satisfaction and hears the ring tone for her phone. The call display shows a private number in Chicago. *Could it be?*

"Georgina Downie? This is Carolyn Beatty, the registrar of the National University of Health Sciences in Chicago. I had a look at your transcripts. The admissions committee will have to confirm this, but I'm reasonably sure they will accept you. I'm the chair of the committee, after all." She chuckles. "I estimate we can give you credit for several core science courses you took at medical school."

Georgie marvels at the speed of this response. "This is such good news!"

"Here's the situation," the registrar says. "We just had two students drop out of the program due to start next week. If you can start this term, I can offer you a place. You would need to be here by the end of the week. Classes start next Tuesday."

It takes Georgie a moment to absorb the offer. "Uh. This term? I am available, but I need more details about the program, the tuition, and accommodation. I live three hours away, so commuting is not possible. Do you have an option for distance education?"

"I am sorry, we don't. I agree you live too far away to commute, and on-campus residence is full, unfortunately. But we keep a registry for off-campus accommodations in the area. I can email it to you right now."

Georgie hesitates, not sure what to say.

"I know this must seem rushed, Mrs. Downie, but I need an answer from you today so we can process your application. We have a waiting list, but so far, no one else has committed to take this place in the program."

The offer is like a dream come true, but the registrar's urgency is akin to high-pressure sales, making it suspect. But Georgie pushes aside her suspicions. *It won't hurt to at least consider it!* "Yes, of course. Please process my application and send me information about accommodation."

Georgie ends the call and her elation fades. Dwayne will give her grief over this, especially about the added cost of accommodation. Still, if she wants to study naturopathy at an accredited school, and not wait another year, this is her chance. *I must make this work!* A few minutes later, her computer dings to notify her of an incoming email. Carolyn Beatty is efficient. Her email includes the course outline, class schedule, tuition fees, and a list of local rental accommodation. Georgie checks the accommodation list, and the rental rates seem steep. Perhaps so close to the start of term, there is no reasonably priced housing left. She groans and puts her head in her hands. *Fresh air. That's what I need.*

She wanders into the backyard, hoping for inspiration or a miracle to deal with her latest challenge. If she wants to avoid an unpleasant conversation with Dwayne this evening, she will need housing in place and something that isn't too expensive. In the next yard, she sees Norma Dodge picking tomatoes. Motioning to Georgie that she wants to chat, Norma ambles towards the fence. *What is she going to complain about this time?*

"Georgie, how is our dear Debbie doing?"

Georgie relaxes, pleased to relay Debbie's success, having a full scholarship and in her freshman year.

Norma's face brightens, replacing her usual dour countenance. Perhaps her time as an occasional sitter made her feel part of Debbie's success. Norma's expression turns serious again. "But Georgie, I'm wondering why you aren't at work. Not sick, I hope."

Georgie smirks. This is more like Norma Dodge, with her overdeveloped interest in other people's business. "Oh, I gave my notice at the clinic. I'm going back to school."

"Oh, that's big news. What kind of school is it?"

Georgie hesitates. What she reveals will be around the neighborhood by the end of the day, but she doesn't care who knows. She really needs to share her woes with someone. "I'm going to naturopathic college, but the closest school is in Chicago. They have a last-minute opening for this term, but I need housing. What I've seen so far is too expensive."

"My, my, that is too bad," Norma studies Georgie for a moment. "Did you know my son and his wife live in Chicago? With their daughter gone, they have an empty bedroom and they've talked about renting a room to a student but hesitated because they want their weekends free. Would this just be Monday to Friday?"

Georgie's mouth drops at this surprising offer, her second one today. "Ah. Yes, I would want to come home for weekends. Can you ask them? I need to arrange for accommodation right away."

"I'll call my daughter-in-law right now," Norma says, retreating to her house with purpose, apparently pleased she might be of help.

As she returns to the house, Georgie chuckles to herself. Norma Dodge doesn't deserve her neighborhood reputation as a busybody. Beneath her nosy neighbor facade is a heart of gold. Even though she stayed with Debbie years ago, Georgie always thought Norma had an ulterior motive—to watch her soaps. She gives her head a shake, amazed at how people can surprise you. Also astounding is that sharing her problems with someone paid off. Her prayer from the previous day was prophetic. *For Your Voice will tell me what to do and where to go; to whom to speak and what to say to them. God, your Voice protects me in all things.*

Georgie enters the lecture hall on Monday morning for her first class of the week, already feeling stressed because she isn't prepared for today's quiz. Her only consolation is today's two one-hour spares that will give her extra study time. A month into the naturopathic program, it still feels like she has entered an alien world with different customs and language. Everything happened so fast after the college accepted her into the program, a flurry of setting up living arrangements, moving her belongings, and catching up on orientation. The other students had a week's head start with their orientation.

Dwayne was livid over Georgie's lack of research on accredited schools. The first twenty-four hours were tense when it seemed he might put a kibosh on her plans because of the added rental expense. Meanwhile, the college registrar was calling repeatedly about the tuition fees and Dwayne was dragging his heels about sending the money.

Norma Dodge came through the same day as their conversation over the fence. Her son Ben and daughter-in-law Sara called to set up an interview about a room rental, and Georgie drove to Chicago to meet them the next day, anxious all the way there. If this didn't work out, she feared Dwayne would nix naturopathic college, perhaps for good.

The location was ideal, only ten minutes from the campus. On meeting Ben and Sara, Georgie had a good first impression of them—pleasant, trustworthy folks. In their mid-fifties, they became empty nesters when their youngest, a daughter, left home in the spring. They showed Georgie a pink bedroom with a teenage décor—prize ribbons and a corsage pinned to a corkboard, posters on the wall, and a well-worn stuffed bear on the bed. Sara surveyed the room with sad eyes and made an assurance they would clear out the room, but Georgie said there was no need---she could relate having a daughter leave home so recently. They agreed on a rental rate for the room, but all the way home, Georgie fretted about how Dwayne would react.

"Hm," Dwayne said, when Georgie reported the weekly rent at the Dodge's. He disappeared into his den and reappeared a half hour later, in a better mood. "My market analysis tells me this is an excellent rate. I don't think you could do any better." Georgie detected in her husband a hint of admiration for her shrewdness in negotiating, but she suspected this was more about "who you know" than her ability to haggle. Ben Dodge had asked her what she could pay, rather than quoting her a rental rate he expected. She had suggested twenty dollars per night, Sunday to Thursday, expecting him to haggle, and was shocked when he agreed. Had Norma Dodge asked her son to keep the cost down? Perhaps it helped that Georgie would be away at school all day, study in her room all evening, and buy her own food. Most people would consider her an ideal roomer.

On her first day at college, the registrar expected Georgie to make a big decision—to choose the fast track or the slow track through the curriculum. She chose the fast track so she could finish the program in three years, but also called home to get her husband's opinion. Although the fast track compressed the cost of tuition fees, Dwayne agreed with her decision, saying, "we need a return on our investment sooner rather than later." But the fast-track schedule is daunting. Once she uses her credits for core science courses, the schedule will be heavy with eight or nine courses each trimester. Each trimester lasts three months, with only a three-week break before the next one starts. It's been seventeen years since she was a student, and she is out of the habit of studying and taking exams. Almost every day in the past three weeks, she questioned whether she could do this, and niggling at the back of her mind was Dwayne's concern about money. *What if I can't finish the program?*

The past three weekends, Georgie made the three-hour drive home on Friday evening. The first two weekends at home gave her respite, but this weekend there was family drama. Dwayne went ballistic when Daphne waltzed in at one o'clock in the morning, well after curfew, not forthcoming about her whereabouts.

"What do you mean by hanging out with friends?" Dwayne asked. "That doesn't tell me where you were or what you were doing."

Daphne responded with an exasperated shake of her head and a quick escape to her bedroom. Instead of studying for her Human Biochemistry quiz, Georgie spent several hours mending the rift between Dwayne and Daphne. It didn't help to remind Daphne she wasn't sixteen until next spring. Georgie wasn't sure how well her talk went with Dwayne, either. He resisted her advice that parenting teenagers requires less shouting and more reasoning.

"Debbie never gave us this kind of trouble," Dwayne said.

"Of course, Debbie was a model child and teenager, but certainly not the norm. Didn't you ever stay out late or defy your parents?" The look on her husband's face showed he had not.

Georgie wanted to get back to school but was concerned about how Dwayne and Daphne would resolve their differences without her there to mediate. Her other concern was the quality of meals Dwayne was serving. Judging by the trash can, it was a lot of prepared, packaged, and frozen entrees. She spent Sunday afternoon making spaghetti sauce and a roast chicken for meals during the week. At least D.J. didn't give any trouble with football consuming all his time and energy.

Georgie preferred driving back to school mid-afternoon on Sunday, but with the drama and the cooking, she couldn't get away until after dinner. By the time she pulled into the driveway at the Dodge residence at nine-thirty, all the lights were out. She knew Ben and Sara were early to bed types, so she let herself in and tiptoed to her room. Exhausted, she collapsed on the bed, reflecting on her first month of managing school and home. Her prayer was simple: *God, give me strength.*

"Vitalism is one of the underlying principles of naturopathy," Professor Blake says in today's class in Foundations of Naturopathic Medicine. "Energetic forces govern our lives and our health as much as our physical environment. In naturopathy, we consider the emotional and spiritual energy of our patients, besides their physical ailments." The professor explains how this principle contrasts with the mechanist philosophy of Western medicine, viewing the human body as a machine to repair with drugs or surgery. "Like a car mechanic, medical doctors attempt to fix parts in isolation from the other parts. But our bodies are not machines; our brains are not computers. We are complex, energetic beings that respond to a holistic approach to healing."

In the first three lectures, the course summarized the clinical theory and framework for naturopathic practice. Georgie finds today's lecture the most fascinating but also difficult to grasp because it is so different from her prior experience and education.

"Vitalism has a long history in natural healing," Professor Blakes says, "pre-dating mechanism that took over as the predominant scientific philosophy early in the twentieth century. The medical community, with its mechanistic view, has vilified naturopathy for its basis in vitalism. But there is hope. Discoveries in quantum physics are bringing more acceptance of the role emotions and thoughts play in our physical health. Still, opinions in the medical establishment are slow to change."

It strikes Georgie that, years ago, the medical specialist thought the source of Debbie's illness was emotional trauma. Even though he took emotions into consideration, it was in error. As she listens to the professor, it seems clear the specialist still had a mechanist approach. He blamed Debbie's illness solely on emotions, so he was still viewing body systems in isolation and attempting to fix one part.

Professor Blake concludes the lecture by explaining how difficult it is for naturopaths to relate to someone with a mechanist approach to medicine. The topic hits close to home because Georgie knows her father holds the allopathic mechanist view of health and healing. No wonder she could not convince her father to accept her career choice. Their philosophies have diverged.

Georgie leaves the class and goes to the library for an hour's spare—an opportunity to cram for her Human Biochem quiz. Right now, her classes are well-spaced from Monday to Friday, with ample time in between for study. Of the eight courses offered in the first trimester, Georgie only has five. As the registrar promised, the school gave her credit for some medical school courses. This term she has another overview course, Fundamentals of Naturopathic Practice, about the regulations governing contemporary practice, which can vary state to state, and an introduction to managing patient consultations. The college required her to take the courses, Spine and the Extremities and Palpation Skills, because there is lab work that medical school did not offer. It surprised Georgie that naturopathic college trains students in physical therapy modalities. These therapies are less interesting to her, but it tells her the curriculum affords grads options for the focus of their practices.

Georgie's fifth course, Human Biochemistry, focuses on the structure and function of proteins, carbohydrates and fats and their reactions in the body's metabolic pathways. She recalls medical school had a four-hour lecture on this subject. In the naturopathic curriculum, the topic merits an entire course of study. A look ahead at the course schedule reveals there are several courses about the science of nutrition and human metabolism. The naturopathic curriculum focuses on how the human body interacts with food and the environment. Medicine focuses more on the diseases and conditions that afflict the human body. It's a fascinating shift in perspective.

Chapter 7

Georgie trudges through the snow to her Friday class after navigating slippery roads on the drive to campus. At least her drive is only ten minutes. Now, in the second trimester, she is more attuned to the life of a student, attending daily lectures and labs and studying most of her waking hours. As she expected, there are several mature students in the naturopathic program, and she got to know two women, Brenda and Katherine, also married with children. The three of them lunch together and, when not discussing course curriculum, commiserate about challenges in balancing school and home. With a full course load since the program's start, Brenda and Katherine have grumbled about the workload. To Georgie, their experience evokes the same anxiety she felt as a med student years ago, but with only six of eight courses in this trimester, she has yet to feel the pressure of a full course load. *How will I ever manage?*

The second last class of the day is Homeopathy I, in which they are learning about the founder of homeopathy, Samuel Hahnemann, and the classical application of homeopathy. The professor is explaining the philosophy behind homeopathy when Rob, a former medical student like Georgie, raises his hand. "Professor, I don't get this 'Law of Similars' and 'like cures like,'" he says. "It seems like you are giving patients a dose of the very thing that is causing the illness. How do homeopathic remedies actually help?"

"You raise a good question," the professor replies. "Homeopathy uses natural remedies to stimulate the body's own healing powers. Practitioners choose remedies based on the patients' symptoms to trigger a healing response. In homeopathy, we consider the symptoms as part of the healing process rather than something to suppress as pharmaceutical drugs do. The dilution and activation of homeopathic remedies promotes healing but, unlike drugs, have no side effects."

Rob nods his head but bears a quizzical look.

The professor nods and looks around the room. "I understand this may be a foreign concept for most of you. No doubt you are more accustomed to Western medicine. However, you will have two more courses in homeopathy, and the concepts will become clearer and equip you to use homeopathy in your practice. Not all grads of the program use it, but after twenty years as a homeopath, I can assure you using these remedies induces healing at the deepest level. You will benefit from learning all you can about homeopathy."

At the end of the class, the professor announces a mid-term quiz next Friday and some students groan. The professor smiles. "We have a lot of material to get through, and I need to know at regular intervals that you are grasping these concepts. What helped me in college was forming a study group of three or four students to quiz each other to prepare for tests and exams. I highly recommend you form study groups."

Georgie turns to Brenda and Katherine, who both nod their heads. There is a one-hour break until the last class of the day, and they gather in the student lounge to talk about how their study group might work.

"What about meeting on the weekend?" Brenda asks.

"Sorry, I go home to Terrance every weekend. If you want to ask someone else, I will understand," replies Georgie.

"I go home some weekends too," says Katherine, who is from Ohio and, like Georgie, rents a room locally.

"No problem. I'm sure we can organize a weeknight," says Brenda, who lives in Chicago. They agree to meet at Brenda's place Monday and Wednesday evenings starting next week. The Homeopathy quiz is looming and studying together will also help with Pharmacology, another challenging course.

Georgie leaves the last class and emerges from the building to biting wind whipping snow in her face. She stops in her tracks. There are already a few inches of snow on the ground and, with the wind, the road conditions and visibility on the interstate will be poor. *How can I drive home in this?* It's a scenario she worried could happen, but prayed would not. Her room rental deal with the Dodges does not include weekends.

Brenda is standing beside her and discerns the problem. "If you don't want to drive home in this weather, you can stay with me tonight. It's a fifteen-minute drive to my place, but at least you won't be on the interstate."

Georgie thanks Brenda and accepts the offer. A call to Dwayne's cell goes to his voice mail, and she leaves a message saying she will be home midday on Saturday.

The unplanned layover in Chicago affords some extra time to study together, but Brenda must wait until her children, aged seven and four, are in bed, which isn't until after eight o'clock. With a glimpse of Brenda's challenge in finding time to study, Georgie's trials seem pale in comparison. Her only challenge today is camping out on a living room couch a tad too short for her five-nine frame.

Before she crashes around eleven, Dwayne calls back. "We were out to dinner, and I had my ringer turned off. I'm glad you didn't drive home tonight. The roads are slippery."

Georgie asks after the kids.

"Same old, same old," says Dwayne.

Too tired to inquire what his comment means and the issues waiting at home, she says, "see you tomorrow." *I hope there is time to study this weekend.*

"Georgie, are you sure you don't want to go to your parents' for Thanksgiving? It's been your family's tradition since I've known you," Dwayne says. His family doesn't have this tradition. They rarely gather as a family, perhaps because his parents still run the hardware store and never take a day off. *Has Dwayne come to enjoy this tradition with my family?*

Georgie must shake off any concern for Dwayne's preferences. "I am sorry, but I don't have the energy and I have to study for finals. The expectations in this program are as high as there were in medical school, and I have a bigger course load now."

As Georgie feared, she feels overwhelmed by the full course schedule of nine courses in the fourth trimester. On her weekends at home, she has massive amounts of reading and studying for in-class quizzes. Classes ended last week to give students a chance to study for final exams and starting next week, she will have to write eight exams over six days. For the ninth course, a lab, there was an in-class exam on the last day of classes. Of most concern are the exams for Nutritional Biochemistry and Medical Microbiology. For nutritional biochemistry, she must memorize details about the how the human body processes nutrients, including energy production in cells. For microbiology, she must know the multitude of infectious agents and their associated disorders.

"If we go to Thanksgiving dinner, I will have to prepare a dish of food, maybe two," Georgie says. "My mother expects homemade, not store-bought. I would have to go grocery shopping and cook, and I just don't have the time. Then my mother will expect us to stay all afternoon to visit. You know how she disapproves of eating and running."

"I'm sure your mother will understand if you don't have time to cook." Dwayne gives a sideways glance. "Are you sure cooking is the reason you don't want to go?"

"Okay, it's not just about the cooking. I don't need family drama right now. Every time we go for a family dinner since I started school, it's the same. My father and sister hardly speak to me or look for ways to provoke me. Like at Easter, Linnie brought up a news story about how a patient sued a naturopath, as if there aren't a multitude of lawsuits against medical doctors." Georgie heaves an enormous sigh and plays her trump card. "And I would like to spend some time with you and the kids this weekend. I hardly have time to talk to you or them. Right now, I don't even know what's going on with them. Couldn't we have a nice at-home dinner?"

"It might upset the kids not seeing their cousins. I'm not sure they'll view an at-home Thanksgiving the way you do. But if you can convince them, I guess I can go along."

"That's curious. From my point of view, the kids spend most of the time at the family Thanksgiving watching football. True, it is with family members, but how is watching football together quality time?"

Dwayne smirks and shrugs his shoulders. "Hey! Thanksgiving and football go together!"

"I'm sure that's not what the pilgrims intended." Georgie laughs to make light of it.

Georgie does not share her family's fascination with football. She will go to a few of D.J.'s games, but just to support him. Because of football, every Thanksgiving after dinner, she has no choice but to spend hours talking with her mother and Linnie, neither of whom cares for the game. She knows how it will be—Linnie will monopolize the conversation, bragging about her kids' achievements or the success of her latest charity fundraiser. Georgie wouldn't mind if she had the same opportunity to share her successes and challenges, but since Linnie aligned with their father against her, there is no pretense she cares about Georgie's life.

"Dwayne, I don't want to ruin everyone else's enjoyment. If you, Daphne, and D.J. want to go, please do. I can beg off because of exams. Melanie always finds a reason not to go, and no one criticizes her. I think my reasons are more valid than hers."

"I guess that might work." Dwayne doesn't sound convinced. "Let's talk to the kids about it."

The Downies gather around the table for Thanksgiving dinner at home. It turned out Daphne and D.J. cared less about Thanksgiving dinner at their grandparents than Dwayne thought. Debbie is not home from school because she is also studying for final exams. Modern convenience came to the rescue when Dwayne found a restaurant offering takeout turkey dinner with all the fixings. It smells just like Claire's turkey dinner, but after a taste of the stuffing and gravy, Georgie judges it palatable but not up to her mother's standards.

During the meal, Georgie enjoys hearing her children's news—mostly it's about their successes in football and soccer. To her surprise, after dinner Daphne offers to clean up the kitchen. "I know you have to study for your exams, Mom."

Did Dwayne put her up to this? Georgie raises her eyebrows and glances at Dwayne, who just shrugs his shoulders. After giving her daughter a hug, Georgie goes upstairs to study at the desk in Debbie's old room. From the family room, she hears whistles and cheering, the unmistakable sounds of a football game.

First thing in the morning, Georgie's mother calls. "I am disappointed you and your family didn't come to Thanksgiving. Your father and I really missed you all."

"Mom! You must have noticed Dad hasn't talked to me for over a year. My presence just upsets him and puts a damper on the affair for everyone else.

And I don't need the aggravation. I need to focus on doing well at school, not repeatedly defending my decision."

"Oh dear, I don't think he means to exclude you. He is just set in his ways. He'll come around, eventually."

That's her mother—always trying to smooth things over.

"But Georgie, I missed seeing you. What about your poor old mother?"

Georgie stifles a laugh at her mother's feeble attempt at a guilt trip. "I am sorry, Mom. I hope it won't always be this way." Her plan to reduce stress by avoiding the family dinner did not work. Now she feels sorry for her mother, caught between her husband and daughter.

The bright spot of the weekend is a call from Melanie. "Hey, little sis! Happy Thanksgiving! How is school going?"

Thankful someone in her family is interested, Georgie says, "overall, good. It's a heavy course load—no surprise there. Believe it or not, Dwayne is getting better at dealing with the kids, and he's even cooking meals."

"That's great, but Georgie, I just spoke to Mom. She's upset you passed on the family's Thanksgiving, but I say good for you. You don't need the aggravation you're getting from Dad and Linnie."

"Thanks, Mel, I appreciate your support," Georgie says a silent prayer for Melanie—the family outcast who understands what it's like to be in her shoes. "But I'm not sure I can handle this much longer. It's almost like shunning, like the practice of some religious sects. My parents invite me to their home, but no one talks to me. It's like I'm not there."

"It's been like that for me for years; I'm used to it. You might say I've formed a family in New York and that's how it is for many people. We don't always jibe with our blood relatives. I think someone once said something profound about that. Hm. If I find the quote, I'll email it to you."

"Hey. Here's my big news," Melanie says, switching topics. "I sold two of my paintings at the Greater New York art show. This sale is going to pay my rent for the next three months."

"Congratulations, Mel! I'm so happy for you." Georgie admires her sister's courage, having no reliable income yet staying true to her dream as an artist after years of struggle and without family support. *At least I have Dwayne.*

Later in the evening, she has an email from Melanie. "I found the quote. It's by Maya Angelou. *Family isn't always blood. It's the people in your life who want you in theirs: the ones who accept you for who you are, the ones who would do anything to see you smile, and who love you no matter what.* But you can always count on this blood relative! Love, Mel."

Georgie types her reply: "Love the sentiment. Thanks, big sis!" She re-reads the quote, wondering if she will have to find a family that isn't blood related. Lisa is the only one who might fit the description but, for now, there is little time for that relationship. Melanie likely sent the quote to be encouraging, but it reminds Georgie how alone she feels.

"Welcome to the University Naturopathic Clinic," says Dr. Miles, the clinic director. "You will spend the next three months in this clinic working with patients, learning how to apply what you have learned in class. I will assign you to a supervising naturopath after you spend a few shifts with me. We like to match students with NDs with similar interests. You will be here eight hours each week, first to observe, and take on more responsibilities for patient care. Questions? No? Good!"

After two and a half years into the program, Georgie is weary of sitting in lectures, learning theories and practice protocols. The prospect of working with live patients is exciting but also anxiety-provoking—this is where the rubber meets the road. In her first two-hour shift, she shadows Dr. Miles in his consultations, intrigued by how he talks to his patients, and the therapies he recommends. One patient has Lyme disease for which the naturopath prescribes several immune supportive remedies and diet restrictions. Georgie studiously takes notes.

The next patient is distraught from constant itching that disturbs her waking and sleeping hours. She is also upset the medical doctor's expensive creams and antihistamines did not solve the problem. It impresses Georgie how Dr. Miles takes his time with the patient going over her health history, diet, work, and family situation. For this patient, he starts with a hypoallergenic diet and a natural anti-inflammatory remedy, then schedules a follow-up appointment to assess progress and determine next steps. When the patient leaves, Dr. Miles asks Georgie what she suspects is the root cause of the itching. It's her first day, and Georgie is nervous about offering an opinion. "Symptoms suggest an allergy," she says. "If the special diet and supplement doesn't make a difference by the next visit, I expect you would explore environmental agents as a probable cause."

"Right," says Dr. Miles, smiling. "I would call the patient before the next appointment. If the itching has not subsided with my initial protocol, I would ask her to bring her cleaning and personal care products to her appointment. With a skin reaction, often it can be something the patient is using every day."

Georgie is a month into her second internship at the free clinic run by the Salvation Army where she spends fifteen hours each week. Most patients using this clinic cannot afford remedies, which means she must focus her interventions on diet changes. It reminds her of what her professor in Clinical Nutrition said, that the first therapy should always be nutrition, finding the right diet for the individual's needs. He warned the class about rushing to prescribe remedies before ensuring diet was ideal. To prove his point, he quoted the Greek philosopher Hippocrates: "Let food be thy medicine, and let medicine be thy food."

To rely on diet changes in healing protocols is a challenge because her clinic patients, so far, have serious health issues: diabetes, Graves' disease, and recovery from a stroke. Today she sees a sixty-five-year-old woman with osteoarthritis who seems embarrassed she cannot afford any supplements or remedies. Georgie recommends an anti-inflammatory diet and explains how this will ease the woman's suffering.

The woman frowns as she reads the diet sheet. "What, no tomatoes or potatoes? That's half of my diet!"

Georgie suggests some alternatives from the diet sheet but, based on the woman's comments, is doubtful she will make the changes.

For the last half-hour of her shift, she goes through her cases with her supervisor, Dr. Rouse. Perhaps Georgie's favorite intern supervisor, Dr. Rouse, is dedicated to using the healing power of foods.

"Georgina, I assure you the anti-inflammatory diet will help the patient with arthritis," Dr. Rouse says. "I have seen it more than once. Often joint inflammation is all about diet."

Georgie nods, reflecting on the patient's stated preference for tomatoes and potatoes, vegetables in the nightshade family known to be pro inflammatory.

"You don't need to jump to remedies until you address diet and nutrition," Dr. Rouse says. "Just appreciate responses to diet changes take time. You will need to be clear with your patients not to expect results right away. Impatience is the primary reason people give up on diet protocols."

After her shift, her supervisor's comment about impatience reminds Georgie of the surprise announcement Daphne made the previous weekend. In September Daphne went to college for liberal arts on a soccer scholarship, but on Saturday morning, only six weeks into the program, she arrived home and announced she was dropping out. Dwayne was furious but did not want to deal with Daphne and left Georgie to reason with their middle child.

"Mom, I understand you believe in higher education, but I just wasn't learning anything worthwhile. I want to learn languages, and you can't do that in a language lab. It will be so much better to travel to countries where they speak the languages I want to learn." Daphne had it all planned out. She would work for four months, save her money, then backpack through France, Spain, and Switzerland to learn Spanish and French from the locals. She would pick up jobs under the table and come home when the money runs out.

Georgie questioned Daphne about giving up on her college program so soon. But, since that no longer seemed negotiable, she focused on the feasibility of her daughter's travel plans. "How do you know there will be odd jobs under the table? What if you don't have enough money to get home? And you're all alone. It will be dangerous."

But Daphne claimed to have it "all figured out." A friend from school would go with her and they would stay at hostels, of which there were many scattered throughout Europe. She stubbornly waved off all her parent's valid concerns for her safety. After one heated exchange with Dwayne, Daphne said, "I'm eighteen in February. You can't stop me then." Even though it seemed like a crazy scheme, Daphne was determined to proceed. Had she inherited her Aunt Melanie's free-spirited ways? Georgie could only hope over the next four months she could talk Daphne out of her travel schemes.

Chapter 8

The house is quiet. Dwayne, Daphne, and D.J. are already out for the day and Georgie stretches out in bed, no alarm to jolt her awake, no classes or timelines to meet. The sun coming through the blinds is welcoming, as if nature is inviting her to a new adventure. The past three years at naturopathic college afforded her few mornings like this. With the unrelenting demands of the curriculum, and more recently, the required internships, she did not have time to savor her mornings. Once she completed the course requirements, she had to study for her licensing exams. It is seven days since she took those exams, and she is still catching up on sleep.

This morning, she looks forward to taking Shadow for a leisurely walk, having had limited opportunities for this while at school. "I'm really out of shape," she says to the dog lying beside the bed. A thump, thump of his tail on the floor suggests he agrees with her assessment. How ironic. She studied to be a naturopath to help others be healthy, and her own health may have suffered.

The chime of the doorbell interrupts her musings. *Who could be at her door so early?* She checks the clock radio—only eight-thirty. Jumping out of bed, she throws on pants and a T-shirt, bounds down the stairs, and opens the door to a courier with a letter requiring her signature. The letterhead on the envelope says: North American Board of Naturopathic Examiners. It will be the scores from her NPLEX license exams that covered four days testing her knowledge on theory and applications in naturopathic practice. On the first day, there was a five-hour exam covering anatomy, physiology, biology, immunology, and pathology. Then there were three consecutive days of exams on clinical application—diagnostics and developing therapeutic plans for twelve different case scenarios using diet, nutritional supplements, homeopathy, botanicals, and lifestyle. Georgie had studied for a month in preparation. In response to Dwayne's inquiry, "how did your exams go?" Georgie had a one-word response: "brutal."

Placing the letter on the dining room table, she clasps her hands, then shakes them out. She retreats to the kitchen to make coffee, hoping her favorite hot beverage will provide strength for the letter's contents. Breathing in the coffee's rich aroma, she takes a sip and returns to the table, regarding the letter that holds the key to her future.

Georgie was the oldest in her class of forty and one of only ten women. Of the women who started the program, only six made it to the end that thankfully included her friends, Brenda and Katherine. She didn't know why the other four women dropped out, but she guessed it was the heavy workload. Georgie studied harder than many of her younger classmates, judging by stories of their weekend exploits. The internships were demanding of time and energy too. In the last twelve months, she spent three to five days a week interning at three different clinics in Chicago. When not with patients, there were long hours of study to identify remedies and protocols. Performance appraisals came from clinic directors, one of whom Georgie found difficult to please, often suggesting a different protocol than she had recommended. Her assessment from her last internship module was not as good as she had hoped. Prior to that, her grades in course work put her in the middle of the class.

Part of her stress while at school was because of the continued estrangement from her father. She has not been to her parents' home in over two years. Her mother calls every week, but her father has not contacted her, leaving her primary sources of support in Dwayne and Lisa. After the first year in school, Georgie realized making time for her friend was therapeutic. On most Saturdays, they would meet for lunch at Henrietta's, a chance to talk about things other than school—the latest news, movies, or hijinks by one of their kids. That was the extent of her social life, apart from Sunday morning worship services.

It took Dwayne a while to embrace parenting and housekeeping responsibilities. Georgie suspects he got the message after her ultimatum eight months into the program—if she had to continue handling crises with their teenagers, she would not pass her courses. Dwayne surprised her by learning to cook a few healthy meals, not just microwaving frozen entrees. That allowed her to focus on her studies on her weekends at home. Were all these efforts worthwhile?

The moment of truth is upon her. With two more gulps of coffee, she plucks up some courage and slits the envelope open. She reads through the letter twice to make sure she is understanding. She passed! Not only passed, but with a grade of eighty-six percent, well over the minimum passing grade of seventy-five percent. All the emotion and tension bottled up from the past three-plus years spills out. She grips the letter and cries tears of joy and relief. With news so momentous, she wants to see the look on her family's faces and bides her time waiting until they come home.

Georgie is waiting at the door when Dwayne arrives. Brandishing her letter, she jumps up and down like an exuberant child and leaps into his arms.

"Well, this calls for a celebration!" Dwayne says. "Let's go out to dinner." He is excited for her, but Georgie also sees relief on his face, likely at the prospect of fewer responsibilities at home.

"Way to go, Mom! I knew you could do it!" Daphne says. "Where should we go out to eat? I know a great vegan place we need to try."

Have her father's meals bored her? They are heavily focused on meat and Daphne prefers vegetarian.

D.J. has tryouts for the summer football league and runs in the door just as they are ready to go out. "Hey, great, Mom! Does this restaurant have burgers?"

The only place that can appeal to both her kids' preferences is Henrietta's. And, as it is her celebration, everyone agrees they should go to Georgie's favorite place. While waiting for their meals, Daphne disappears and returns with a smug look on her face, closed-mouthed about where she was. The mystery is soon solved when three restaurant staff appear singing a congratulations song and serving Georgie a cupcake with a candle in it. "The best we could do on short notice," the owner says to Georgie.

Back at home after dinner, Georgie takes time to reflect on her family. With little time for them over the past three years, have they sacrificed for her career goals? Debbie is okay. She is in teachers' college and practice teaching in Fort Wayne. Georgie is not worried about her oldest, but the other two give her pause.

Perhaps if Georgie had been at home, she could have talked Daphne out of her trip to Europe. True to her word, Daphne worked from November to March, saved enough for plane fare and lodging, and then flew to Paris in April. With only sporadic emails from Daphne to assure her parents she was okay, Georgie had worried. She was furious about the distraction at a time she needed to focus on her final internship and studying for her licensing exam. Two weeks ago, Daphne returned after two months touring France and Switzerland, claiming success in finding work in a restaurant and at a farm. When she returned, she was clear about her intention to work for as long as it takes to save money for another trip. The second day home, she landed a job at a local pub and spends her off hours in online chats with Bridget, her travel companion, about where they will go next.

D.J. remains focused on sports, playing basketball, football, and baseball. While at school, Georgie only made it to one or two of his games. Is D.J. resentful? It is difficult to tell because he now has a young man's bravado—it's not cool to admit needing one's mother at games. In the coming fall, he will be a senior in high school and still unsure what he wants to do. Dwayne has been after him to think about college, but D.J. has resisted the pressure, saying: "Just let me enjoy my senior year. There's lots of time to decide on college. I could work for a while until I figure out what to do."

Throughout high school, D.J. has been a star on the football team, but his grades remain below average. His chance for a college scholarship for football faded after he let his grades slip this year. Dwayne was livid and railed at his son. "You're spending too much time partying. You need to keep your grades up if you want a scholarship. That's how I made it to college." But the message seemed lost on D.J. He continues to be focused on the moment, enjoying all the adulation high school culture gives to football players.

During Christmas break, Georgie reminded D.J. about the importance of education, but he had an answer ready. "Mom, you first went to college years ago, and it didn't work out for you. Why can't I take some time to decide?" Georgie had no basis to argue the point and, with a twinge of guilt, realized her false start at med school may have provided her son an excuse to avoid post secondary school. She never talked to her kids about why she left medical school because it might sound like she regrets having kids. She doesn't! Recently, Georgie made the tough decision to stop pushing D.J.

about college, recalling how the pressure her father placed on her turned out. Still, Georgie remains concerned only one of her three children is interested in higher education. She sees postsecondary education as a necessity. They seem to think of it as one of many options.

It's Sunday and Georgie is eager for some time in prayer and reflection with her church community. Today, Pastors Rick's message is about letting go of judgment, which leads Georgie to confess to herself that she has been judging her children's choices. As her children grew up, she expected parenting would be easier, but it has turned out to be a balancing act between providing guidance and allowing her kids to find their way, even make mistakes. When she has time, she wants to talk to the pastor about this dilemma. *Do a lot of parents struggle with this?*

Lisa is at church, too. At fellowship time, Georgie shares with her friend the good news about her licensing exam. Lisa gives Georgie a lingering hug, saying, "I knew you could do it!"

"But Lisa, something is really bothering me. Neither Daphne nor D.J. are following in my footsteps in higher education. Daphne might still get back to college, but I'm worried D.J. will never get there because of his grades. He's going to get a job when he graduates. Have I indulged him—not demanded enough of him? Was I so focused on my education that I didn't encourage him enough?" She doesn't wait for an answer. "Of course, I put some blame on those football scouts who made him believe he would have a scholarship, but never warned him about the grade requirements. With so-so grades, he has no chance of a scholarship. If he wants to attend college, we can't afford the tuition, at least not until I can get my practice going."

Lisa cuts in. "Georgie, what D.J. does is not all because of you. Look at my Kim. She's taking a break after college, working menial jobs and enjoying her leisure time. I'm not blaming myself, and nor should you. As for D.J., working before college might be just what he needs. He'll find out how hard it is to make a living without a degree or training. Better to learn that sooner rather than later!"

Georgie waggles her head from side to side and purses her lips. "Perhaps, but it seems so obvious to me that college is essential."

"Sure, but some kids should take a break after high school. One of my clients' kids went to college right out of high school, and in his sophomore year, changed his major. He had to start all over again and, with the added tuition costs, I don't know how the parents are managing."

Georgie sighs, recognizing the truth of what her friend is saying. Lisa always makes good arguments. She would have made an excellent lawyer.

Lisa lays her hand on Georgie's arm. "In the end, kids don't do what you say, they do what you do. And you and Dwayne are superb role models. They'll find their niche, eventually. It just may not be when you want it to happen."

Georgie gives a nervous laugh. For a moment, she feels some sympathy for her father's disappointment in her own choices.

The house is empty when Georgie returns home and she takes the dog for a walk in the woods. Her senses drink in the verdant scene of the forest canopy, birdsong bringing the woods to life and the sweet fragrance of wildflowers and fresh growth. As she strides along the path, she breathes in rhythm with her steps, trying to still her mind. But worries about her kids niggle into her thoughts. They aren't youngsters anymore, and she has little control over them. She can only hope Lisa is right, that her kids will eventually follow her example.

On Monday, Georgie's mother invites her over after lunch. Georgie sits in her car for a few minutes, reluctant to go in, wondering how her father will receive her.

Claire greets her at the door. "Your father wants to speak with you."

Here it comes! Georgie follows her mother into the living room, where her father is seated waiting for her.

"Congratulations, Georgina." Her father nods with a fleeting smile. "Though I disagreed with your choice of education, I am proud you saw it through and that you did well."

Her mother has obviously passed on the news about her licensing exam. Georgie gapes at her father, that he is even talking to her. "Dad, thank you for saying this. You know, I worked hard for my grades."

"So, what's next?" her father asks, leaning forward.

"I'm getting my head around building a practice," Georgie replies, uncertain how much to share for fear her father will have an opening to criticize. "You may not know this, but setting up a naturopathic practice will differ from a medical practice. I won't have patients lined up right away when I hang out my shingle."

"I know. That is one reason I didn't want you to study naturopathy. But now you've done it, and you'll have to make the best of it."

There it is! Her father has not changed his tune. Perhaps her mother pushed him to give his congratulations, but what he really wanted was to pour cold water on her career choice again. Georgie's heart sinks. She excuses herself with a vague reference of "things to do at home," but before she leaves, she can't resist giving some attitude of her own.

"You may not see much of me. I expect I will be as busy as I was at school—out there trying to make the best of it!"

To distract from the distressing encounter with her father, Georgie busies herself with some spring cleaning that may not have happened last year, judging by the grime on the windows and the dust bunnies under the furniture. Often busy hands help push aside worries, but not this time—she can't stop fretting over her father's criticisms.

Dwayne arrives home, makes his usual martini and sits at the kitchen island watching Georgie prepare dinner. A smile of satisfaction replaces his usual serious expression. "Are you ready for the next step? Finding a clinic to set up your practice?"

Georgie senses his comment has an undertone, "finally, you can start contributing to the family income again!" She bristles at the pressure coming so soon, less than a week after hearing she passed her exams, but she tempers her irritation. Dwayne has made many sacrifices. The expense of her tuition and lodging meant three years of no vacations, no new car, no new anything!

After dinner, Georgie gets on her computer to search for clinics within an hour of Terrance. That is Plan A: Find a clinic seeking a new associate. Plan B is setting up a private practice but that will require considerable investment, which Dwayne is unlikely to support. She will have to find a clinic in need of a new associate. By bedtime, she has compiled three packages with a résumé, her license exam results, and a cover letter for naturopathic clinics within an hour's drive.

Perched on a stool at the kitchen island, head in her hands, Georgie feels like the world is crashing down around her. In the past two weeks, she learned none of the nearby clinics were looking for new associates. Fearing Dwayne's displeasure, she lacks the courage to give him this news. She calls Lisa to cry on her shoulder.

"Come on over," Lisa says. "I have a few business details to finish up, and then we can talk over an espresso."

Georgie heads over to Lisa's right away and waits a few minutes in the hallway. Lisa works from home, an arrangement Georgie envies—no commuting required. After a few minutes, Lisa appears. "Sorry, I had a last-minute phone call, a client in a rush for their order, you know how it is with…" She stops mid-sentence, noticing Georgie's crumpled face. "What is going on? Did somebody die?"

"Nobody is dying… except my career… and before it's even started," she says through sobs. "There are zero opportunities for me. Dwayne is going to have a fit."

Lisa finishes brewing the espresso, hands one to Georgie, sits down next to her with a hand on her arm. "Hey, there is always hope. You know what they say—it's who you know. I'm going to call my new naturopath Philip Rice and put in a good word for you. He purchased the practice from Dr. Young, who retired last year. The practice is busy, so maybe they could take you on. I assume you called there."

Georgie shakes her head. "I called that clinic first, and I didn't get past the receptionist."

"Dr. Rice may not even know you called. I'll get in touch with him and, even if he can't take you on right now, you could ask his advice about how to get your practice going. He knows a lot about that. He had a practice in Chicago for fifteen years before coming here."

Georgie peers at her friend. "Are you sure? I don't want to put you in an awkward position."

Lisa waves her hand. "It's no trouble. I will mention you to Dr. Rice. I'm sure he can help."

"Thanks! I do hope so. My options are practically nil."

Lisa excuses herself to take a business call, and Georgie makes her way home, feeling despondent. If the clinics don't need new associates, perhaps there is not enough demand for naturopathic doctors. Plan B no longer seems like an option. Even if she could afford to open her own clinic, there may be a limited demand for naturopaths in the area. Otherwise, the existing clinics would have openings. Her only other option is to approach clinics at a distance, but that would mean a daily commute of an hour or more each way, not something she welcomes. And she can predict word for word what Dwayne will say. "Georgie, how could you spend all that time and money on college without considering the opportunities in the profession? I thought you did market research on this!" And he would be right.

Chapter 9

Georgie arrives for her interview with Dr. Rice, impressed that it only took a week for Lisa to set this up. The clinic is in a strip mall on a busy street near the commercial district. Over the door, a plain white and black sign reads: Naturopathic Clinic. She enters to a waiting room with three chairs, a small reception desk, and down a narrow hallway, spies three office doors and a meeting room towards the rear. The color of the walls is a nondescript gray. Dingy and depressing are the words that spring to her mind—not the ambience Georgie would choose for a health care office. The only sources of cheer are the large schefflera plant by the window in the waiting room, and soft music playing. This office space is not the one Georgie recalls from when she took Debbie to Dr. Young. Lisa mentioned that Dr. Rice moved the clinic location after he took over.

Dr. Rice welcomes her into his office. He has a stocky build and a receding hairline—he looks to be in his fifties. Peering over his glasses with a serious expression, he reminds Georgie of the stereotypical demeanor of a doctor. He asks her the standard interview questions. Why did you get into this field? Where do you see yourself in five years? Georgie is expecting such questions and hopes her prepared answers will impress the clinic owner. His deadpan expression gives her no sign. Next, he asks about her time as the office manager in Dr. Randall's medical practice. Surprised by the question, she gives a few details about her eight years in the role.

Dr. Rice smiles with a magnanimous air. "I have an offer for you. What would you think about taking the office manager position at three-quarter time and slowly building up your patient roster? We can put your name and credentials on the door and the website, so your name gets out there. It's a way to ease into your practice and have some income while you are doing it."

Uncertain what to say, Georgie gapes at him while he explains how his office manager quit last week with no notice. No doubt she was the one Georgie spoke to when she called the clinic about an opening. She was brusque, almost rude—perhaps she had one foot out the door.

Georgie doesn't want to appear ungrateful, but this is not the offer she is seeking. "Ah, I will have to think about it, Dr. Rice. I have just started my search for a position. Can I take some time to think about it?"

Dr. Rice grimaces and shakes his head. "I'm not sure how much time I can give you. I'm in great need of a new office manager now. Dr. Thom and I are taking turns covering the front desk, which means we must reduce our patient consultations. I really need an answer in a couple of days."

Georgie promises to give him a decision by Friday. As she leaves his office, her heart is heavy, her spirit crushed. This offer feels like a step backward, as if the past three years of study, stress, and sacrifice are meaningless. How would she sell it to Dwayne? And her father? She would never hear the end of "I told you so." Back at home, she stews over it for a couple of hours, no closer to knowing the right move. *I need another opinion.* She calls Melanie.

"I can't talk long. I have paint all over my hands, and my phone doesn't have a hands-free option," Melanie says. "Right now, I'm creating phone art. Maybe it's a new thing!" She chuckles. "What's up?"

"There's only one clinic opportunity in Terrance, but they want me to be their part-time office manager while building up my practice. I don't know whether to take it or continue my search, which would have to be out of town. The clinic director only gave me a couple of days for my answer. What do you think I should do?"

"Hm. Here is what I know. When I started as an artist, I had to compromise—work at jobs I didn't like so I could afford art supplies. Hey, at least you'd have some income."

This isn't what Georgie wants to hear. Next, she calls her mother.

"I watched your father build his practice, and it was a while before we had enough money to live on," Claire says. "I took in children to babysit. You wouldn't remember because it happened before you were born. Often it is best to take something than wait for the ideal situation that may not exist."

"But, Mom, this situation is a lot less than ideal. It's like taking an office clerk's job when you're qualified to manage the office."

"If you take the job, do you want me to tell your father? I can be vague about the details of the position—give you some time to get your practice going."

Georgie has always thought her father ruled the Novak household, but it is clear her mother does behind-the-scenes management. She thanks her mother and ends the call. Staring at the phone, she searches for a source of optimism. *Maybe I will get some patients before Dad finds out I am back in an office manager's job.*

While waiting for Dwayne to come home from work, Georgie rehearses how she will break the news about her unusual offer and her only option.

"Hm. I suppose it's a start," Dwayne says, when Georgie tells him after dinner. "Of course, it's up to you, but just be sure it's the best offer out there. I will not object for now because it will help the finances."

Georgie's disappointment is palpable. The three family members she always relied on for support have said, at least indirectly, she doesn't deserve more than a return to being an office clerk. After spending Thursday morning rechecking with all the clinics within driving distance, Georgie has no choice but to accept Dr. Rice's offer.

The situation at the clinic has been a source of discontent for a while. Georgie asked to speak to Dr. Rice, and he gives her a few minutes between patients.

"Dr. Rice, it's been almost six months, and I've only had five patients. I ran ads in the local newspaper with minimal response. Even though my name and credentials are on the door, I suspect patients view me as the office manager, rather than a qualified naturopath. And there is something else that bothers me. You and Dr. Thom have full appointment schedules, yet neither of you refer any patients to me."

"It's not up to us to give you patients. It's *your* practice and *you* will have to promote yourself."

"Dr. Rice, you have a good practice, there's no doubt. I've noticed you have a lot of word-of-mouth referrals. People call the office asking for you all the time. Very few people call who are not direct referrals to you or Dr.

Thom. That means I must promote myself outside the clinic. Do you have advice on how to market myself?"

"Every new practitioner must figure out how to promote themselves. No one explained to me how to build a practice."

Georgie stares at her clinic director, exasperated by his attitude, like he has trade secrets he won't reveal. But she can't leave it there. "There was a course on marketing at college and there are different strategies I could try, but I would appreciate hearing what worked best when you started your practice."

Dr. Rice eyes her as if measuring her resolve. "Promotional talks—at least one every week."

Georgie's jaw drops and shakes her head. *Why hasn't he mentioned this before?* It confirms what she suspected. Dr. Rice likes her in the office manager role, and if her naturopathic practice grows, he will have to find someone else to run the office. For the rest of her workday, she goes through the motions of her job. She leaves the office for the day with a heavy heart. *I'm wasting my time here.*

In the evening, she checks the naturopathic association website, something she does regularly to keep abreast of new openings. To her delight, a clinic in Indianapolis has just posted an opening for a new associate. She doesn't stop to think about the commuting distance—seventy-five miles—and emails her application. There is no need to tell Dwayne yet. Nothing may come of it, anyway.

Georgie arrives at the Caroll Clinic for her interview as a clinic associate. It is only six days since she submitted her application, and it's encouraging things are moving along so fast. The clinic is on a well-traveled road near the downtown in a converted three-story home likely once considered stately. Two mature trees shade the front of the house, a rustic wooden sign inscribed with Caroll Clinic the only outward evidence this is not a family home anymore. The parking lot is at the rear, taking up what used to be the backyard. Georgie enters the front door to a large front lobby, noticing no more traffic noise from the street—the walls of the old house must be thick. Surveying the scene, Georgie admires the restored oak trim, oversized windows, and high ceilings, décor that exudes confidence and permanence, like the clinic has been there for a long time.

Because it is after office hours, there is no receptionist, but within minutes a man strides towards her from the hallway, smiles, and shakes her hand firmly. "Welcome. I'm Mark Caroll, the clinic owner." He is of average height with an athletic build and sports a buzz cut. Georgie guesses him to be in his late forties, but he could be older. When someone is in good physical shape, they can appear younger than they are. She likes his personal greeting—first name, no doctor title—indicative of a man who does not need to aggrandize his accomplishments.

To Georgie's surprise, Dr. Caroll takes her on a tour of the clinic before her interview. This seems out of order, but gives the impression he genuinely means his "welcome." Beyond the spacious waiting room are four large offices plus two smaller treatment rooms with massage tables, perhaps for acupuncture. Georgie read on the clinic website that one practitioner offers this therapy. On the stairway to the second floor, there is a lift for those with mobility issues, a sign of care and concern for patients. Upstairs, Dr. Caroll shows her a conference room with a kitchenette and a large room with ten recliner chairs, what he calls the cancer therapy room. Both rooms feature natural light from tall windows and skylights, the result of opening the ceilings into the third storey of the house.

They settle into padded swivel chairs in the conference room, and Mark Caroll asks Georgie a series of questions about her background, professional interests, and goals. He doesn't seem deterred by her lack of experience and seems more focused on getting to know her as a person. To his question about what she has done so far to build her practice, she admits "just a few ads."

"Here's what I know," he says. "It's all about making connections with potential patients. Early in my practice, I did promotional talks in the community, and joined local clubs and organizations."

Georgie's eyes widen in amazement at his willingness to give helpful advice during an interview. It bodes well for the support she might have should she join the clinic. To prepare for the interview, she read the clinic's website and learned of Dr. Caroll's credentials. He has been in practice for over twenty years, much of that time specializing in complementary cancer care. She also learned the clinic has two other naturopaths who offer other therapies. Knowing it is impressive to have her own questions ready, she asks why he is seeking a new associate and how busy a new associate could expect to be.

"All three of us have waiting lists," Mark Caroll replies. "The new associate will receive patient referrals from the other naturopaths on day one."

At hearing this, Georgie has trouble containing her excitement. *Don't get ahead of yourself. He isn't offering you the position yet.* Next, he asks if she has other questions.

"Not a question, just an admission. If you invite me to join the clinic, I won't be moving to Indianapolis. But I am okay with commuting."

Mark Caroll nods and smiles, giving no hint whether this would factor into his decision. Georgie prays this detail won't hurt her chances, but it's better he knows this before he makes an offer.

On the way out, Dr. Caroll introduces her to the other two naturopaths, Pam Samuels and Roger Brownlee, who apparently stayed late just to meet Georgie. The two naturopaths couldn't be more different. Pam smiles and shakes Georgie's hand. "So nice to meet you, Georgina." She appears to be in her late forties, a sturdy build, with short, prematurely gray hair. Roger is distinguished looking with gray hair at the temples and bears a solemn expression. "Good to meet you," he says, offering his fingertips to shake. Mark Caroll escorts Georgie to the door and says, "I'll be making my decision in a couple of days. I'll be calling you." The last thing he says immediately strikes Georgie as a sign she is a front runner, or perhaps already has the position.

While driving home on the interstate on a rainy evening, she tries to imagine doing this commute five days a week. If she joins this clinic, it will mean a one hour drive each way, perhaps more in rush hour. She is leery about driving alone on the busy road, especially in winter when storms can come up without warning. But she likes the clinic owner and the atmosphere in the office. *Dare I hope for an offer?*

Georgie's cell phone rings as she is leaving the Rice Clinic at the end of her workday. The call display reads Caroll Clinic. Her breath quickens as she rushes to her car to take the call in private. It's only been two days since her interview.

"It's Mark Caroll, calling. Georgina, I would like to invite you to join our clinic. Are you still interested?"

"Yes, I sure am!" Georgie hopes she doesn't sound like a schoolgirl being asked to the prom.

Dr. Caroll quotes the rent for the office space and other organizational details that Georgie can't recall after the call ends. She is too excited. Of course, she must get Dwayne on board.

After dinner, she takes Dwayne aside in his office to tell him of the offer from Caroll Clinic. Before he can say anything, she makes a sales pitch—mentioning the clinic's success and her favorable impression of the clinic owner.

Dwayne rocks back in his chair, his expression unreadable. "Hm. I know you're not progressing at Dr. Rice's clinic, and you need to get your practice going. If this clinic is your only opportunity, I guess you should go for it. I mean, I'm not keen on your driving on the interstate and the long hours you will be away, but what choice do we have?"

Dwayne's guarded approval is disappointing, but Georgie doesn't let that dampen her enthusiasm for what is her first big break into her chosen field.

On Georgie's first day at the Caroll clinic, while she is organizing her office, Pam arrives at her door with the files for ten referrals. They chat a moment and Georgie learns Pam has been in practice for six years, working mostly with older adults. Georgie likes Pam's smile and the impression she gives of being calm, confident, and wise—likely how she gains the trust of her patients. Dr. Caroll has a busy practice in complementary cancer care. From him, Georgie already received two patients who need onetime coaching on an immune-supportive diet. Since he seldom has time for nutrition coaching, he said he will have more referrals like this. Roger, the third naturopath, practices Chinese medicine, uses acupuncture, and assists Dr. Caroll with cancer patients. He offered no referrals, saying, "my unique specialties make referrals inappropriate." However, in Dr. Caroll's offer to join the clinic, he promised Georgie most of the new patients at the clinic unless they are older adults, seeking cancer care, acupuncture, or Chinese medicine.

Georgie spends a few hours going through the files for Pam's referrals and discovers most of the patients have multiple health issues, which will require some research on alternate therapies. She sets up appointments with three of the patients for the following week. Karen, the office manager, advises her that Mark's cancer patients, who need nutritional counseling, have appointments with her on Friday. Georgie opens the files for these patients to acquaint herself with their health history.

In the afternoon, with nothing else to do for patients, she takes Mark Caroll's advice and works on crafting a promotional talk. She has never given speeches or seminars before, nor done any sales or marketing. There was one course in marketing at naturopathic college, but knowing and doing something, she now realizes, are two different things. After several hours, she makes little progress in developing a promotional talk. Frustrated, she takes her concerns to Dr. Caroll, who is so busy she must wait until the end of clinic hours when he is about to leave.

"Dr. Caroll, I'm struggling with topics for my presentation. As a new practitioner with less than a year's experience, I'm afraid I won't impress anyone with what I have to say. How can I promote my services with so little clinical experience?"

"That is always a challenge for new practitioners, but Georgie, you have something going for you—your passion for healing. It's the primary reason I brought you into the clinic."

"Thank you for the vote of confidence. But will a passion for healing be enough to attract new patients? Don't they want to know that I can help them?"

Dr. Caroll motions to Georgie to join him in his office, opens a file cabinet and pulls out a big folder. "Here are copies of my presentations from twenty years ago when I was new to the profession. You are welcome to use whatever material you want from these."

Once again, the clinic director impresses Georgie with his willingness to help, a stark contrast to her former clinic director. Except perhaps for Dr. Brownlee, everyone at the clinic has been welcoming and helpful.

The next day, Georgie spends several hours reading Dr. Caroll's presentations. They are interesting, but most focus on his area of interest—immune suppression and cancer. One of his talks he titled, Why Naturopathy? highlighting the philosophy and benefits of naturopathic medicine. She already knows that, for many people, it is a leap of faith to consult with a naturopath, just like she did with Debbie years ago. Even now, most people's experience is with a medical doctor, and they don't know what to expect from a naturopath. Georgie decides she can use this topic.

Arriving home at eight-thirty, Georgie is tired and discouraged after giving her first promotional talk at the public library. It took her two months to secure the space at the library, but only five people came, and no one asked about a consultation. It's of minor consolation, but perhaps the cold and threat of bad weather kept people at home. Her drive home seemed longer than usual as she pondered what she could have done better with her presentation.

The house is quiet except for the sound of some sporting event on TV, where she finds D.J. sprawled on the couch, munching on a big bag of chips. There is no sign of Dwayne. "Don't you have homework or some studying to do?" Georgie yells over her shoulder as she peers into the nearly empty refrigerator.

"Nope," comes the reply.

D.J. will finish his senior year in a few months and, in Georgie's view, should be more concerned about his studies. She shakes her head, still searching for something to eat. The sandwich wrap she had at five o'clock would not see her through the evening. What did D.J. eat for dinner? There are no dirty dishes, so she must assume it was just chips, but maybe she can't blame him. The fridge doesn't have much to offer. She finds one tired looking apple and starts munching on it just as Dwayne comes in the door.

"Where have you been?" Georgie asks. "I doubt D.J. has eaten a proper dinner."

"I'm running a business! Today, a client demanded his financials right away, and I had to take care of it or pay someone else for the overtime. I don't need you coming at me, too."

"I know, I know. So, we both have demanding careers. But I have a tiring commute at the end of my day."

Dwayne glares at her. "And whose fault is that? And for what? Your fees barely cover your expenses, or perhaps you didn't think I would notice." He stomps into his study and slams the door.

Georgie now understands the source of her husband's outburst. It's money, again! But for her even-tempered spouse, this churlish behavior is out of character.

Dwayne announces on Saturday morning he has "work to catch up on," and disappears into his den. It seems a thinly veiled excuse and more to do with his discontent from two days ago. Georgie is left with all the grocery shopping, laundry, housecleaning, and cooking, and it occurs to her while fighting the weekend crowd in the grocery store that Dwayne was more supportive while she was in college. Now it's like he's had enough of helping her, even though she is toiling to build a practice, and commutes over two hours every day. *How am I supposed to do all the household chores, too?*

Georgie recalls what Lisa has said many times. "All women's liberation has done for women is to give us the right to do it all—career, child-rearing, and running a household. We've earned the right to be *more* stressed than men!" Georgie always thought this sentiment to be an exaggeration but now she sees the truth of it. She takes a break from housecleaning and calls her mother to complain about Dwayne's lack of help at home.

"Georgie, this career is what *you* wanted," Claire says. "What did you think would happen? Men are just not cut out for domestic responsibilities, no matter what they might say."

In the past, Georgie would have laughed at her mother's antiquated ideas about gender roles. She's not laughing now. Now it seems to be her reality.

To complicate life at the Downie residence, Daphne returned home from Europe yesterday after being away for four months. She ran out of funds, and once again she's home to earn money for her next trip. Daphne's claim is that travel is helping her "find herself," but sees nothing wrong with relying on her parents when convenient. To Georgie, this is a double standard.

When Daphne breezes in the door at dinner, the drudgery of Georgie's day doing domestic chores has worn her patience to a frazzle. "It must be nice to live rent-free at home to save money for self-indulgent travel. Most people can find themselves at college, you know. And you *will* need a degree to find a rewarding career that pays well."

"Mom! Traveling is a great education! Do you really think all your schooling has helped you? It just seems so difficult for you. You're working far from home, and you've been at it almost a year with little progress. Why do you think I didn't stay at college? I know too many people with a degree who are working in a grocery store or a pub. Higher education is no guarantee of anything."

Georgie frowns and shakes her head. Daphne is espousing a negative view of higher education to lend credibility to her wayward lifestyle. Georgie wants to point this out, but doesn't want further confrontation. Instead, she defends her career progress, saying "any worthwhile endeavor requires a lot of effort."

Daphne gives her a dismissive look and disappears into her room.

This exchange casts a pall over the evening, which may account for Georgie's fitful sleep. In the middle of the night, she wakes up in a sweat from a nightmare. In the dream, she was climbing a steep mountain with no ropes or gear, lost her footing, and started falling, and as with such dreams, woke just before hitting the ground. The dream felt so real and she has heard dreams mean something. *Am I afraid my career is going to fail? Or that I have no support from my family? Likely both!* Usually, waking up from a bad dream would be a relief. This time, waking reality is almost as terrifying as the nightmare.

Chapter 10

Georgie arrives at Lisa's house on a Saturday afternoon for a consultation about marketing. After three more promotional talks, Georgie is even more discouraged. It seemed like her audiences were there out of curiosity, or seeking free advice, with no serious interest in a consultation. In frustration, she called Lisa for advice on how to promote herself. While building her health food business, Lisa has learned practical marketing strategies and, as she has often joked, "what not to do."

Lisa has the espresso made, and they settle into her home office, full of houseplants and a bookshelf covering one wall.

"Georgie, it's good you're getting in front of people, making a personal connection. But you need to be strategic—find those who are looking for your services. To build my business, I had to figure out who my best customers would be. I marketed to practitioners in alternative health and health stores. Now think, who might be your best customers?"

Georgie thinks for a moment. "My situation is different. I don't have a product to sell."

Lisa shakes her head. "No, but you have a valuable service: natural healing. Who might connect with that?"

"I'm not sure, perhaps many people. I don't know." Georgie slumps in her chair, wondering if enough people are interested in natural healing. The need for it seems so obvious to her because of her personal experience and education.

"Think of it this way," Lisa says. "Who do you want to help most?"

"Women like me. Women with children. Those who had an unpleasant experience with the medical system. But how do I find them?"

"Perhaps you don't have to find them. I'm thinking you just need to get in front of a group of women. There are sure to be some women there who've had a similar off-putting experience with doctors. It's more common than you think. Also, there are women's groups who meet regularly and bring in outside speakers. This gives you a ready-made audience with no advertising required from you."

Georgie nods, eagerly scribbling notes.

"And, for your talk, I think you should share your ordeal with Debbie's health problems," Lisa says. "People connect with real-life stories about overcoming challenges."

"Hm. At college, they told us not to talk about our personal issues with patients."

"Of course, not during a consultation. But anyone new in business uses personal stories in their promotion. When I started out, I talked about how my greens supplement helped me with my asthma and kept my daughter from getting colds and flu. You can speak from the heart about Debbie's ordeal, how it affected her and you, and how the naturopath helped you. Tug on a few heartstrings! Most people make buying decisions based on emotions rather than logic. Case in point: Most women buy clothes and makeup for emotional reasons."

"But I had envisioned my promotional talk would give information about health conditions and naturopathic therapies. Won't people expect solutions to their health issues?"

"Of course, people want solutions to their health concerns. The point of your talk is to assure them you *will* have the answers *if* they become your patient. You can't give free advice during a public talk."

Back at home, Georgie gets on the phone to Debbie to make sure she doesn't mind her personal ordeal being shared with strangers.

"Mom," Debbie says. "Of course. If you can help other kids and parents to avoid what we went through, please share our story."

It's been a month since Lisa's pep talk on marketing and there is room for optimism. Georgie found it easier than she expected to craft a presentation about Debbie's ordeal and opted for a dramatic title: How Naturopathy Healed My Daughter. Promotion of this title resulted in ten people at her monthly library talk. Because she was an alumnus of UIndy, the University Women's club agreed to have her speak at their meeting. The response from these two events was more promising. She gained three new patients.

Today, Georgie is in consultation with one of those new patients, Carrie, who has multiple health issues—chronic fatigue, a heart condition, and severe allergies. Before seeing Georgie, Carrie consulted with two medical doctors with no significant improvement in her health. The desperation shows on her face. But the combination of ailments and Georgie's lack of clinical experience will make it challenging to help this patient. She advises Carrie on a few dietary changes and pledges to follow up with a therapeutic protocol in a few days. After escorting her patient out, she returns to her office to research health conditions and treatments. This is the pattern of her workday so far—one to two hours of study for every hour with a patient. It means she can't take very many patients, which limits her income. She asked Dr. Caroll for help, but he was so busy she had to make an appointment with him for two weeks away.

Slumped over her desk, head in her hands, Georgie notices Pam leaving her office. Georgie has already gathered that, of the three naturopaths, Pam is the most sympathetic to the struggles of a new practitioner. Much like Georgie, she went back to school in her late thirties, but for a different reason. When Georgie first joined the clinic, Pam took her out to lunch and shared her personal tragedy, losing her husband to a fatal stroke when he was only thirty-eight. That experience led her to study naturopathy and specialize in the health issues related to aging.

Georgie calls out to Pam, asking if she has a few minutes to talk. They settle into Pam's office, where Georgie relays her challenges in devising protocols without doing a lot of research.

"I know how difficult the first few years can be," Pam says. "What helped me was a good reference book, so I had information at hand for complicated cases. I'm sure you have a lot of textbooks from naturopathic college, but they are likely dedicated to a specific modality—nutrition, botanicals, or homeopathy." Pam pulls out a thick book from her bookcase. "This book provides all the therapy options for hundreds of ailments and conditions. There's also a section on contraindications between pharmaceuticals and natural health products. I can loan you my copy for a couple of days."

"Thank, Pam. This is so helpful!"

The next day Georgie buys her own copy of Pam's reference book, a four-hundred-page tome, at a cost of two hundred dollars. She can already hear Dwayne's complaints when he sees the credit card statement.

With two hours between patients, Georgie has time to reflect on the mixed results from the past two months of promotional talks. On a tip from Lisa, Georgie developed an evaluation form for her presentations, and comments showed she was not always clear in her message. She gained a couple of new patients, but Georgie considered her efforts to attract them unsustainable. Sometimes it feels like she needs a marketing degree and, more than once, she considered calling the naturopathic college to suggest they beef up the one marketing course they offered.

After a two week wait, Dr. Caroll found the time to meet with her and he suggested joining local business groups to build her contacts in the community. He recommended the networking events at the Downtown Business Association and the Chamber of Commerce. By attending two of these events, she lined up speaking engagements at a mom's and tot's group and a Rotary Club. Still, she has had only a trickle of new patients from those talks.

Dr. Caroll walks through the office on a rare break between patients and pops his head into Georgie's office. "How is it going since we talked last?"

Georgie shakes her head and sighs. "So-so! I was hoping for more new patients from my presentations and community involvement. My consulting fees are still barely covering my rent and my gas to get here every day."

Dr. Caroll enters Georgie's office and sits down. "Tell me more. How do you feel during your talks? Is your audience engaged?"

Georgie shrugs her shoulders. "I'm not sure how to tell whether my audience is engaged."

"Hm. If you're not getting enough new patients from your talks, it could be your presentation style. People always respond more readily to interesting speakers. If the response is not there, it could be about how you've organized the talk or how you interact with your audience."

Georgie pauses, hoping he will explain further so she won't have to admit she does not know *how* to be interesting or interactive.

Studying her carefully, Dr. Caroll slowly nods his head. "If you are unsure about your speaking skills, I suggest you join Toastmasters. It's a voluntary organization with an excellent training program in public speaking. I've been a member of a local club for ten years. Why don't you come with me to the next meeting?"

Since joining Toastmasters three months ago, Georgie realizes Dr. Caroll was right about the organization. The training manual has excellent instruction on effective speaking, and the weekly meetings provide regular opportunities to give speeches. There is an atmosphere of mutual support that translates into constructive feedback on how to improve her presentation skills. Now, with several prepared speeches completed and helpful comments from club members, her confidence in engaging an audience has grown. Another bonus from her Toastmasters membership has been making more new contacts in the community. Some club members became her patients, and another member invited her to speak at a weight loss group, resulting in more new patients.

The Toastmasters meetings are every Monday evening, which means a twelve-hour day with a drive home after nine o'clock in the evening. She is reminded of her comment to Daphne a while back: "any worthwhile endeavor requires a lot of effort." Before she got into naturopathic medicine, she knew this in theory. Now she can attest to its truth. The cost of building her practice continues to be a hefty investment of both time and money.

Georgie arrives home on a Saturday afternoon at five o'clock to find Dwayne sitting in his easy chair, arms crossed. "Nice of you to roll in! You worked six days this week, and you're gone for ten hours each day, sometimes more. I've hardly seen you. I might as well be a bachelor!"

Dwayne's vehemence catches Georgie off guard. Apparently, his resentment from some months ago has been festering under the surface. She slumps on the couch opposite his chair, tired after a full day of patient consultations. Dr. Caroll suggested she schedule appointments on a Saturday to build her patient roster. For those with busy work schedules, like the women she wants to attract, Saturday appointments can be the only option. The other three naturopaths are busy enough they don't have to work on Saturday.

"Hey! I'm not naïve," Dwayne says. "I recognize what it takes to build a business. But I need to know this will not be the norm from now on, that there is an end in sight. You're working all these hours, but I still don't see the payoff. I started my accounting firm knowing there would be a market for my services. Companies need accountants." He gets up and starts pacing the room. "Are you sure people *need* a naturopath?" He points his finger for emphasis. "Do the other naturopaths in your clinic have busy practices? At what point is it realistic to have a steady income? You could earn more at your old job as a doctor's office manager. And I am concerned about you commuting on that busy road every day and driving late at night alone. It's dangerous!"

Dwayne's barrage leaves Georgie speechless. She stares at him, jaw dropped, not knowing which question to answer, or if she even has answers.

"Let's face it! You're barely home before you head back to work," Dwayne says, his voice rising. "Plus, when you are here, you're too tired to do anything. We have no social life—something I expected we would get back after you finished school. But apparently not…" Dwayne's voice trails off. He rises from his chair, throws up his hands and stalks into his study. Georgie follows him and shuts the door, not wanting D.J. to overhear. Dwayne is sitting, arms crossed, with his office chair swiveled away from her.

"I understand it's tough right now, but it won't be forever," Georgie says. "By working today, I got three new patients. And there is a good reason to be in the clinic Monday to Friday, even if I don't have a full appointment schedule. Often people call the office to speak to a naturopath for fifteen minutes—it's a free service the clinic offers to help people who aren't sure they want to book an appointment. By taking those calls, I am the practitioner the caller chooses."

"Well, I'm glad you think it's worthwhile, because it seems like you are abandoning us here."

Georgie's patience is waning. "Dwayne! You are forgetting a bit of history. While building your business, you worked twelve to fourteen hours each day while I had a full-time job and the care of three children, with little help from you. But did I complain or tell you to give up your business and get a job?" She wants to say he's being sexist, applying a double standard—that it's okay for husbands and fathers to be hyper-focused on their career, but not for wives and mothers. He has boasted in the past how liberated he is about gender roles, but are these his true colors? She is about to accuse him of being sexist. Instead, she opts for an argument to which he can relate.

"You must know I'm working long hours, so you get a return on your investment in my education. Would you rather I coast along just hoping I can make it?"

He turns his chair towards her.

Encouraged, Georgie addresses Dwayne's other concerns. "I understand you're disappointed about my progress, but the other naturopaths at the clinic are doing well in their practices. They've just been at it longer, six years or more. And haven't you always said it takes any new business five years to get established? I've been practicing for just over a year, and the first six months were at the Rice Clinic." She watches for a sign he is softening in his stance, but he still has his arms crossed.

"The promotional talks and the Toastmasters meetings have me out a few evenings, but they are critical to building my practice. Dr. Caroll assures me these activities will work, but I can't predict how long it will take."

Dwayne shakes his head. "This is very disappointing. I'm not sure how long I can support this. D.J. may want to go to college once he realizes working at the sporting goods store won't get him anywhere. As it stands, we can only afford tuition at the community college. You and I both know he won't go for that. If he goes to college, he'll want a Division 1 school so he can play football. Tuition at those schools is more than we can afford right now."

Georgie clenches her jaw, resentment rising in her throat. D.J. didn't apply himself in high school, which is why he didn't get a football scholarship. Now Dwayne is placing the resulting financial burden of college tuition on her shoulders. But she doesn't want to talk about their issues with D.J.

"Dwayne, all I ask for is the same courtesy I gave you. I sacrificed for your career working full time at a job I didn't want. And that went on for almost eight years." She stops, seeing Dwayne's color rise again. *One of us needs to de-escalate this situation.* "Don't get me wrong! I was all for your working hard to build your accounting practice. It made sense. We focused on the long-term benefits of being a business owner. Now I'm in that situation, and my patient caseload is increasing. I'm sure I will have a stable income soon."

Dwayne shakes his head, his brow knitted. "I hope you're right."

Despite her assurances, she is not sure when her income will satisfy Dwayne. While her work with patients is fulfilling, by the end of each day, she is exhausted. It helps somewhat going to bed early, eating well, and taking vitamins, but she suspects the source of her energy drain is the daily commute on the busy interstate. She didn't mention this challenge to Dwayne. Based on his mood, it would surely trigger more accusations of how she is failing him.

Chapter 11

"It all happened so fast," Georgie says to the police officer. "I never saw the truck until it sideswiped me, and the next thing I knew, I was upside down in my car."

"Well, Mrs. Downie, you rolled your car twice," says the officer. "You're lucky to get off with a few scrapes." He jots something down in his notebook and excuses himself.

Georgie doesn't feel lucky. Her neck is stiffening up, and the gash on her forehead is deep. The emergency room doctor arrives carrying a big needle and suture materials.

"You need a couple of stitches," he says. "Now, this won't hurt a bit."

Georgie groans. *Why do doctors say it won't hurt a bit when it always does?* Ironically, it's the needle with the anesthetic that hurts. As the doctor sutures her wound, all she can think is, how long will she be off work? This couldn't come at a worse time!

Just as the doctor finishes the stitches, Dwayne rushes in. "Are you okay? The police told me you were in a collision, but gave me no details."

He is out of breath and as anxious as Georgie has ever seen him. She nods weakly as tears well up in her eyes and Dwayne takes her in his arms, allowing her to cry. Regaining her composure, she says, "I'm sure I look worse than I feel. They say I'll be fine—just a stiff neck for a few days."

Dwayne bends down and peers into her eyes. "Okay. Let's just get you home."

Within twenty minutes, the doctor declares Georgie passed the initial concussion protocol, allowing her to go home if someone monitors her for the next twenty-four hours. Dwayne holds her around the waist and guides her to the car. A welcome wave of comfort washes over her, despite her splitting headache. On the way home, Dwayne says nothing about the accident, for which she is grateful.

The next morning, she feels like a truck hit her, which it had. During the night, as part of the concussion protocol, Dwayne woke her up every couple of hours, so today they are both overtired. Still, Dwayne is attentive, making coffee and serving her fresh fruit and an omelet. He announces he is staying home for the day to continue monitoring her for signs of a concussion. When she is finished eating, he sits down facing her and takes her hand.

"Georgie, this accident is what I feared when you went to Indy and it's a warning you shouldn't be commuting. Next time, you might not be so lucky."

Georgie interjects, "But it wasn't my fault! The police said the truck driver swerved into my lane. A good Samaritan saw the whole thing and waited with me until the police got there." She doesn't remember what happened except for the kindness of the man who stopped to help. His eyewitness report is likely why the police absolved her of any blame for the collision. Now she regrets not asking for the man's name and contact information so she could properly thank him.

"I don't care whose fault it was," Dwayne says. "That busy highway is too dangerous, especially after you've worked all day. Who knows? Maybe you were too tired to concentrate on the road, and that's why you didn't notice the truck swerve." He grasps both of Georgie's hands and peers into her eyes. "I need you to promise me you will search for a position at a local clinic."

Too stiff and sore to argue, Georgie nods half-heartedly even though she doubts her chances of landing a position locally. Right now, there are other priorities. She calls Karen to cancel all her patient appointments for Friday and Saturday. She sends a prayer of thanks that the accident happened on a Thursday evening to allow her an extra day to recover. Hopefully, she can return to the clinic on Monday.

Just to keep Dwayne off her back, she calls some clinics closer to home, but there is only one clinic in Terrance, and she just left there last year. It is unlikely Dr. Rice would take her back. Lisa told her he had trouble finding a suitable replacement for the office manager's position. When she calls, it is no surprise he is not available to speak to her.

Claire arrives on Friday afternoon, all flustered and attentive, after Dwayne called her about the accident. Dwayne takes her visit as an opportunity to go to his office to check in with his staff.

Clair fusses over Georgie's facial injury. "Are you sure you're okay?"

Georgie nods with a weak smile.

"Georgina, dear, this commuting is going to get you killed. I hope you see that now. Just think how much your children still need you, and it's not fair to Dwayne."

Georgie shrugs her shoulders.

"You need to find something closer to home, or better yet, take a break from what you're doing."

"Mom. There are no opportunities in Terrance, and I can't just give up my practice at the Caroll Clinic. If I do, everything I've done so far will go to waste."

It hurts Georgie that her father doesn't call to ask how she is, but that's how it is—he's still shunning her. After her mother departs, Georgie calls Lisa for another opinion, one less influenced by disapproval of her career choice.

"I don't think you should commute either, but maybe you don't have to quit the clinic," Lisa says. "I know someone who works at quite a distance from home. His solution is to take a room near his work Monday to Friday and go home on weekends. I have contacts in Indy, and there's a good chance I can find you a room or a small apartment to rent. It might cost you more than commuting, but at least you won't be risking your life on the interstate every day. You were lucky this time. It could have been a lot worse!"

Georgie shakes her head and purses her lips. "Ooh, I doubt Dwayne would agree to that. He's been at me for months about how I'm never home and he's already disappointed with my income. I can't imagine he will be okay with me being away even more and with a rental expense."

Dwayne arrives home from the office with takeout for dinner, announcing that Georgie must rest for the weekend—no housework or cooking. With nothing to do, she is left with her thoughts, and disturbing questions surface about her priorities. *Is it my career? Is it my family?* She considers Lisa's idea about staying in Indianapolis on weekdays, but in all her imagined scenarios, her relationship with Dwayne would suffer. The more she ponders, the more problems she envisions to the point of despair about her situation. Her career is driving a wedge between her and everyone in her family—mostly Dwayne. *How can I be on the right path if there is so much dissension?* All she gets from these thoughts is a throbbing headache, which the doctor warned might result from the accident.

On Saturday afternoon, Georgie is lying on her bed with a cold cloth on her head, considering whether doubt about her career is contributing to her lingering headache. On her bedside table, she spies the self-help book she picked up at a mall kiosk a few weeks before. The title jumped out at her because it was about how to handle change—something she has been dealing with a lot. She opens the book and soon becomes intrigued. So much in the book speaks to her problems—how to embrace change as an opportunity and handle new situations and challenges without doubt or worry. There is even a section on self-sabotaging behavior and how to recognize it. When Melanie accused her of self-sabotage, she dismissed the notion, but now? There could be something to it. While in med school years ago, she had trouble maintaining the expected grades, but quitting was not an option because of her father. Was getting married and having kids an easy way out of her struggles at medical school? Is choosing to work out of town sabotaging her career now? Should she have stuck it out at the Rice Clinic?

By Sunday night, Georgie is almost grateful for the accident, given the outcome was no serious injury. The time to rest, read, and reflect was just what she needed—to step back from her frenetic life and seek perspective. She has an inkling much of her stress is self-inflicted, from wanting assurances her choices will turn out okay, that she has control over what happens. The accident reminded her no one has such power.

The time in reflection also brings home to her the benefits of daily prayer. Of late, she used her busyness as an excuse not to pray. On Sunday evening, she prays for a good half hour and a saying comes to mind: *You always pass failure on your way to success.* A quick search online reveals, to her surprise, the source of the comment was the actor, Mickey Rooney. If it's true, she wonders how much more failure she will have to endure.

Georgie is the first to arrive for the monthly clinic meeting. This month, as a change of scene, Dr. Caroll opted to meet at a local restaurant with a private meeting room. Georgie checks the calendar on her phone and realizes she is a half hour early. *How did I get the time wrong?* The peppermint tea she ordered arrives, and she breathes in the sweet fragrance, warming her chilled hands on the mug. With time to kill, she reflects on the last three months since she made the brave decision to live in Indianapolis during the week. Lisa had worked her magic and found a small loft apartment at the estate of one of her business associates. The apartment over the garage was once the chauffeur's quarters when wealthy people had live-in servants. Her landlords travel often and like to have someone around which could explain the nominal rent, reasonable enough to ease Dwayne's distaste for the arrangement.

The loft is perfect—tastefully furnished, with a private entrance and, best of all, overlooking a city park. Georgie can relax and recoup her energy, and the proximity of the park provides easy access to invigorating walks. It's only a five-minute drive to the clinic, twenty minutes if she walks. Because she moved just before winter, she avoided the risks of driving on icy or snow-covered roads for a second year. It dawns on her she hasn't felt this rested since starting naturopathic college. While commuting, there was never enough time to rest and recuperate. Now she has more energy and welcomes each day at the Caroll Clinic.

Perhaps it is her imagination, but since moving to Indy, she sensed more support from her clinic colleagues. Perhaps they viewed her move to the city as a firm commitment to the clinic. Both Mark Caroll and Pam Samuels offered more advice on growing her practice, most recently urging her to identify a specialty. They explained how a specialty would set her apart from other practitioners and create less competition for patients with her clinic colleagues. They pointed to three significant benefits to her practice—enhanced expertise, more efficiency working with patients, and attracting more patients. To Georgie it seemed counterintuitive. How could a specialty appealing to fewer people bring her more patients? But her colleagues' success seems to prove the point. Dr. Caroll's specialty in cancer care keeps him busy with a long waiting list. With her focus on health issues related to aging, Pam always has a full appointment schedule. Roger's niche as the only practitioner in the city specializing in Chinese medicine means he never wants for patients. To Georgie's questions about identifying a specialty, her colleagues suggested it would reveal itself naturally with some clinical experience. The key, they said, was to follow her passion.

She has been using her evening walks in the chilly late winter air to stimulate her thinking about a potential specialty. What was her passion? She struggled to answer that question, so she considered a different one: Why did she choose naturopathy? Primarily, it was disenchantment with medical practice and her personal experience as a mother of a sick child. She doesn't want other parents and children to have the same challenges she and Debbie had. That realization may have led her to a specialty which she will test with her colleagues today.

Dr. Caroll has been running clinic meetings for years for practitioners to share their successes or challenges with their patients to support each other's practices. As a new practitioner, Georgie appreciates her colleagues' willingness to share their experience, adding to her knowledge of protocols and remedies.

Everyone else arrives at the appointed time, and while waiting for their dinner to arrive, Dr. Caroll gives a status update about the clinic. "We are one of the busiest clinics in the city, with four practitioners who have a full appointment schedule and waiting lists."

Georgie is thankful he doesn't point out she's doesn't quite have a full schedule yet, and certainly not a waiting list.

"Patients come from all over the state for our complementary cancer care," Dr. Caroll says, continuing his pep talk. "Roger, I like what I hear about your work in Chinese medicine and acupuncture, and I appreciate you backing me up when the cancer patient load gets heavy. Pam, you're serving the older adults that, with the aging population, is a growth area." He chuckles at his weak attempt at humor. "We have specialties that are complementary rather than competing." He turns his attention to Georgie. "Dr. Downie, have you given any thought to your specialty?"

"I plan to specialize in women's ailments," Georgie says, trying to sound confident. "The stress women face these days takes a physical toll on their health—hormonal imbalances, sleep issues, digestive problems, and depression. I am also considering a secondary specialty in child development. What do you all think?"

All three nod and smile at her. "Hm. Sounds promising," Dr. Caroll says. "They are definitely complementary to the rest of us. I suggest you focus on one specialty to start—the one that excites the most passion."

Georgie nods, seeing the wisdom in that. *Definitely women's health.*

At each clinic meeting, the associates have the option to talk about their practices, new therapies, or case studies. Dr. Caroll leads off. "I typically have thirty to forty patients each week receiving high-dose vitamin C intravenous therapy." He turns to Georgie. "Dr. Downie, I'm not sure you know. This type of IV therapy remains controversial among most medical oncologists who believe it interferes with chemotherapy. But their opposition stems from a misunderstanding about how vitamin C works when administered intravenously. When taken orally, high doses of vitamin C could promote cancer cell growth, but intravenous therapy, which goes directly into the bloodstream, has the opposite effect—the death of cancer cells."

Georgie had one college course about intravenous therapy but had no practical experience with it. She asks Dr. Caroll to talk about his patient outcomes.

"For early stage cancers, we regularly see full remissions," he says. "Stage 4 cancer care is about improving quality of life, perhaps giving the patient more time. I see more Stage 4 cases than any other because by then most oncologists discontinue chemo and radiation and we are their only treatment option." He shakes his head. "If I had more patients in the early stages of their cancer, I could help even more people. But at Stage 1 and 2, people are more apt to take chemo and radiation, and some medical oncologists advise them against IV therapy."

The clinic director's comments remind Georgie of her father's warnings about medical doctors opposing naturopathic medicine.

Dr. Caroll's face brightens. "I have an exciting announcement about the investment I've made in a new therapy. We are now one of a few clinics in the Midwest with a hyperthermia device. It focuses high heat on tumors to slow their growth. The therapy was developed in Germany and is relatively new in the U.S. There is solid research that hyperthermia shrinks tumors when applied in coordination with medical oncology treatments. Because the therapy works synergistically with both chemo and radiation, very few oncologists will be opposed. Having this device will put our clinic on the map."

With their meal orders served, the practitioners agree to pause the presentations and reports. Georgie is first up after everyone finishes eating. "I'm seeing more women with hormonal imbalances—adrenal fatigue, underactive thyroid, PMS—most often related to undue stress or poor diet. My recommendations typically include B vitamins, adaptogenic herbs, an organic diet, and strategies for stress relief. I also have several patients who are under twelve years old with stomach aches, rashes, or behavioral issues. Treating children is tricky because it involves persuading parents to stick to my protocols, and children are not always compliant. But thankfully, most parents are patient in expecting results, knowing their child is not following the protocol as closely as they should. Some parents are now referring their friends and family to me."

Dr. Caroll nods and smiles. "When you get referrals, you are on your way to a successful practice. I look forward to hearing some case studies at the next clinic meeting."

Georgie revels in his encouraging words and has a bounce in her step after the meeting. It is now almost two years since graduation, and of late, she has worried less about whether she could build a successful practice. She still makes promotional talks regularly at service clubs, church groups, and support groups—weight loss, parenting troubled teens, autism, and rheumatoid arthritis. From each talk, she typically picks up new patients. Some patients only need one or two consultations, and such turnover means she must continue her promotional talks, at least until she can rely on word-of-mouth referrals.

Now that Georgie isn't commuting every day, she has the chance to develop a social life, befriending Sandra and Marina—two women she met at the Toastmasters club who teach at the university in psychology and sociology. They often go out to dinner on Monday evenings before Toastmasters meetings when they commiserate over their work and the challenges in balancing career and home.

While her professional life is going well, Georgie can't say the same about her relationship with her father. Her mother calls her every couple of weeks to ask how she is doing, but the questions and comments aren't supportive or encouraging. She has the sense her mother is gathering information for her father. He won't call himself, but still wants to know what is going on. Surveillance is the best word to describe her parents' interest, almost like they are waiting for her to fail. *Will I ever be able to talk to my father about my practice?*

Among the many changes in Georgie's life, there is yet another. After years of Saturday lunches with Lisa at Henrietta's, they had to move it to Sunday after church. Saturdays are no longer possible because Georgie is seeing patients all morning and seldom arrives home before mid-afternoon. Today, they had to reserve a table because the café is a favorite lunch spot for church goers.

Georgie orders the chicken falafel, a new menu item, and Lisa chooses her usual veggie wrap.

To Georgie's accounting of two recent successful outcomes with patients, Lisa says, in a lackluster voice, "I'm glad you're doing well."

"What's up with you? You sound a little down."

"Oh, John is having some financial trouble." She says no more, which also is not typical. Usually, she is open about her personal life.

After catching up on family news, Georgie circles back to Lisa's admission and gently pries out of her friend what is going on.

"John had a business loss," Lisa says with a sigh. "He sometimes takes too many chances with his investments and now we're in some financial trouble because of it. I'm furious with him!"

"Oh, Lisa. That must be so difficult for you. I could talk to Dwayne; he knows some good financial advisers. I'm sure he would pass on their names to John."

Lisa shakes her head. "Thanks for the offer, Georgie. I'll mention it to John, but his pride is apt to keep him from accepting any advice because he fancies himself as a brilliant financial mind, too. I'm certain he believes he can recover from this on his own."

Georgie studies her friend with concern. Lisa is always upbeat, so this situation must be dire. "Perhaps I can help in some other way, through your business. I will ask my clinic director if you can make a product pitch to the other naturopaths. They should recommend your greens supplement to their patients who are nutritionally deficient, like I do."

"Good of you to offer! I tried to get into your clinic a few years back, but they didn't want to switch product lines. But, with your endorsement, I'm sure I will have more success. You're the best!"

As the newcomer to the clinic, Georgie hopes she hasn't overstepped her authority and raised Lisa's hopes by offering something she can't deliver.

Chapter 12

The Sunday morning conversation begins with a perfunctory exchange of "G'morning," but Dwayne's tone is anything but good. He sits hunched over at the kitchen island, gripping his coffee cup and grim-faced, while Georgie whisks eggs for an omelet.

"Georgina," he says, without looking up. "I've had a lot of time to think. When you had your accident, I hoped you would find a position in this city, not move out. This is no kind of life with you living in another city and breezing in here for thirty-six hours each week. Unless you can be home more, I don't see how we are going to make this work."

Georgie stops mid-whisk, puts the eggs aside, and turns to face him, processing his implied threat. "I know it's difficult for you and D.J., but I'm sure it won't be forever. And I didn't move out."

"Well, it sure feels like you did. How do you expect things to get better if you stay at this clinic in Indianapolis? I'm not moving there! You need to work at a clinic closer to home. Otherwise…"

Georgie is momentarily speechless, not daring to ask what comes after "otherwise." "Well, let's keep an open mind. You never know what will happen." The platitudes sound lame as soon as they come out of her mouth.

Dwayne shakes his head but says nothing, disappearing to the garage to get his golf clubs out for his Sunday morning game. *He wouldn't miss that!* Georgie wants to say something about his religious zeal for golf, how that is okay, but her dedication to her career is not. Her complaints about golf have fallen on deaf ears in the past, so saying something seems like a waste of breath.

Dwayne returns from the garage. "I'm late. I'll eat at the club."

Georgie winces at the slam of the door and pours the eggs into the omelet pan, wondering how she will eat it all herself.

D.J. bounds down the stairs. "Something smells good!"

It's early for him. Georgie raises her eyebrows at him as she dishes out the omelet onto two plates.

"I'm working today," he replies to her unspoken question. He slides on a stool at the kitchen island, digs a fork into his omelet, and shovels it in his mouth.

Georgie sits down on a stool beside him. She hasn't talked to him alone for a while and inquires about his school plans.

D.J. rolls his eyes. "I'm working on it, Mom. Don't worry! I need a college with a business program and a good football program. You may disagree with the football part, but it's important to me. I visited Indiana State and talked with some guys there, but I'm leaning toward Illinois State, in Bloomington. They have highly rated programs in both business and football." He checks the time and finishes his omelet with three quick bites. "No more time to talk—I'm due at work by nine. When you work in retail, Sunday is a big day. I make commissions on my sales now."

As Georgie readies herself for church, she reflects on the conversation, however brief. She is encouraged D.J. has finally decided on a major and is taking initiative to choose a college.

Georgie arrives at the worship service, harboring some guilt because she hasn't been for a while. The pastor's message seems meant for her—discerning your mission in life and using your talents to help others. *That's what I have been doing! Why is it causing so much strife?* There seems to be no right answer to her challenges in balancing career and the expectations at home. At fellowship time after the service, a few church members ask about her career and applaud her for being adventurous. When Georgie shares her living situation, the church matriarch raises her eyebrows, a reminder of how unconventional Georgie's life has become.

Lisa waits until the well-wishers drift away, and she suggests a new vegan restaurant for their weekly lunch. Georgie likes the ambiance with tables well-spaced apart and big potted plants for privacy. At Lisa's suggestion, they both have a quinoa salad with black beans and cilantro. Georgie finds the dish a little bland but can't put her finger on what is missing, like she can't remedy what is missing in her home life. When the meal ends, Georgie is reluctant to go home. She should spend more time with Dwayne, but their conversations always devolve into disagreements over her work. When she seeks more time with her husband, it just brings more stress.

By midafternoon, Dwayne is still not home, and Georgie relaxes on the back deck with the dog who lays his head on her lap, his way of begging for a walk. Georgie pats his head. "Good boy! At least you're happy to spend time with me." Unable to resist his pleading brown eyes and wagging tail, she takes him for a leisurely walk in the woods. It's a sunny spring day. As Shadow romps along the path, sniffing at every tree, Georgie revels in the sights and smells of spring growth, pushing aside worries about what Dwayne said. Better to focus on how she and Dwayne could navigate these troubled waters. As she walks, she prays, *Dear God, how can my passion for healing others be detrimental to my family? I need your guidance and wisdom.* A thought comes to mind, which could be an answer to her prayer: *Any attack is a cry for love.* Is it her rambling thoughts, or is it God speaking to her? Then it comes to her—it is a lesson in A Course in Miracles. Some passages, like this one, have stayed with her. *Is Dwayne making veiled threats as a cry for love? Is he afraid of losing me?*

Once home from her walk, she takes the time to prepare Dwayne's favorite meal—roast beef dinner—as a peace offering. At dinner, she plans to be attentive to his concerns.

"So, tell me how it is for you two bachelors? How do you manage meals?" she asks.

"A lot of takeout!" Dwayne says.

D.J. is focused on devouring his meal and does not comment. Perhaps takeout is okay with him.

Georgie turns to Dwayne. "No wonder you're fed up! Takeout food is full of crap. It's a slow, salty death. That's the first thing they taught us in nutrition class." She laughs and gets a chuckle out of Dwayne.

"How about I stay here this evening and make some meals ahead for you? I can drive back to Indy tomorrow morning."

Dwayne shrugs his shoulders as if her offer won't make a difference.

After dinner, Georgie busies herself cooking three meals—lasagna, a roast chicken, and stew using the leftover roast beef. Dwayne watches Sunday night football, but at half-time, comes to the kitchen to help her cut vegetables for the stew. As they work side by side, Georgie senses an easing of the tension between them and it occurs to her there is another concession she could make. "Can I call you during the week? Maybe at a set a time each evening? It would definitely help me keep going."

A smile crosses Dwayne's face. "Okay."

They set nine thirty in the evening as their call time and retire to bed to rekindle some physical intimacy, a rare occurrence of late.

On Monday morning, before she leaves for Indy, Georgie asks D.J. if she could text him every day. Without looking up from his cell phone, he says, "Okay, whatever." Georgie will take it. Eighteen-year-old boys are unlikely to admit they need a daily text from their mother. Her drive during rush hour is stressful, but she believes it a worthwhile sacrifice to tend to her family's needs.

Dwayne phones around five o'clock well before their appointed time. "Daphne called from the airport. She flew in this afternoon and didn't have your cell number to get in touch with you. Can you pick her up? She wants to stay with you for a few days."

Daphne is home earlier than they expected. While driving to the airport, Georgie wonders if something happened and her suspicions grow when Daphne greets her with an overly long hug.

Daphne enthuses over the loft apartment as they relax in the sitting room overlooking the park. Georgie asks about the reason for the premature return.

"Mom, I just missed home. You can only take so much of hostels and one-star inns. I'm going to take a job in Terrance and live at home while I plan my next trip."

Georgie hesitates to voice concerns about this lifestyle because Daphne will dig in her heels to criticism. Instead, she asks Daphne about her travels and why she enjoys it so much. Daphne eagerly expounds on all her adventures and the fascinating people she has met.

Georgie decides it's time to weigh in. "You may learn some things about the world, but I'm worried you will spend too much time traveling and develop no career. You can't put "travelled Europe" on a résumé."

"Mom! Don't be such a worrywart. Lots of people travel before they settle on their careers—find out who they are and what they want to do. There is no right time for settling on your life's work. Look at you! Did you see yourself as a naturopath when you were my age?"

Georgie must concede the point. "Of course, you are right, in a way. But at your age I was in school with a career goal that, I'll have you know, contributed to where I am now. Please consider how your travels will help you in the long run. It seems to me more like self-indulgence." As Daphne throws her head back and rolls her eyes, Georgie holds up her hand. "I know you're an adult, and it's your life. I just worry. That's what moms do!"

Whenever Georgie feels the urge to push Daphne about her career plans, she recalls the pressure her father placed on her. She doesn't want to make a similar mistake with her daughter and risk alienating her. She changes the subject. "Tell me about your time in Italy."

"Mom, it was so great." Her face brightens. "I picked up some Italian while I was there. So now I have that along with French and Spanish, my fourth language! And I am learning so much about the world and other cultures. Most kids my age have no clue about the world outside the U.S. Their views are so narrow!"

"I suppose you are learning something and it's great you are going to be multilingual. I'm sure that will help you down the road." Georgie considers how to offer advice without sounding critical. "Maybe you could see yourself in a career in the foreign service or as a translator." Georgie peers at Daphne, expecting resistance.

Daphne hesitates, head cocked. "Well, it's something to think about, Mom. I'm sure I'd need a college degree for those positions, but they're not completely crazy ideas!"

"Sure, just something to keep in mind." Georgie leaves it there. Her free-spirited daughter is better off thinking something is her idea.

Friday after clinic hours, Georgie and Daphne drive home to Terrance after four days spent together. Daphne is preoccupied listening to music in her headphones, giving Georgie time to contemplate significant interactions with both Daphne and Debbie during the week.

Georgie couldn't take time off work, so Daphne amused herself during the day like a tourist checking out the many museums in the city—sites you don't visit when you are a local. They met for lunch at some trendy cafés and watched chick flicks in the evening. Eat, Pray, Love was a big hit. Daphne commented on the scenes in Italy, "Mom, it is just like that! Italians savor their food in the company of friends and family. Americans barely taste their food and eat on the run!" Georgie laughed but admitted some truth to Daphne's insight, evidence her travel was providing her valuable lessons, after all.

On Thursday evening, Debbie called, something she does once a week. For the first part of the phone call, the sisters talked, sharing their news. Then Daphne passed the phone to Georgie. Their conversation was memorable.

"Mom," Debbie said. "Lately I've been thinking about when I was sick. I appreciate how you stood up to doctors who thought my illness was all in my head. I shudder to think where I would be today if you had not looked elsewhere for answers. When I was a kid, I didn't understand what you risked by taking me to the naturopath. Gramps would have been horrified. Have you ever told him?"

Georgie admitted she had never told her father about the naturopath, that he wouldn't understand. Debbie commiserated about how difficult it must be not being on good terms with one's father. The compassion in Debbie's insights almost brought Georgie to tears.

While reflecting on this interaction from the previous evening, it occurs to Georgie her relationship with Debbie has evolved. It wasn't long ago Georgie was giving all the support and advice. Now the relationship with her oldest is one of mutual support, more like she expected to have with an adult child. Debbie understands why her mother is in naturopathic medicine and the costs of that decision to her family relationships. For a twenty-three-year-old, Debbie is more mature than her years. Georgie would like to take credit, but she suspects her daughter's health challenges played a role. To endure a time of trial can build strength of character, or so Georgie has heard. The thought gives her hope—that her current problems would one day strengthen her, too.

Georgie is looking forward to today's clinic meeting when she will present two patient cases. She has the choice of sharing cases with successful outcomes or ones that are challenging. If she chooses a success story, it would be for the edification of the other practitioners—the assessment tools and remedies that were effective. To present a challenging case is meant as a request for help. So far, Georgie has brought cases to seek advice from her more experienced colleagues, and in two instances, she passed the patients to Pam or Roger because their specialties were more suited to the patients' health conditions.

Georgie is still learning how best to apply her knowledge—identifying the most effective protocols and estimating the time it will take for her patients to achieve the desired results. Her colleagues are helpful in recommending protocols but estimating healing time will come only with more experience. Her college internships taught her how to set up protocols for many ailments, but she did not have enough long-term contact with patients to see results. To confidently predict a timeline for healing, she needs to guide more patients to a resolution of their concerns. It is important because she has noticed some patients are more compliant when they have a clear expectation of when they will feel better.

Recently, she came across other reasons for patient non-compliance. She recalls Judy, a patient who came for her follow-up appointment, having made few changes, complaining Georgie had not provided enough guidance. Judy wanted sample menus and in-depth explanations for why she was to avoid certain foods. Another patient, Annabelle, came for her follow up consultation admitting she was overwhelmed by the diet recommendations and couldn't seem to implement any changes. This reminded Georgie what an internship advisor said about tailoring recommendations for two distinct personalities—the generalists and the detail-oriented types. The generalist, who would get lost in the details, needs guidelines and a few priorities to follow. The detail-oriented person needs lots of information and step-by-step protocols. Georgie makes a mental note to ask future patients about their preferences for details.

Georgie's spirits are buoyed by something she feels she has going for her. Her experience as the mother of a sick child allows her to put herself in her patients' shoes. She has wondered if her ability to relate is the source of some positive outcomes with patients. Whatever the reason, experience, or ability to relate, she looks forward to sharing some of these successes at today's meeting.

To change things up, Dr. Caroll organized today's clinic meeting over breakfast on a Saturday morning, so Georgie had to move her Saturday appointments to the afternoon. But it turns out to be a non-issue. Dwayne is away all day today with D.J. visiting Illinois State. They are negotiating an offer for a partial scholarship for football and going today to see how partial the scholarship will be. Dwayne will be in his element, Georgie muses, talking about dollars and cents.

Georgie has a light breakfast—yogurt and granola with fresh fruit. The others order cooked items—omelets or breakfast sandwiches—so she must wait for the others to finish. She uses the time to look over her presentation notes, so she doesn't forget any details. The waitress clears the plates away and Dr. Caroll nods to Georgie to start her presentation.

"I have two cases to present today in which the patients are doing well," Georgie says as an introduction. "The first case is a woman aged forty-five who was in a terrible state when I first saw her six months ago. Several medical specialists could not resolve multiple issues—headaches, bloating, premenstrual syndrome, and fatigue. It's my impression she consulted with me as a last resort with little hope for a resolution. I assessed she had chronic adrenal exhaustion related to undue stress and a fast-food diet. I set her up on hypoallergenic diet, a greens supplement, and, for adrenal support, a vitamin/herbal formula and a homeopathic remedy. At her three-month follow-up visit, the patient reported significant improvement—more energy, very little bloating, and fewer headaches. Yesterday was her six-month follow-up, and she reported no more headaches, good digestion, and more energy. Her PMS symptoms were minimal."

Pam asks about the homeopathic remedies Georgie used. Mark Caroll smiles, nodding a few times, and Roger Brownlee takes notes. Georgie would have liked more reaction from the male naturopaths, but perhaps it is not surprising. This case is outside their specialties.

Georgie turns to her notes for her second presentation. "My second case is a twelve-year-old boy with attention-deficit/hyperactivity disorder. His medical doctor had prescribed a medication for ADHD, but the boy had significant side effects to the drug—digestive problems and low affect. The parents reported while their son was on the medication, his mind was always in a fog, taking no pleasure in anything. They felt forced to choose between the son in a fog or the hyperactive one, neither state being ideal. My diet assessment revealed the boy ate prepared foods and snacks full of preservatives and artificial food dyes. It was difficult for the parents, but they cut down on their son's intake of such foods. After two months, the parents reported marked improvement in his behavior without the prescription drug. These parents were so pleased they told some other parents whose kids have ADHD, and I've had two new patients by referral."

Dr. Caroll's smile broadens. "I recall you shared some frustration about patients giving up on their protocol before seeing results. Did you do anything with these patients that helped them keep on track?"

"For the female patient, I told her she could email me whenever she had questions. If I didn't hear from her by Friday each week, I would send her a check-in email—just a quick 'how are you doing?' For the boy, I called his parents every other week. I think making contact helped because often, they had challenges and hadn't thought to ask for help. I've wondered if they were embarrassed to call me because they felt like they were failing." Georgie eyes the more experienced practitioners, nervous about offering her views on why patients don't reconnect.

"You raise a good point, Dr. Downie," says Dr. Caroll, nodding his head. "Perhaps they were not following your recommendations to the letter and didn't want to admit it. I don't have that happen with cancer patients, but then their conditions are life-threatening. Pam, Roger, do you have thoughts on Georgie's question?"

Roger shakes his head, but Pam nods. "Some of my patients have given up on my protocols. Most of them are seniors and perhaps their old habits die hard. There's another dynamic I've noticed. For some people, it's easier to give up than to complain to a health practitioner, so I like what you're doing with your follow-up calls. It's time consuming, but it should help your patients keep on track."

Georgie smiles at Pam, appreciating the validation. Encouraged by the spirit of cooperation, Georgie asks her colleagues if Lisa could make a presentation about her greens supplement at the next clinic meeting, adding a testimonial for the product's benefits. Pam and Roger turn to Dr. Caroll. This is the clinic owner's call.

"We don't have sales talks very often," Dr. Caroll says, "but I think we can have a listen since you think so highly of the product."

Georgie leaves the meeting elated the clinic owner approved her suggestion. She has two other patient success stories to share, but to control the length of meetings, Dr. Caroll limits each practitioner to two presentations.

These will have to wait until next month's meeting. An excellent problem to have! Her other two successes affirm the reasons she wanted to practice naturopathy. Linda, a twenty-seven-year-old woman, had a medical diagnosis of irritable bowel syndrome but could not resign herself to the doctor's prognosis: "you'll have to live with it." Diagnosed at age twenty-five, Linda had already suffered for a few years. Georgie gave Linda some hope at the first consultation, saying, "IBS does not have to be a life sentence." Assessing potential causes—diet, food sensitivities, gut flora imbalance, stress—Georgie determined the root causes of Linda's IBS to be a diet high in sugar and low in fiber, and a suspected intolerance to dairy products. At first, Linda was skeptical but proved it to herself by eliminating milk, yogurt, and cheese for two weeks and experiencing a rapid return of her symptoms after having ice cream. She expressed her surprise at what simple diet changes could do and promised she would tell everyone she knew how Georgie helped. That day Georgie's hope for her practice soared.

Her other success was a ten-year-old girl with severe digestive problems that started after the family returned from a Caribbean vacation. Georgie recognized the symptoms as eerily similar to Debbie's, and sure enough, testing confirmed an intestinal parasite. An anti-parasitic protocol of herbs and homeopathic remedies brought the child back to full health within four weeks. Of Georgie's successes, this outcome was the most gratifying. Who knows? She may have prevented prolonged suffering by the child and her parents.

One of Georgie's ongoing frustrations is for her patients who have suffered needlessly. They stayed with their medical doctor's treatment even when there was no improvement, often taking years before they sought another opinion. As Georgie sees it, the problem is that many people consider a naturopath as an alternative rather than a primary care provider. If people knew how naturopathy supports healing, they might consult with one earlier and avoid unnecessary pain and anguish. More must be done to build the reputation and credibility of naturopathy, but it is a daunting task for a newbie like herself. For now, she must focus on what she can manage, and that is to help each patient.

Chapter 13

Georgie escorts her last patient to the clinic door and returns to her office to wait for the clinic meeting to start. She is tired but satisfied, at least with her career progress. With a full schedule of patient appointments four days each week, she now has a steady income. Recently, Dwayne stopped complaining about her absences. Apparently, he can handle her being away through the week if there is enough money coming in. Even on the weekends, their time together is limited—just a few hours on Saturday and Sunday because Dwayne started visiting D.J. at school on Saturdays. It is apparent Dwayne plans to make the two-hour journey to Bloomington every Saturday until December, the end of football season. Dwayne won't go with her to church, and he golfs on Sunday until mid-afternoon. She sighs. *I'm not sure what is worse: Dwayne's nagging or his absence.*

Now that Daphne returned to Europe again, Georgie and Dwayne are "empty nesters," but their relationship is not as she imagined, having watched friends whose kids left home. She expected they would once again have time to enjoy each other as a couple, but now their lives barely intersect. Dwayne's threats about the state of their marriage weigh on her mind, but it does no good to dwell on it. There is little she can do differently. For now, her career is in another city.

Her musings are broken by the after-hours doorbell. It's Lisa, here for the clinic meeting to make her sales pitch to the Caroll Clinic naturopaths. Georgie greets her friend with a hopeful expectation that her colleagues will see the value in Lisa's greens product.

Lisa speaks with knowledge of her product's health benefits and why she selected specific ingredients—sprouted grains, sea and land vegetables, plant oils, herbs, and botanicals. Georgie admires her friend's effectiveness in promoting her product and herself as someone committed to health and well-being. After the presentation, Georgie gives a testimonial about how Lisa's greens helped her patients and Debbie during her illness. The other naturopaths ask Lisa about her formula, ingredients, and sources, and take some information but make no verbal commitment, even though Georgie senses Lisa's presentation impressed them. As Lisa leaves the meeting, Georgie gives a thumbs-up, optimistic her colleagues will add her friend's product to the clinic dispensary.

The clinic meeting continues with practitioner reports. Georgie planned to present her success cases—the woman with irritable bowel syndrome and the girl with parasites—but weighing on her mind are patients who did not do well under her guidance. She can't shake a suspicion these disappointing outcomes reflect her lack of skills as a practitioner. Perhaps her colleagues can detect where she went wrong with one patient she failed to help.

"I had a fifty-year-old patient who is menopausal and overweight—in reality, obese," Georgie says. "She came to me for weight loss with a history of losing and regaining weight several times since her early twenties. I marked 'Yo-Yo dieter' in my notes. She asked me which diet pills worked the best, saying she tried all the diets, and they never worked. I took some time to explain why diet pills are not the solution because they don't address the root cause of her overweight. When I asked about her eating habits, she was vague, but when I pressed for details, she admitted to snacking when stressed."

Pam interrupts, asking if the woman was on any medications. Georgie checks her case notes. "Yes. She was taking three prescription meds for depression, anxiety, and for joint pain." Georgie pauses, and, having no other questions, she continues.

"My protocol included a probiotic, digestive aid, vitamin supplements, a diet plan to support weight loss, and regular exercise. The woman came for a follow-up visit, had lost no weight, and once again asked me for diet pills, claiming diet changes would not work for her. I repeated my stance that diet pills are not part of natural healing and urged her to follow my recommendations. The patient did not return for her next appointment, and now I can't reach her to find out what happened. I must assume she gave up. What could I have done differently?"

The three naturopaths are silent for a few minutes, mulling over everything Georgie said.

"In my early days of practice, I tried specializing in weight loss and found it too difficult," Pam says, shrugging her shoulders. "There were too many variables in patients' lives that, as a practitioner, I could not control. To me, your patient may be difficult to help."

Georgie is about to ask why, but Pam continues. "I see several things working against weight loss with this patient, the anti-depressant medication, for one. Stress is likely elevating her cortisol levels, which will promote fat storage instead of fat burning. She sounds like an emotional eater, and for most people, that means too many sugars and starches. Her mindset is about finding a quick fix—diet pills, so it's no wonder she wouldn't follow a diet or make lifestyle changes. This is not the type of patient you want to hang your reputation on."

Georgie stares at Pam in disbelief. "So, you're saying there are some patients we shouldn't take on? Some we can't help. That's not what I signed up for. This woman was desperate for help. How could I turn her away? Isn't there something else I could have done?"

Mark Caroll nods. "Georgie, as Pam says, there are variables in a patient's life you cannot control, and those variables can work against healing. I understand. As a new practitioner, you want to help everyone. Otherwise, you wouldn't be in the profession. But you will learn there are some you just can't help."

Pam is up next with a presentation about how she helped a patient with high cholesterol who could not tolerate a statin medication. The woman lowered her bad cholesterol on Pam's protocol of anti-inflammatory diet, a plant sterol supplement, and herbs to support the liver. Georgie makes mental note of the protocol, but for the rest of the meeting, she has trouble focusing. She appreciates her colleagues' advice, but rails against it. *Why should I be okay with not helping some people? There must be something I can do.*

After the clinic meeting, Georgie pores over her case notes for the patient in her presentation. The woman had never seen a naturopath before, which means she may not understand how naturopathy works. Perhaps the woman thought a naturopath would be like a medical doctor, but use natural supplements instead of medications. After all, she wanted diet pills to do the work, much like a prescription medication would. Georgie recalls giving the woman her usual spiel about the natural healing process: "the longer you have a condition, the longer it will take for results." Perhaps this was not enough to highlight the differences in approach between naturopathy and medicine.

This situation reminds Georgie of other patients who did not follow her guidance. Often, the reason for their non-compliance was a mystery. Was it a lack of willpower? Impatience? Or something else? She does a web search on "naturopaths" and "patient compliance" and finds an article about a well-known clinic in California. Their solution is to hold seminars for new patients to introduce them to naturopathic practice and how it differs from the medical approach.

When leaving the office for the day, Georgie floats the idea with Dr. Caroll. "We could offer a seminar for new patients to explain how naturopathy works with the body's natural healing processes, the time it takes, and how our approach differs from medical doctors. The seminar would provide our patients with a consistent message on what to expect from us. Most important, patients wouldn't have unreasonable expectations for resolving their health problems, and we might lose fewer patients."

Mark Caroll checks his watch, apparently in a hurry to leave. "I used to hold new patient orientations, but after twenty years, I don't have to worry about patient retention. But you can pursue the idea if Pam or Roger are interested."

Somewhat discouraged, Georgie goes to Roger's office. He shakes his head, saying as the only Chinese medicine practitioner in the city with a long waiting list, he has few concerns about patient compliance. By the time she gets to Pam's office, she is shy about sharing her idea, but Pam listens, smiles and nods her head. "I'm interested in exploring this idea with you. My patients are older adults more used to medical doctors, and I suspect they don't understand how naturopathy works and may have unreasonable expectations. Sometimes I've struggled to make them understand."

The seminar for new patients is ready to launch. Georgie surveys the clinic conference room, counting twenty people in attendance, including patients and their spouses. Over the past four weeks, Georgie and Pam worked together to craft a forty-minute presentation they call The Naturopathic Way. In the presentation, they included some history of naturopathic medicine, a comparison to medical practice, an outline of the naturopathic assessment, and an explanation of natural healing. They also described Caroll Clinic's collegial approach and its benefits to patients.

Georgie gleaned ideas for the seminar from Dr. Caroll's old promotional talk, Why Naturopathy, but Pam's experience was also invaluable, applying the principles of the profession to everyday practice. Despite Georgie's urging that the seminar would be more impactful coming from an experienced naturopath, Pam was not keen on leading it. Georgie agreed to facilitate, hoping her Toastmasters training would compensate for her relative inexperience in practice. There was another challenge—how to convince patients to attend. From her promotional talks, Georgie knew how difficult it was to attract an audience, even when the event was free.

At Georgie's weekly lunch with Lisa, she asked her friend for ideas on promotion.

"Even if you promote the seminar as beneficial," Lisa said, "it helps to include a perk—a tangible benefit from attending. What about giving participants a service or product?"

They brainstormed the products or services to offer. A discount on the consultation fee was one idea, but Georgie settled on a free product as less costly. Lisa offered samples of her greens supplement she uses as giveaways at trade shows. They agreed it would be a win-win—free for the clinic and an enticement for the clinic practitioners to include Lisa's products into their supplement protocols.

"What, she no-showed again? Did she give any reason?" Georgie asks Karen, the office manager, who shrugs her shoulders. It's the second time this patient missed an appointment and Georgie expects one missed appointment could be an emergency, but to reschedule and not show up again must be something else. She recalls a couple of other no-shows last week, which were confounding because they had all attended the first Naturopath Way seminar just a few weeks ago. There is the other possibility—concern about the consultation fee. Not everyone has health insurance covering naturopathic services. Could it be that? That was one of Dwayne's initial concerns about her choice of profession.

Puzzled, she pulls out the case file for today's patient to study it for clues to explain the no-show. At the first follow-up appointment, Georgie's notes read:

"patient has not changed her diet and only took supplements intermittently." *Is something holding her back?* She turns to her initial assessment notes and reads the patient's report of a troubled relationship with her spouse, possibly abusive, and hints she suffered child abuse. One of Georgie's case notes stands out: "Patient carries a lot of guilt and self-recrimination for the abuse inflicted on her by others." Money should not be an issue with this patient, who had commented about her husband, "at least he is a good provider." Georgie keeps studying the file to identify what is different about this client and finally, it hits her: abuse. *Could this patient's emotional trauma make it difficult to make changes, even healthy ones?* She recalls learning about the effect of emotional trauma on physical health in one course at naturopathic college. She hasn't referred to the course materials since she graduated, but has them at her loft apartment.

During the evening, Georgie reviews her course notes and the text about how emotions interact with physical health. The complexities of mind-body interactions are astounding. When people are depressed or suffer from anxiety, they can become physically ill but it can also work in reverse—people with a chronic illness can suffer from mental health issues. Comorbidity is the medical term used to describe such conditions. The course explains how to assess patients for these unhealthy emotional patterns, and some of her patients have all the signs. During the course, she recalls there were introductions to mind-body therapies—hypnosis, meditation, behavior modification, and biofeedback—but there was no training provided. Either she must refer patients to other practitioners or take additional training in at least one of these disciplines. But Dwayne is likely to object to her spending any more on education. *How can I help these patients if I don't?*

Before considering additional training, Georgie resolves to read more about mind-body connections. After leafing through her course materials, she finds a reading list for independent study, identifies two likely book titles she did not have time to read in college, and downloads the E-book versions. Being alone in her loft apartment in the evening, she certainly has time for extracurricular reading.

Georgie reads the first book in two evenings, intrigued by the notion that physical ailments can have emotional connections, such as fear of the unknown, worry about the future, guilt about the past, and resentment towards others for perceived wrongs. She considers how common these emotions are and wonders why everyone isn't sick, including herself. Later in the book, the author clarifies that physical illness occurs only when negative emotions are dominant over positive ones.

The following afternoon at the clinic, Georgie studies the files of five patients who were no-shows or fell off their protocols. She discovers some commonalities, and it doesn't appear to be the lack of funds. They all have long-term physical health issues, a history of trauma, and emotional problems.

Delving into the second E-book in the evening, she reads something more alarming. The author theorizes that people who suffer from a long-term illness can become so identified with being ill they unknowingly resist healing. There can be a seductive power in a long-term illness because family and friends may offer extra care, attention, and sympathy. For the person with the illness, an irrational belief can take hold—their recovery will mean the end of others' care, attention, and sympathy. Taken to the extreme, the chronically ill person identifies with their illness so much they don't know how to live without it. They may believe they want to get better, even say they want to get better, but their psyche works against them. Could some of her patients be in this state? Is that what Dr. Caroll meant when he said, "you can't help everyone?" *I don't want to give up on patients, especially if they don't know why they can't heal.*

The saying "physician, heal thyself" pops into her head and Georgie takes a hard look at her health issues, assessing them for mind-body connections. She has suffered for years from headaches almost every week, and while they could be quite debilitating and annoying, she had become resigned to them. Her mother has them too, and Georgie has long thought she inherited the tendency, but the books on mind-body issues forces her to re-think this assumption. *Could my headaches stem from emotional stress?* To verify this possibility, she pledges to track her headaches—when they happen and what transpires just before their onset. *If I'm going to help my patients, I need to know the source of my headaches.*

From her reading, Georgie is aware of a New Age notion that if one expresses a specific need or desire, the universe provides the opportunity. She wonders if this is something like having answers to one's prayers, but whatever the mechanism, it works! Days after deciding she wants to learn about mind-body therapies, she notices an online ad for a local meditation group, one of the mind-body therapies she wants to explore. Starting this evening, the group meets weekly for six sessions at Community Church.

Curiosity leads her to attend the first session of the meditation group, just to check it out. Sally, the group leader, impresses Georgie with her soothing voice and calming presence. Sitting comfortably and breathing deeply along with the group, Georgie experiences her first guided meditation—Be Present. After the meditation, Sally explains the benefits of being present: fewer regrets about the past and less anxiety about the future, bringing more peace. The session concludes with a sung meditation chant, "Be still and know that I am God," based on Psalm 46.

The next morning, before clinic hours, Georgie bursts into Pam's office, eager to share her experience at the meditation group. Pam had politely turned down the invitation to come along.

"The meditation was so relaxing! Last night, I slept soundly and woke up refreshed. It's been a while since that happened. As holistic practitioners, I think we all would benefit from meditation as a daily practice."

Pam glances at Georgie but returns her attention to a patient file. "Hm, that's nice. Should you maybe finish the six sessions before you make a judgment? And how do you know *all* practitioners need meditation?"

Have I offended her? "Of course, you have a point. I only know what it did for me." Georgie leaves it there for now.

In the second group session, the meditation practice is about letting go of judgment—negative assessments and criticism—of others and herself. For Georgie, this meditation has an unsettling effect. Before heading home, she sits in her car, head in her hands, thinking about Dwayne, her father, and even her two youngest children. *How much judging have I been doing? Is judging others exacting a toll on me?*

At the sixth and final meditation session, Sally concludes with a talk emphasizing the health benefits from daily meditation—stress reduction, hormone balancing, and even slowing down aging. "The anti-aging benefit from meditation has something to do with preventing damage to telomeres, special proteins that protect DNA," she says.

Georgie supposes the meditation leader is closing the series with this information to encourage people to continue meditating on their own, and many participants, middle-aged or older, appear impressed. Georgie already knows damage to DNA is one reason we age, but has never heard meditation could prevent such damage. Back at her apartment, she checks online for scientific studies on telomeres, DNA, and meditation, and finds three studies that seem legitimate. But is there evidence in clinical practice? Georgie resolves to ask Pam if she knows about this.

"I heard something about such benefits from meditation," Pam says when Georgie approaches her the next day. "But there are so many theories on how to slow aging. Not all of them can make their way into my patient care. I have to avoid recommending things, like meditation, that patients might see as foo-foo."

Georgie chuckles at Pam's use of the odd idiom.

"Don't laugh," Pam says. "I hear this response from some older patients who are skeptical of things they believe are New Age. I suspect many would view meditation as something yogis do in ashrams, not for a seventy-year-old living in Indianapolis. Georgie, I can't recommend therapies that are too far ahead of where my patients are."

"I understand, but please keep an open mind. Before I went to the meditation group, I was wary about it, too. I went to the first session just to check it out, but I believe it's helping me. You likely need to try it yourself." The conversation ends there because they both have patients waiting. Georgie mulls over their conversation during her workday and, when leaving the clinic, approaches Pam to join her for guided meditation some mornings before clinic hours. Pam seems like she is going to say no, and Georgie pulls on some heartstrings. "My meditation group ended, and I need a meditation partner. It's so much better than doing it alone. Please, at least give it a chance."

Pam gives Georgie a long look and a sigh of resignation, but agrees to try it, and they set a time to meet at Georgie's loft the following morning.

Chapter 14

Pam has just left Georgie's apartment after a meditation session that left Georgie feeling calm and ready for her workday. As she changes into her work clothes, she reflects on her meditation experience over the past two weeks. Pam overcame her initial hesitancy and continued to join her for meditation, at least a few days each week. On days she meditated by herself, Georgie's experience was less satisfying and she's still not sure why that is. The phone breaks her meditation-induced calm.

"Georgie, don't you listen to phone messages?!" Dwayne says. "I called you last night at ten-thirty. It's D.J.! He took a nasty blow to the head, playing football. He's at Bloomington General, unconscious."

Georgie gasps and her throat tightens. "I'll be there as soon as I can!" Leaving a quick message with Karen to cancel her appointments, she dashes to her car and drives well over the speed limit to Bloomington, praying the state troopers aren't out today. Thankfully, the weather forecast for freezing rain is wrong. Her hands cramp from gripping the wheel too tight, and she shakes her hands out one at a time while taking some deep breaths, saying meditation mantras on each breath. Still, her anxiety grows as she imagines worst-case scenarios from a head injury. *This is when meditation should help!*

Rushing into the emergency, she finds Dwayne in the waiting room, his head in his hands. She places her hand on his shoulder.

"Oh!" He jumps at her touch. "I thought you were the doctor." He groans, runs his hands over his face, and slumps back in his chair. "They just took D.J. into emergency surgery to relieve pressure on his brain. The MRI showed an epidural hematoma from the hit to his head." Tears form in Dwayne's eyes. His hands are shaking.

"Oh! Dwayne!" Georgie's knees buckle and she collapses into the chair next to Dwayne, gripping both of his hands. "Did the doctor give a prognosis?"

Dwayne just shrugs his shoulders. "No. He's been vague, except that it could have been worse—a subdural hematoma, he called it."

Any type of brain hematoma is serious. Georgie doesn't voice this, seeing that Dwayne is already so shaken—more than she has ever seen him. With nothing comforting to say, she keeps holding his hands and bows her head, repeating a silent prayer: *Please God, guide the surgeon's hands and help my son come through this.* Dwayne just sits, staring at the clock as if that will bring news faster.

"I'm sorry I turned off my phone and missed your message," Georgie says. "Have you been here all night?"

"I got here last night at around ten, I think. It's a bit of a blur." Dwayne's disheveled hair and bags under his eyes suggest he hasn't slept.

Georgie's parents arrive. Claire rushes over and holds Georgie in a long embrace, rubbing her back, then hugs Dwayne. George skips the pleasantries and goes to the nurse's station. "I will make some inquiries," he says over his shoulder. "The staff may give me more information than they will you."

He returns a few minutes later, perturbed his doctor status afforded him no inside information, but he managed a private waiting room for families of patients in surgery. Thankfully, they are the only ones in the room, and they wait together in silence, Claire with her arms around Georgie, Dwayne pacing the room, and George sitting stoically in a straight-back chair. Georgie keeps checking the clock, but the time doesn't seem to change. Waiting is excruciating.

Around noon, the surgeon appears, looking haggard, his expression unreadable. He greets everyone by nodding at them one by one, then he smiles. Georgie takes a sharp intake of air. She hasn't breathed since the doctor arrived.

"Good news, folks! D.J. is out of surgery. We had to drill a small hole to aspirate the hematoma, and we did another scan to confirm there was no further bleeding. I expect he is out of danger. We will keep him in hospital for a few days to monitor him—make sure the bleeding doesn't recur."

Georgie puts her hand to her throat and lets out a sigh of relief. "Thank you, doctor!" Her father and mother echo this almost in almost unison. Georgie and Dwayne embrace.

"What are the odds of a complete recovery?" Georgie's father asks the surgeon.

"The odds are good. But I wouldn't want to speculate," the doctor replies. "You never know with these injuries, but he has youth on his side. The next few months will tell the tale."

Georgie and Dwayne agree to take turns staying with D.J. in the hospital, she with the day shift, and he taking over after work. "No sense in both of us sitting here," he says. "And we have a big contract to fulfill this week."

Georgie is too stressed about D.J.'s situation to object or remind Dwayne she doesn't have the option to work. She had to cancel her appointments for the rest of the week, three days' worth, but he will have the more demanding shift—overnight, sleeping in a recliner chair in D.J.'s room. The long drive back and forth between Terrance and Bloomington will be another stressor for both of them.

With D.J. sedated to support his recovery, Georgie has little to do. She left Indy in such a hurry she didn't bring any reading materials, and the hospital gift shop only has light reading, nothing to intrigue her. Bouts of anger and resentment toward Dwayne and D.J. interrupt her attempts to meditate and pray. *I warned them! Football is dangerous. Now, look what's happened!*

Late in the afternoon of the second day, her father's arrival interrupts her prayers and recriminations. She expresses surprise he would make the two-hour trip from Terrance again.

"I came to consult with D.J.'s attending physician to check on my grandson's care, and I am satisfied with what I heard. Thought I would come in and sit awhile with our patient."

"That is nice of you, Dad." She puts a finger to her lips. "Sh. Apparently, he needs to keep still, but they only gave him a mild sedative. I don't want to wake him."

They fall into silence which, after a while, hangs heavily in the room. "How are you doing, Dad?" she asks in a hushed tone. "Are you still practicing full-time? Mom said that you were going to cut back on your patient load."

"Oh, I think I'll just keep practicing until I can't do it anymore. I don't know what I would do with myself if I quit."

More silence. They sit at opposite ends of the room, staring out the window.

"And how are you doing, Georgie? Apart from worrying about D.J. right now?"

"I'm doing well, Dad."

"I hope you appreciate that D.J. might not be alive if it weren't for medical expertise. This is the medicine you think isn't worth anything, that you won't deign to practice."

Georgie stares at him in disbelief. *There it is again! Does he see every situation as an opportunity to criticize me?* Dwayne arrives to take his turn by D.J.'s bedside, and Georgie bolts from the room—saved from a confrontation. Once in the elevator, the tears come. With the strain of the past few days, her father's comments are just too much, and it takes a half-hour sitting in the hospital coffee shop to compose herself before she can drive home to Terrance. By the time she is home, her head is pounding. Even Shadow's wagging tail cannot break through her dark mood.

After a five-day stay, the doctor releases D.J. from the hospital with strict instructions to rest at home for two weeks at least. He isn't home an hour before he takes the stairs two at a time, and Georgie must spell out what "resting" means. It feels like she's tending to a five-year-old again.

Dwayne arrives home from work and reports on his lengthy phone conversations with the dean at D.J.'s college. "Because he missed three final exams, he could lose those credits. He may need an additional semester to finish his degree."

"That is unfortunate," Georgie says. "But this is the chance one takes when playing a full-contact sport."

Dwayne gives her a withering look.

Georgie returns his look but says no more about it. Instead, she announces she needs to get back to work. She has already called her mother, who agreed to come over to check on D.J. and make sure he has lunch. At Dwayne's look of displeasure, Georgie grimaces and shrugs her shoulders. "No consultations, no income!"

"Of course." Dwayne gestures a backhand wave. "Do what you want."

Georgie stares at him, waiting for him to say more. Hearing nothing, she can't help but analyze his comment. Does he mean, "I don't care that you're going" or "I don't care about you?" She has heard trouble can bring families closer together but, so far, this has not been the case with Dwayne and her, and certainly not with her father. Foreboding accompanies her on the long drive back to Indianapolis.

At her weekly lunch with Lisa in Terrance, Georgie shares her recent experiences with meditation and prayer. After her meditation group ended, Georgie took the leader's advice and set up a meditation space in her loft. "It's near the big window that overlooks the park. I have a comfortable chair, a candle burning, and soothing music playing. Sometimes Pam joins me, but when I'm alone, it's not as satisfying as meditating in a group. I've wondered what I'm doing wrong. But I just started with another group at Community Church about the power of prayer in health and healing."

"Ooh. That sounds interesting!"

"It is! The group leader introduced us to five elements of prayer: worship, gratitude, blessings to others, confession, and requests for help. I was embarrassed to admit my prayer life has been all about asking God for help in times of trouble. Lisa, it's like I treat God like a complaints department or an order desk: Dear God. One miracle, please!"

Lisa giggles at Georgie's rare attempt at humor.

"But other people in the group admitted similar limitations. It turns out none of us had instruction on how to pray."

"I get that. I spent years going to church before I learned much about how to pray. It's wonderful you found that group."

"Lisa, I didn't give enough credit to the power of prayer. Now, after praying, I feel more balanced, more peaceful. And I have needed more peace with all the worrying about D.J.'s health. My goal is to learn how to use meditation or prayer with my emotionally unbalanced patients. I'm just not sure where to start."

Georgie joins about one hundred others for a seminar at one of the convention centers in the city. She shakes her head in wonder how it happened for the second time. She had an interest in learning something, and the opportunity presented itself. A woman in her prayer group shared a notice about a seminar on mind-body medicine being held right in the city. Amy

Morningside, the presenter, is a university professor and the author of a book on mind-body medicine that she is promoting by giving free seminars.

As the session goes on, Georgie gains insight into why some of her patients don't heal from traditional medical therapies or even her natural remedies. She notes several physical and mental health interactions that remind her of some of her patients. Included in the professor's case histories are examples of how people benefit from mind-body therapies. Georgie leaves the seminar with the professor's book and enthusiasm for new possibilities in her patient care.

On arrival home late Saturday afternoon, Georgie is still enthused about what she learned and tells Dwayne about how it could help grow her practice. He listens for a few minutes, but just says, "huh." She's not sure he gets it, so she calls Lisa.

"Georgie. I missed our lunch today. I hope your seminar was worth it."

"It was! What I learned today confirms what I suspected. Some of my patients are so stuck in their negative thoughts and emotions they can't heal. Consciously, they desire health, but subconsciously they have no identity outside their illness. They emotionally invest themselves in being ill."

"That sounds strange!"

"At first, I thought so, too. It can start innocently enough. A person with chronic illness can get a lot of attention and care from others. Over time, they can become afraid, not consciously, that if they get better, no one will care for them anymore."

"Wow! People can get so screwed up!"

Georgie laughs. "Well, maybe not screwed up, but their emotional awareness is certainly flawed. Anyway, this might be the key to helping some of my patients. I'm still working on putting it into practice, but I thought teaching them positive affirmations could be a first step, to help them see a role for themselves apart from their illness. At the very least, affirmations can get them out of negative self-talk, which is detrimental to their health."

"Hm. You sure are exploring a lot of spirituality lately. Affirmations? I'm sure they don't teach that at Naturopathic College."

"Perhaps this approach is… out there, but it may be the only way to help these patients."

Their conversation turns to family news—how their kids are and issues with family. Georgie laments over her recent upset with her father and her growing suspicion their ongoing rift is triggering her headaches.

"So, what are you doing to heal your relationship with your father?" Lisa asks. "If your suspicions about your headaches are correct, you need to work on mending the relationship. I'd hate to see you end up like one of your patients."

"You have a point. But there's not much I can do. I won't change professions, and he refuses to come to terms with my choice."

The conversation with Lisa reminds Georgie how challenging it will be to help others heal from physical ailments triggered by emotional issues. If Lisa is right, she has yet to deal with her own issues. After the call ends, Georgie does an online search and finds an affirmation to reframe her father-daughter angst: *The love between my father and me is stronger than our misunderstanding.* She repeats it a few times and must admit it feels better than focusing on what is wrong with their relationship. *But will simply saying the affirmation change anything?*

The practitioners at Caroll Clinic gather for the monthly clinic meeting in the upstairs conference room after clinic hours. Again this month, there is no time for a dinner out; they are all too busy, which Mark Caroll declares "a good thing!" He springs for a big fruit tray, scones, coffee, and tea, and they load their plates to eat from during presentations.

Georgie already planned to talk to her colleagues about exploring mind-body medicine as one of her specialty areas. During her presentation time, she gives a five-minute overview of how she believes mind-body healing will help her patients.

"Perhaps you should take training in spiritual counseling," Pam says, "and I know of a continuing education course that a former classmate took. I can connect the two of you if you like."

"It is possible that this training could help your practice," Dr. Caroll says. "But I'd like to know about the course before you register—make sure it's not some fly-by-night course with questionable credentials. What you do reflects on the clinic."

As usual, Dr. Brownlee has nothing to add. He just nods at Dr. Caroll's suggestion.

Following the meeting, Georgie reaches Pam's naturopath contact by phone, and based on what she learns, makes a snap decision to take a spiritual counseling course. She registers for an online course on prayer without letting Dr. Caroll know. If he disapproves of the course, she expects to find some benefit personally, and the investment is small—two hundred dollars for the course fee and book. There are six other courses for the full certification as a spiritual counselor, but, for now, she will take it one at a time.

With satisfaction, Georgie re-reads the email congratulating her on a grade of ninety-five percent in her first spiritual counseling course. As an online program, she could progress at her own speed, and she finished it in two months, even though four months was the expected time for completion. The material was so fascinating she spent most of her weekends on it, and, while she did not mind giving up her free time, Dwayne grumbled about it.

Most significant to Georgie was learning an approach to prayer to suit different faith perspectives, even atheists. She hopes this will help her reach patients like the one from a few months ago, an avowed atheist, who reacted to her mention of the healing power of prayer, calling it "the p word." She must accept not everyone believes in prayer, perhaps including her clinic colleagues. However, she remains determined to introduce her patients to prayer as a healing therapy, at least for those open to it.

To promote mind-body counseling as part of her practice will require a stamp of approval from Dr. Caroll, and the chance to make her case is at today's clinic meeting. Georgie finishes her presentation, and Dr. Carroll looks at her quizzically. "I am concerned that this will divert you from your current specialties, in which you have been effective. If people want spiritual support, can't they just talk to their pastor?"

Georgie detects criticism from the clinic director, perhaps because she took the spiritual counseling course without his blessing. Still, his words of praise about her current specialties are encouraging. "Fewer people are members of a church community than in the past. Anyway, my intervention is not about encouraging someone in their faith. It's about using spiritual practices to support healing."

"Hm," Dr. Caroll says, tilting his head. "It's your practice, but I suggest you make this a minor focus until you complete more courses."

Pam smiles. "The naturopath I know who uses spiritual counseling in her practice is having positive outcomes. But, when she first started, she had trouble convincing people to engage in the counseling. Apparently, it took off after she brought in a speaker on mind-body healing." She pauses and glances out the window. "Maybe you could do the same—hold a seminar at the clinic to introduce the concept."

The mind-body seminar is due to start in fifteen minutes and Georgie checks the mike and sound system and makes sure the speaker has everything she needs. It all came together in one month with help from Pam. Georgie congratulates herself on securing as a speaker, Amy Morningside, the professor from the seminar she attended some months before. Amy asked for a small honorarium to cover travel from Chicago, and the opportunity to promote her book. Georgie views it as an ideal fit. If her patients buy Amy's book, it will legitimize the role of mind-body connections, and, since Amy is not a practitioner looking for patients, it will allow Georgie to promote her counseling services at the event.

To accommodate a larger audience than the clinic meeting room would hold, Georgie rented the auditorium at Community Church. She covered the cost of the speaker and the space, believing it money well spent to promote her practice. Pam suggested they ask participants to pay a small fee with all the proceeds donated to charity because "people put more value on something they pay for." They agreed to donate the proceeds to the local food bank, one of Pam's favorite charities.

Most of the promotion for the event was to clinic patients and their families—an open invitation with no pre-registration required. *Was that a mistake? What if not enough people come?* Community Church also promoted the event to their members, and Georgie hopes that will pad the numbers. At the seven o'clock start time, her anxiety dissolves as she counts heads—fifty-five people. An acceptable turnout.

Amy speaks for forty-minutes about the history of mind-body medicine, mind-body issues, and case examples of how various techniques promote healing. Georgie checks the faces in the audience a few times to judge their response, noting some nods and smiles, a sign that those people are receptive. After a question-and-answer period, Georgie gives a testimonial for Amy's book and announces her plan to offer counseling in mind-body healing at Carol Clinic. "Anyone who is interested in more information about this therapy can leave their names with me."

Several people line up to purchase Amy's book and Georgie notices some are writing their names on the sign-up sheet for counseling—existing patients plus others she does not recognize. Pam and Georgie smile and nod at each other, signaling their agreement the event went well.

Once again, the Carol Clinic's monthly practitioner meeting is on site after clinic hours. For dinner they get takeout—assorted meat, egg, and veggie wraps and salad. Georgie picks at her salad, having little appetite because she is apprehensive about Dr. Caroll's request for a report on her progress with mind-body counseling.

"I had eight counseling patients this past month," Georgie says in her report. "Half of them embraced the counseling and seemed to respond positively. Two seemed interested, but they made little progress. Two others had one session and did not continue."

"Have you determined why those two patients discontinued the counseling?" Mark Caroll asks.

"I can't be sure, but based on what they said, I suspect they resisted the idea their emotions were controlling their physical health." Georgie doesn't share how one patient took offense, saying she didn't come to a naturopath to be psychoanalyzed. All she wanted was to get rid of her stomach pain.

"It's a good start," Pam says, "but I feel you need an approach that is effective with more of your patients. And you need to define what a successful outcome would look like."

Georgie admits she is still working on that.

"I recommend you finish the spiritual counseling certification before continuing this form of therapy," Dr. Caroll says.

Georgie's colleague's responses are deflating and she is close to giving up, but for one unexpected benefit. By taking a course and counseling others, she confirmed her suspicions about how her emotions affect her physical health. She has headaches whenever someone is critical of her or challenges her, usually her father but lately Dwayne, too. And she has a surprising realization; she's had fewer headaches in the past few months. *Could this be a benefit of daily meditation and prayer?* This is the awareness and benefit that she wants for her patients.

It's a hot, muggy day in July. Georgie strolls through the park at dusk to avoid the worst of the heat, but a recent source of frustration weighs on her mind, making her time in the outdoors less satisfying. Her latest attempt at mind-body work was to recommend meditation to patients with anxiety and emotional issues. Without the training to lead group meditation herself, she referred her patients to the local meditation center, but few followed through. Could Pam be right? Perhaps meditation is not for everyone. There are other mind-body therapies—yoga, relaxation techniques, and tai chi—but Georgie knows little about them, which means she can't make definitive recommendations to her patients.

Near the end of her walk, she has an aha moment based on her own breakthrough in understanding the source of her headaches. Perhaps her intervention can be less about the therapy, whether it be meditation, prayer, or yoga. Perhaps her focus should be more on increasing her patients' awareness, how their emotional responses can trigger health issues, and how toxic emotions block healing. Such in-depth understanding of oneself is critical but challenging to achieve, as she discovered in her first attempts at counseling others. Her colleagues are right—she is not ready to include mind-body counseling as a specialty in her practice. She must put it on hold until she has a reliable approach to raise her patients' awareness of their emotional barriers to healing.

Chapter 15

"Georgina, your father has... had a... stroke. He's in... the hospital," Claire says between sobs. "And I can't reach Linnie." Georgie is about to return to Indianapolis mid-morning on Monday when she receives this call. Instead, she speeds to the hospital in Terrance and rushes into the Intensive Care Unit to find her mother pacing the floor. Her father is sitting up in bed, even though he is hooked up to a heart monitor and has an IV running. He is a pale version of his usual self.

"I'm going to be fine," he says, waving one hand. "They just have me here for observation as a precaution. If I had another event, they would be afraid I might sue them! I'll be fine, just fine."

Typical bravado of a doctor. They have trouble seeing themselves as a patient.

The doctor in charge of her father's case arrives. "Dr. Novak, preliminary tests show the stroke left you with minimal use of your left arm and leg, but no evidence of mental impairment. You may regain some movement in time. If not, you could end up in a wheelchair. I'm sorry I don't have better news."

"But there is always a chance of full recovery," George says.

"Of course, but I assess it's a slim chance," says the doctor.

George seems to take the news in stride, perhaps preferring to hang his hopes on the "slim chance." Claire gasps, stumbles, and leans against Georgie, who steadies her with one arm and steers her to a nearby waiting area where they sit together, hands clasped.

"Your father will not be a good patient," Claire says, fighting back tears. "He'll fight the wheelchair. I'm sure of that! And I'm not sure I can handle him at home. My back is bad." Her eyes widen and her hand flies to her mouth. "Oh, no! He won't be able to keep his practice going and, without his fees, our savings will soon be gone. And I know our medical insurance will not cover all the medical bills and therapy he may need."

Georgie puts her arms around her mother. "Whoa, Mom. Don't get ahead of yourself. The doctor said he might recover some movement on his left side. But if you need therapy or help at home, Dwayne and I could help with the costs. Or maybe you could ask Linnie. Her husband is doing very well."

Claire shakes her head, tears now streaming down her face. "All those years he worked in his medical practice. We didn't save enough money, and now we have to accept help from our kids." She fumbles in her purse for a tissue and dabs her eyes. "I can handle this, I suppose, but not George. His pride will get in the way. If he knows that you or Linnie are helping, he might not accept it. Then what will we do?"

Georgie studies her mother, scrambling for something to say that will console her. "Mom, what about this? You keep the books, so how is he to know who is paying for what? He's likely better off not knowing."

Claire nods weakly, her eyes glazed over. It alarms Georgie how frail and lost her mother looks. Perhaps neither of her parents is up to managing this new reality.

Upon release from the hospital, the doctor confirms George will be in a wheelchair, at least for a while, and daily therapy will be essential. Claire seemed too distraught to make any preparations, so Georgie took charge and contacted an agency to arrange for additional care at home. Claire was also reluctant to call Linnie to ask for financial help. After several unanswered calls, on the day her father is released, Georgie reaches Linnie, who is just returning home from a vacation.

"Georgina, I can take care of any additional costs for Dad's home care," Linnie says right away. "We can afford it, and I want to do this for Mom and Dad. Why have a lot of money if you can't help your family?"

Georgie stifles a snort. Her sister's value on money has made it difficult for them to be close, but this time she doesn't care about Linnie's eagerness to flaunt her wealth. Dwayne has repeatedly reminded her they are tapped out from the cost of D.J.'s college tuition, and the commitment will increase because of the three lost courses.

Georgie arrives at her parent's home on Saturday afternoon, her father's second day home. He is sleeping in his easy chair, so she joins her mother in the kitchen for a cup of tea. Georgie notices there is no fresh baking—her mother obviously has no time for that. Her mother's haggard appearance is also alarming. Usually, she would be neatly dressed, her hair styled, but today it looks like she just got out of bed.

Besides the strain of her husband's ill health, Claire talks about the challenges she has had the past week negotiating with local doctors to take over the care of George's active patients, at least temporarily. "Each doctor can only take on a few patients, and some are picky about who they will accept. It's been difficult." She peeks around the corner. "Good, he's still asleep and won't hear me. Georgina, I worry those patients will prefer to stay with the other doctors—they're younger and more up to date on the latest treatments. By the time George is practicing again, if he can, he may not have any patients left." She dabs her eyes with a tissue. "Part of his retirement plan was to sell his practice. Now he might not have a practice to sell."

Georgie embraces her mother but has few words of assurance. It is something she and Dwayne know full well. They are both self-employed with no company pensions.

"Georgie, I hope you are putting some of your income aside in investments, so you have a retirement fund. We put some away, but not enough."

Her mother must have read her thoughts. "Yes, Mom. Dwayne has it all in hand. He *is* an accountant, after all. But we can't put a lot aside while we're paying for D.J.'s tuition." She has a sudden pang of guilt. Years ago, her parents paid for two years of her medical school tuition, that her father now views as a waste. Those funds would certainly help her parents now.

Georgie is about to leave when her father wakens. Beneath his bravado, George Novak is a man desperately trying to hide a personal defeat. He planned to keep his practice going for a few years more, like many doctors who work well into their seventies or eighties. He is now seventy-six, and his plan is in doubt.

"And how are you doing with your practice?" her father asks, shifting the focus from his health status. "Are you able to make a go of it? My greatest fear was that you would not make a living as a naturopath. After all, in my day, the medical association considered naturopaths as nothing more than quacks, pushing unproven treatments and giving people false hope. I can't imagine that would make for a successful practice."

Her father's objections sound like a broken record. He is talking to her, at least, but in a familiar critical tone. She opens her mouth to defend herself but stops when her father puts up his good hand.

"I know. You're going to tell me you're not a quack, and your mother seems to think you're helping some people, but it may not matter if you help a few patients. Old attitudes are slow to change."

If all doctors are as stubborn as you, attitudes will never change. Georgie cringes at the depressing thought.

"I hear a couple of medical doctors run this quackery website," her father says, wagging his finger. "If you're not careful, they will put you on their quack list. That'll shut you down for sure!" He turns away, a tear forming in his eye. "And you could have avoided all this if you went into medicine. You could have done so much more being a proper doctor. It's the biggest regret of my life."

I can't fight with him right now. He's not well enough. "Let's not talk about that right now. You shouldn't be worrying so. You need to rest so you can get back on your feet."

"Sure, sure. I'm resting, but I'm also praying that you will see the light!"

"And I've prayed you will respect my right to choose my career, and I'm still waiting for an answer to that prayer." She gets up to leave. "Take care of yourself, Dad. I'm afraid I can't visit again for a while. My presence upsets you too much."

On the drive back to Indianapolis, Georgie practices deep breathing and meditation chants but can't restore calm. Once at her apartment, she drinks two large glasses of wine. As she finishes the second glass, it hits her that drinking is another unhealthy response to stress. *Why won't my father let this go? And why do I let him get to me?*

On Monday morning, Georgie wakes up with a headache and she drags herself to the clinic with her father's warnings ringing in her ears. It seems so unfair that even if she helps her patients, she could face censure from some doctors whom she has never met, who know nothing about her work. Until now, she has not dared look at the quackery website, but curiosity gets the best of her. She types "quackery" into the search engine, alarmed that the website comes up first on the list. After reading through several pages, she finds what she dreaded—an article specifically mentioning mind-body medicine as quackery. A shock runs through her body. *If I list mind-body medicine as a service, this website could label me a quack!*

Georgie scans the quack list on the website and sees a practitioner she knows—her clinic director, Dr. Caroll. *How unfair*! He is a Fellow of the American Board of Naturopathic Oncologists, an accreditation only for practitioners with recognized experience and proven expertise in cancer care. Based on the case histories Dr. Caroll presents at clinic meetings, he has excellent outcomes with his patients. Just recently, he had a Stage 3 breast cancer patient achieve full remission without chemo or radiation. The IV room is at capacity every day, and he had to hire a nurse to help administer infusions. He has published several journal articles about complementary cancer care and given several presentations at integrative health conferences. Georgie estimates he is in the top ten in his field in the country, but somehow, that makes him a quack. *How does he handle this?*

Distracted by troubling questions and her lingering headache, she struggles to be effective in her patient consultations. At the end of clinic hours, she approaches Dr. Caroll. "I saw your name on the quackery website. Were you aware of that? How do you keep going in the face of such opposition to your work?"

A wry smile crosses his face. "Yes, I was aware of that listing. But I have to keep my focus on my patients' health and not let the irrational doubters distract me." Georgie stares at him in admiration, wondering how she could be as brave as her clinic director.

On a rare morning off from seeing patients, Georgie is taking a leisurely shower after returning from her morning walk in the park. The phone rings, but she can't get to it in time. Throwing on a robe, she listens to the message on her voice mail. "This is Dr. Caroll. Dr. Downie. You had better get into the office right away." It's the first time he has called her at home, and his tone is ominous. The short drive to the clinic seems to take forever. *What is so urgent?*

Mark Caroll is waiting at the clinic door, his brow furrowed. He directs Georgie into his office, motioning her to a chair. "You'd better sit down."

Georgie sits on the edge of the chair, her hands tightly clasped.

"I had a call from the coroner's office early this morning," he says. "Your patient Rosemary Polaski passed away a few days ago, and they are doing an autopsy. They somehow know she was your patient, and that she was not seeing her medical doctor anymore. It sounds like there will be a police investigation into her death."

"What? How terrible!" Through her shock at losing a patient, Georgie digests the other part of the news. "She stopped seeing her medical doctor! She didn't tell me that." Georgie's mouth goes dry, and she wrings her hands together.

Dr. Caroll's frown deepens. "Did you ever discuss her medical treatment or suggest she discontinue it?"

"No, no, of course not. I never suggest naturopathy can replace a medical doctor's care and I'm careful to say that my care is complementary."

"Well, I hope your case notes back up what you're saying. Prepare yourself for questions!"

As Georgie leaves his office shaken by Dr. Caroll's questions and demeanor, he says, "An investigation like this can blow up in the media, especially when a patient abandons medical advice. This could renew calls from the AMA to discredit our profession."

Georgie retreats to her office and flops into her chair, feeling sick to her stomach. How could this have happened? Of course, her patient's unfortunate demise is upsetting, but an inquiry would hurt her reputation even if she did nothing wrong. And the press would be all over this! Her office phone rings. It's Karen from the front desk.

"The police are in the office lobby asking for you," says Karen, her voice shaking.

Before Georgie gets off the phone, a burly officer, rigged with his gun and nightstick, appears at her office door. "I am here for the patient records of Rosemary Polaski," he says. "This is part of a police investigation into her sudden death."

"Of course. Anything to help." Georgie's fingers fumble as she rifles through her file cabinet. With the patient's file in hand, ready to give to the officer, she asks: "Do I get these files returned?"

The officer folds his arms and frowns. "No. You'll have to make a copy. And I will have to watch while you make that copy."

The copier is behind the front desk in full view of the waiting room. As Georgie feeds papers into the copier with the officer hovering at her elbow, she scans the room, thankful there are no patients there. At least, for now, patients won't know about this.

For the rest of the day, Georgie struggles to bury her fears and focus on her patients, but she feels scattered, more than once asking a patient to repeat what they said. At night, she lies in bed for hours, staring at the ceiling, and wakes up in the morning with a fuzzy head and a queasy stomach.

A second day goes by with no contact from the police, and Georgie suffers another sleepless night. She considers talking to Dwayne and Lisa but doesn't want to sound any alarms, not until she knows more.

"This is the coroner's office. You need to come down to the police station to answer some questions."

It is three days since Georgie heard of her patient's untimely death when she receives this call. Fighting off her alarm, she plucks up the courage to ask, "Am I charged with something? Should I call a lawyer?"

"No. Just routine questions," says the caller.

Georgie recalls from TV dramas, police giving this assurance, but the questions never turn out to be routine. They just say it is routine as a ruse to catch people off guard. Indecision has her sitting at her desk for a while. *Do I need a lawyer? But having a lawyer might make it seem like I'm guilty of something.*

Georgie ends up going to the police station on her own. An officer ushers her into a room furnished only with a long table and three chairs, much like the interrogation rooms she has seen on TV. Two men arrive. One introduces himself as the coroner, and thanks Georgie for coming in. The other man says he is a detective. Georgie immediately forgets their names. The arrangement of chairs is disconcerting, with Georgie seated in the middle and the two men sitting at opposite ends of the table. They take turns asking her questions, requiring her to make a one-hundred-and-eighty-degree head swivel each time. *If they're trying to make me feel uncomfortable, it's working!*

The men pepper Georgie with questions about her case notes and her supplements. She is thankful she followed the procedures naturopathic college taught to detail everything in case notes. Her note on a protocol sheet, a copy of one given to the patient, might make all the difference: "Recommended in conjunction with current medical treatment." Still, at the end of the two-hour interview, she feels shell-shocked, and alarmed when the coroner says they may have other questions after the autopsy is complete.

She would prefer returning to the refuge of her apartment, but stops in at the clinic, having promised Dr. Caroll to speak to him right away about her interview. He motions her into his office, where she collapses into a chair.

"There were two men—interrogators, really. They asked me about my remedies, the probabilities of side effects and interactions with the patient's medications. I heard the same questions several times, but worded differently, like they were trying to catch me in a contradiction. It felt like they were bent on proving my remedies caused that poor woman's death."

Worry lines Dr. Caroll's forehead. "Were you comfortable with the way you answered?"

"I think so. I hope so! Near the end, I got a little steamed, and asked if they were looking into the side effects of the medications my patient was taking. After all, I told them, medications have serious side effects, and they affect everyone differently. The coroner kind of made a face. I hope I didn't make things worse."

Dr. Caroll asks to see Georgie's case notes and treatment protocol. "Your protocol is mostly based on diet and lifestyle changes, with just two vitamin supplements and a homeopathic remedy, all fairly benign. But you had better make sure you have consistent answers about contraindications if they question you again."

Georgie nods, panic tightening her throat.

She returns to her apartment and calls Dwayne right away. There were reporters outside the police station and if the inquest makes the news, she wants Dwayne to hear about it from her first.

"Dwayne, I had to speak to the police today after a patient of mine died unexpectedly. Nothing to worry about—just routine questions."

"What? I don't like the sound of that! Are you sure it's just routine?"

"Yes, yes. Standard procedure when someone dies suddenly." Georgie struggles to keep her voice calm. It may not be standard procedure, but it sounds plausible and might keep Dwayne from overreacting. *Change the subject. That will divert his attention.* "So, how is D.J. doing?"

"Just okay. I got a call from the college dean today. D.J.'s grades from the last term are not good enough for football eligibility, and just when the doctors cleared him to return after his head injury."

Of course, Dwayne's concern is more about football! "Dwayne, are we really going to be upset if he can't play football anymore? Does D.J. have some future in the game? And given his injury, is it even a good idea?"

"I'm surprised at you, of all people, saying he shouldn't pursue his dream. Listen to yourself! It's okay for you to pursue your dream, but his is not worthwhile. Keep it up and you could push him away just like your father did you."

Georgie cringes at Dwayne's accusations. *Is that what I'm doing?* "Of course, I don't want to discourage him, but this situation is different. Sure, he may have a dream to play professional football, but that doesn't mean he has the ability."

"Well, he's young. I think we can give him some time to figure out if he can do it. Hey, the football scouts will soon tell him, so we don't need to say anything."

To Georgie, Dwayne is shirking his responsibility. This is a situation in which their son needs parental guidance—his future could depend on his decisions now. She wants to continue pushing against her son's participation in football but senses it will fall on deaf ears. She heaves a sigh. "At least, can you talk to him about improving his grades?"

"Oh, I already called him earlier this evening. He knows he needs to buck up so you don't have to say anything. And please don't! You could make it worse by badgering him about it."

"It just upsets me we keep having this conversation with him. He's smart, but he won't apply himself."

"And you knew everything at his age? Lighten up!"

It's a sour way to end their conversation, but Georgie feels powerless to say more because Dwayne now seems to be the parent with more influence. As she stews over this development, she realizes all her recent conversations with Dwayne were about their children, and they seldom agreed on a position to take. They seemed to have little else to talk about, which means most of their interactions were acrimonious.

Before bed, she meditates for a while and turns to an affirmation that has helped in the past. *Today, I will seek balance in my life. I will re-frame this negative situation into a positive experience—an opportunity for growth.* The claim about affirmations is that if you repeat them enough times, they come true. She wonders how many times is enough.

Chapter 16

The investigation into Rosemary Polaski's death is still going on. The only upside is that, even though two weeks have passed, the news media has not linked Georgie to the investigation. Her efforts at meditation and prayer have not controlled her anxieties over how things will play out. It doesn't help that her clinic colleagues appear to be tiptoeing around her, like her troubles could be catching. Are they afraid her legal issues could harm their own reputations? Dr. Caroll suggested she take time off from seeing patients, but Georgie declined, preferring to keep busy and focus on what is going well.

Today she has a follow-up appointment with Katrina, a woman who consulted Georgie two months ago with a mysterious onset of asthma. Medical doctors had not identified the cause, and so far, Georgie wasn't sure either. At the second consultation, a month ago, Katrina had little relief in her symptoms, and Georgie changed the supplement protocol. Katrina also mentioned her children were experiencing similar health issues, to which Georgie suggested the involvement of environmental toxins in the home. They planned to explore this at the next visit, which is today.

Georgie half expects Katrina to cancel the appointment, but she arrives with a smile on her face, brandishing a piece of paper. Because of Georgie's comment about toxins, Katrina's husband arranged for an air quality test in their home that identified a high count of mold spores concentrated in the bathroom. When they looked behind the drywall, they discovered black mold. The mold has been removed, but Katrina's asthma is still troublesome. Georgie explains it will take a while to restore health and recommends immune-supportive supplements and anti-fungal remedies. Katrina is effusive, expressing her relief at having a diagnosis and a treatment plan. It is just the tonic Georgie needs—a reminder of why she is practicing as a naturopath.

Sitting in her office, waiting for her next patient, she receives the call she has been expecting and dreading. The results of Rosemary Polaski's autopsy are in. It was a heart attack. Georgie shakes her head, mystified how a woman of forty-eight, with no apparent risk factors, could suffer a fatal heart attack. Another call comes in an hour later asking her to come to the police station around five o'clock.

Ushered into the same meeting room, two different investigators ask what seem like the same questions as the first interview. Georgie struggles to control her irritation while she repeats the answers she already gave. Having taken Dr. Caroll's advice to be sure about her remedies, both the benefits and risks, she provides copies of the research on her remedies to back up her claims of safety. But privately, she has her own questions. *Did I miss something in my assessment of this patient? Did I miss signs of an impending heart attack?*

Georgie leaves the interview, discouraged and exhausted. The uncertainty and worry over the investigation are taking a physical toll—her headaches have returned, and she has lost her appetite. She must have lost some weight because her pants are loose, and the other day Pam commented how gaunt she looks. Weary to her bones, she arrives home and climbs the long flight of stairs to her loft. The phone is ringing—it's Lisa. Almost every evening, she has a call from Lisa or Melanie or both. *Bless them for trying to keep my spirits up.*

"How are you faring?" Lisa asks. "Any news?"

Georgie fills her in on the autopsy report and the grilling she took during a second two-hour round of questions.

"Georgie! This must be so unsettling for you."

"It's freaking me out. I'm having headaches almost every day, bad enough to cancel a day of appointments this week."

"Oh, poor you. Are you still meditating? It was giving you so much peace."

"Yes, every day. Sometimes it helps, sometimes not. Even though I did nothing wrong, the judgment on my remedies could come from a medical examiner who has a bias against naturopathic practice. It feels like the cards are stacked against me, and there's nothing I can do about it."

"Hey, if you did nothing wrong, I'm sure it will work out," Lisa says with what sounds like forced optimism. "But if you decide you need a lawyer, call me. I know a good one in Indy, the ex-husband of one of my best customers."

"Thanks, Lisa. I appreciate it, but I hope I won't need a lawyer." Georgie shakes her head, astounded by how Lisa always comes through in a crisis. They end the call and the phone rings again. This time, it's Melanie.

"What did Dad say when you told him?" Melanie asks.

"I haven't told him yet because I'm not sure what to say that won't set him off. He's bound to judge this as a failure and start lecturing me. I can hear him now: 'This wouldn't have happened if you had gone into medicine.' It won't help to remind him medical doctors get investigated too, and likely more often than naturopaths. Did you know medical errors are the third leading cause of death?" She doesn't wait for Melanie to answer. "But I can't mention that to him, either. That would surely enrage him, and Mom says we can't upset him."

"Does Mom have enough help? I thought you arranged for home care."

"Yes, the home health aide comes in each day, helps Dad with personal care and does physio with him, but it's only for four hours. Mom has to manage the rest of the day, and there's not much I can do except visit Sunday for a couple of hours. Linnie comes over a few times each week, but Mom is still struggling. I gather Dad is not a good patient. He's become more and more irritable, likely because he expected to recover from his stroke."

"Well, you need to tell Dad what's going on. It won't be pleasant, but putting it off won't make it any easier and you don't want him hearing something on the news."

Georgie sighs. "I know."

"Just tell him. How bad can it be? No worse than it's been for past six years."

It's Sunday afternoon after church. While driving to her parents' house, Georgie rehearses what to say about the investigation that won't unduly alarm them. She is surprised her father greets her at the door, then shuffles back to his chair, holding on to the wall and furniture along the way.

Her mother calls out from the kitchen. "George, I hope you're using that cane!"

A mischievous smirk on his face, he puts one finger to his lips: "Sh! Don't rat me out!" Grabbing his cane, he plops into his easy chair just as Claire comes into the room. Georgie hugs her mother and they both sit on the couch together opposite her father.

"Nice to see you, stranger," her father says in a familiar accusing tone.

She could remind him she visited last Sunday, but he won't appreciate a comment about memory loss in the wake of his stroke. "Well, Dad… Mom… things have been a little crazy. There is something I need to tell you." She takes a deep breath to steady herself. "One of my patients died suddenly, and I had to give statements to the police. Nothing to worry about, but I didn't want you to hear it from someone else."

Her father frowns and leans forward. "That's serious! Police don't question doctors unless there is something seriously wrong. Obviously, I haven't had that happen, but I had a colleague who was once under investigation. What happened to your patient?"

Georgie relays the sequence of events, and her optimistic assessment that no one could implicate her remedies in her patient's death.

Her father frowns and wags his finger. "I hate to say it, but this was always a risk. Many in the medical world are skeptical or downright antagonistic toward naturopaths. It's one reason I tried to talk you out of this career."

Georgie rolls her eyes. "You have said this over and over, but I can't see how there will be concerns about my therapies. The chances of vitamins and a homeopathic remedy causing a heart attack are almost nil."

Her father grimaces and shakes his head. "Hm. I hope you're right!"

Georgie doesn't share how difficult it was dealing with the police questions that felt more like an interrogation. Before this, she thought she understood what mental fortitude meant, but this experience is at a whole new level.

Back at home, Georgie is cutting up potatoes for Sunday dinner when the phone rings. It's Debbie.

"Sorry I haven't called you in a while, Mom. Teaching takes up so much of my time."

"Debbie! Dear, it's so good to hear from you!"

"Mom, I have big news. I wanted to tell you in person, but I can't get home right now. Are you ready?"

"Yes, of course. I hope this is good news. I sure could use some!"

"Mom. Craig proposed! I'm getting married."

"How wonderful! I'm so happy for you! I don't know Craig well, but he seems like a nice young man." Georgie met Craig just once when Debbie brought him home for Thanksgiving. They met at college, but now they are in different cities. Debbie is teaching in Fort Wayne and Craig is at law school in Indianapolis. Georgie recalls a similar situation with her and Dwayne when they were planning to be married. "Where are you going to live? Your work is two hours away from Indy."

"Oh, we'll figure it out. Craig will have one more year in law school after we get married, but I can't think practically right now. I love him and that's all that matters. But with my teaching experience, I can likely get a position in Indy."

Debbie goes on for another twenty minutes about Craig and their wedding plans for the following summer. It is a relief to Georgie when Debbie says she wants to "keep it simple"—a reception in the family backyard. Georgie doesn't need more things on her plate right now.

"Whatever you want, dear. I'm so happy for you!" Georgie may be happier than most mothers because there was a time when she feared Debbie's health issues would prevent her from having a normal life. "This is the best news I've had in a long time!" she says.

In response to Debbie's inquiry about Georgie's practice, she talks about her recent success with patients, not wanting to burden her daughter with her legal woes.

On Monday morning, the coroner's office calls and requests a meeting for the following day. This is the third time they have called her in. Not a good sign! Georgie is ready to call David Longhurst, the lawyer Lisa recommended. On his website, it says he offers "fifteen minutes of free advice," and just before noon, she reaches him by phone to take advantage of the free service and get a sense of the man. He spends ten of the fifteen minutes asking her questions before giving an opinion.

"I believe the coroner is considering an inquest," Longhurst says. "Otherwise, he would not be calling you in again. If I'm right, he will ask you to make a formal statement and, given the interest in you, I expect he would call on you to give evidence at the inquest. If you wish, I can come with you to meet with the coroner, off the clock. That way, I can determine if you need a lawyer."

"Thanks for going with me, but, ah, won't they think I'm guilty of something if I bring a lawyer?"

"No," Longhurst replies. "Not necessarily. But for this interview, I would just be there to listen."

I hope he is right!

The next day, Georgie meets David Longhurst for the first time outside the police station. He could be a poster boy for the expression tall, dark and handsome, plus he is well-groomed and exudes confidence. She berates herself for being impressed by the superficial—his good looks and expensive suit—but his confidence is something she needs right now. They enter the interview room together to meet with the coroner, who makes no comment about Longhurst's presence. They nod at each—no doubt they already know each other.

"Dr. Downie, I am calling an inquest into Rosemary Polaski's death," says the coroner. "I am advising you because you are a person of interest in the inquest. Do you know what that means?"

"No… I don't." Georgie's words catch in her throat and come out in a whisper.

"In an inquest, a person of interest has relevant information to give about the matter under investigation. Today we will set an appointment for you to make a statement and, at the inquest, I will call on you to give evidence and answer questions. I preside over the inquest. This is not a trial, just an inquiry into the circumstances of a sudden death."

Georgie stares at the coroner, her tongue tied. She knows little about inquests except what she has seen on TV, where everything is overdramatized, and someone ends up being charged with a crime. She shudders at the thought.

David Longhurst steps in. "Ralph, can you tell us more about the reason for the inquest?"

"Some circumstances about this death are unexplained, but I'm sure Dr. Downie has shared this with you already. The family of Mrs. Polaski claims to have information that needs to be heard, and I agree there are enough unanswered questions to warrant an inquest."

Georgie's throat closes, and she gasps for breath. *This can't be happening!* The coroner sets a date for Georgie to make her formal statement and the meeting is over. As she descends the stairs outside the police station, her head swims and her knees wobble.

"Ooh! Let's get you off your feet," says Longhurst. He takes her arm and steers her to a nearby coffee shop, where she orders a chamomile tea to calm her nerves.

Longhurst explains the inquest process, repeating some things the coroner said. "Dr. Downie, you are not on trial."

Georgie likes how he speaks to her, in soothing tones, unlike his businesslike manner while meeting with the coroner. She takes a few sips of tea and regains some composure. "Please, call me Georgie. I need less formality right now."

He smiles, displaying dazzling white teeth. "Okay, Georgie, if you call me David." He leans back in his chair in a manner that is both confident and casual. "I understand this is all new to you. Here is my legal advice. You will benefit from having a lawyer with you at the inquest to pose questions to the others who give evidence. By studying the statements from the other persons of interest, I can have questions ready. The family will no doubt retain a lawyer who could challenge your version of events, and I can prepare you for what he or she is likely to ask. Checking for precedents in previous proceedings is another part of my service. Half of my success in court proceedings comes from advance research." He hesitates, perhaps noticing her deer-in-the-headlights look. "Too much information?"

Georgie nods, her eyes wide.

"You look like you've lost your best friend, and I'm wondering why." He lays a finger to his lips and studies her. "This is always a delicate point, but I have to ask. Are you concerned your treatments are connected to your patient's death? Is there something you need to tell me?"

Georgie snaps out of her funk. "No, no, not at all. That is not the reason I'm concerned. Who else is apt to give statements at the inquest? Who am I up against?"

"The medical examiner who did the autopsy, someone from the family, and the medical doctor who treated the deceased most recently. There might be a medical expert, too."

"That is my concern—two or three persons of interest who are medical doctors. The medical profession does not look kindly on naturopaths, and some try to discredit us. Are you aware of the website quackery.com? A couple of doctors operate the website to smear the reputation of naturopaths and alternative health practitioners, trying to drive us out of business. I have done some work in mind-body medicine, something they label as a quack therapy."

"I heard something about that website from a colleague. A few years ago, an alternative health doctor launched a slander suit against the guys who operate the site, but I can't recall the outcome." He nods his head, his mouth set in a thin line. "This confirms that you need legal counsel. I have experience with inquests, and I can represent your interests. And by the way, the coroner is the one who makes the final judgment, and he is not a medical doctor. He's a trained investigator."

"Well, that at least is encouraging. Now, before retaining your services, I need to know something. What is *your* opinion of naturopaths?"

"I would say favorable. My mother had naturopathic treatments when she had lymphoma ten years ago and she's still going strong. She's likely in better health than me." He places both hands on his abdomen as if he is carrying extra weight around the middle.

If the situation were not so distressing, Georgie would laugh. David Longhurst appears to be in excellent health, fit though not overly muscular; in short, a magnificent specimen. *Focus Georgie!* She drags her attention back to the matter at hand—deciding whether to hire this lawyer. Leaning back in her chair, she crosses her arms and studies him as her father's repeated warning, "never trust a fast-talking lawyer," flashes through her mind. But what David Longhurst said made so much sense. *Even though I just met him, I feel I can trust him.* Her gut reaction wins out over her father's old advice, and she makes a snap decision to hire him.

As soon as Georgie gets to her apartment, she calls Dwayne to tell him about the inquest.

"What? That doesn't sound good," he says, his voice rising. "Don't inquests usually end up with someone getting charged? Are you in trouble?"

"No. The lawyer assured me inquests rarely end in charges; that's only on TV shows. Still, I'm convinced I need a lawyer. Lisa found me a good one here in the city."

"How much?"

"It's no chump change, but I don't have a choice. My professional reputation is on the line, and I know nothing about how to represent myself."

Dwayne asks about the lawyer fees and his trial record, but agrees, grudgingly, with her decision to hire him. Georgie isn't sure what he is most concerned about—her reputation or the lawyer's fee. She suspects it's the latter.

During her evening meditation, Georgie cannot push aside her worries and focus on her mantra. The looming inquest has her unnerved, but she also has a sense of dread about recent interactions with Dwayne—mostly discord over money or their children. *I don't remember the last time we had fun together. Is this what our relationship has become?*

Chapter 17

Georgie leans forward on the edge of the hard courtroom seat, waiting for the inquest to begin. She takes a quick look around and counts twelve people in the room and relaxes a little. The case seems to have attracted little attention—no incriminating headlines in the local news. Beside her, David appears unusually relaxed, and she turns to him. "How can you be so calm?"

He smiles wryly. "It's a lawyer thing. Never let on what you're thinking or feeling."

"I'm tied up in knots." She wrings her hands. "It is my first time in a courtroom."

"Don't worry. Everything is under control." He squeezes Georgie's hand. His touch sends an infusion of positive energy through her, though she wonders how he has so much confidence. *How is everything under control?* She does some deep breathing while waiting for the proceedings to start.

The coroner sits at the judge's bench, but without a judge's robes. He announces the four persons of interest in the inquest: the medical examiner, Mrs. Polaski's medical doctor, Gwen Wright, who is Mrs. Polaski's daughter, and Georgie.

The medical doctor is first up. "Four months before Rosemary Polaski's death, I diagnosed her with high blood pressure and prescribed a calcium channel blocker. She was to see me again in two months to assess her response to the medication, but she canceled that appointment. I was not aware if she even started on the medication. It happens all the time. Not everyone takes a medication even when it's prescribed. I also was not aware she had consulted a naturopath."

"Are there any risks from taking a calcium channel blocker?" the coroner asks.

"I haven't seen a reaction in any of my patients."

"May I approach? I have a question," David says, rising from his chair. The coroner nods his assent. "Doctor, are you aware that one side effect of calcium channel blockers is heart palpitations?"

"Well… yes, but it is extremely rare."

"And if Mrs. Polaski did not take the medication as prescribed, could that increase the risk of such a side effect?"

The doctor shifts in his seat, one hand to his chin. "I suppose, ah, it is possible."

David returns to his seat with a slight grin on his face, as if to say, point scored.

Next is the daughter, Gwen Wright, a woman in her early twenties, with an elaborate hairdo and heavy makeup. As she walks to the front of the courtroom, her heavy perfume wafts through the room, and before taking a seat in the witness stand, she glares at Georgie. The coroner asks about Rosemary Polaski's state of mind leading up to her death.

"My mother told me she had lost confidence in her family doctor. That was a few months before she died. It was odd because she had never said that before. When I asked her why the change of heart, she told me about her naturopath, this Dr. Downie." She makes a dramatic jab of her finger at Georgie. "My mother claimed this woman was helping her more than the doctor ever did. Now, understand, my mother would never consider going against her medical doctor. I think this Downie woman unduly influenced her." With an affected flourish, she wipes a tear from her eye.

Unnerved, Georgie turns to David, who doesn't look up, but scribbles something on his notepad. The coroner asks if either lawyer has questions, and David rises, strolling to the witness stand.

"Mrs. Wright, you said your mother would never consult a naturopath. How do you know that? Did she expressly say this? Did she write it down, say, in an email?"

The daughter seems surprised by the questions. "Well, not in so many words, I guess, but it was clear to me. Our family doesn't go in for wacky treatments that our doctor doesn't approve of."

"So, you would never go to a naturopath?"

"Oh, no. That's not for me."

David cocks his head and turns away from the witness stand. "What makes you so sure you would never consult with a naturopath?"

"Well, I trust proper doctors, medical ones. I saw what my mother brought home from the naturopath and it seemed like hokum to me. I wouldn't be surprised if one of those concoctions killed her." Once again, she glares at Georgie, and everyone in the courtroom stares, too.

Georgie cringes under the scrutiny, wondering how this woman can be so negative about a profession when she's had no personal experience with it. How can naturopaths gain credibility when there are people like this with such irrational opposition?

"One last question," David says. "For the record, what is your profession?"

The daughter looks down and fidgets with the tissue in her hands. "I'm a hairstylist."

"So, no background in health care, then?"

The daughter shakes her head no.

"No more questions." David turns and strides back to his chair. Georgie stares at him in horror, but he whispers behind his hand. "Don't worry. I established she has a bias against naturopaths but is completely uninformed. She can't prove what her mother was thinking, either."

Next, it is Georgie's turn to give a statement about her assessment and recommended therapies for Rosemary Polaski. When she finishes her statement, the coroner asks about her qualifications and her length of time in practice as a naturopath. Georgie is thankful she attended an accredited school rather than the one in Indianapolis, but her three years in practice don't sound impressive.

"Can you tell me the purpose and risks of nux vomica, one remedy you prescribed for the deceased?" the coroner asks.

"This homeopathic remedy is useful for many maladies," Georgie replies, "but for Mrs. Polaski, it was for adrenal support and insomnia. The only contraindication is for those with liver disease, which she did not have."

The family's lawyer rises and motions to the coroner. "I have a question," he says, glancing down at his notes. "Doesn't nux vomica contain strychnine? A poison?"

This is the question Georgie is dreading. She swallows hard and struggles to keep her voice steady. "There is a trace amount, but it's at a level designed to promote healing. This is the principle governing homeopathy, which has been practiced safely for hundreds of years."

"But strychnine *is* a poison. What are the risks of taking nux vomica?" the lawyer asks.

David prepared Georgie for this very question, which, she gathered, involved him doing extensive searches of medical and court records. She stares steadily at the lawyer and says, "there are no reports of harm from taking nux vomica at the dosage I prescribed." She sneaks a look at the coroner's face, but his deadpan face reveals nothing about how he received her evidence.

David motions to the coroner that he has questions. He asks Georgie to read from the informed consent document the deceased patient had signed.

"The consent form reads: 'It is vital that you inform your naturopath immediately of any disease process that you are suffering from and, if you are on any medication or over-the-counter drugs.'"

"And did Mrs. Polaski sign this document?" David asks.

"She did," Georgie replies.

"Can you read the patient intake form that she completed, in which she reported all her medications?"

Georgie holds up the form and reads: "She wrote: 'calcium channel blocker and an occasional non-prescription pain medication.'"

"And as far as you were aware, Mrs. Polaski was still under the care of her medical doctor?"

"Yes, that was my understanding. I told her my therapies are complimentary, not a replacement for her doctor's care. I also wrote this on her protocol sheet and advised her to tell her medical doctor everything she was taking."

She leaves the stand feeling encouraged.

Next, the coroner calls on Dr. Collins, the medical examiner, to give his statement. "The autopsy found that Rosemary Polaski had no prior evidence of heart disease or physical heart defects, leaving me to consider three possible causes for her death—ingestion of a poison, an interaction between one or more medications, or an overdose of one or more medications."

"Dr. Collins," says the coroner, "Your report shows there were medications and supplements found in the deceased's home following her death.

In your expert opinion, could any of these substances increase the risk of a cardiac event?"

The medical examiner checks his notes, taking his time to respond. "The deceased had several bottles of medications—over-the-counter cold medicine, over-the-counter pain medication, a generic antacid, two vitamin supplements, the homeopathic remedy, and over-the-counter sleeping pills. She had one prescription medication for high blood pressure, the calcium channel blocker. If she was taking all these remedies and medications, there is a slight risk of an adverse cardiac event."

"In your autopsy, could you determine if she had taken any of these medications the day of her death?" asks the coroner.

"Yes, she did—the prescribed blood pressure medication, the pain medication, and the sleeping pill. We couldn't detect whether she had taken the antacid, the vitamins, or the homeopathic remedy."

"And in your expert opinion, were there any contraindications from the medications found in her system?"

"There is a remote possibility. I had the occasion to research the valerian in the over-the-counter sleeping pill the deceased was taking. There is a moderate contraindication between valerian and pain killers. The risk increases when also taking an antacid regularly. It all depends on how much the deceased took of these medications and how often. If she was taking them for a long time, it could put her at risk."

"Is there anything else that could have caused her sudden fatal cardiac arrest?"

"Nothing I could determine from the autopsy."

The coroner motions to both lawyers if they have questions.

The family's lawyer rises to question the medical examiner. "Dr. Collins, can you please comment on the risks of the remedy nux vomica?" Georgie holds her breath. This was one of her fears—a medical doctor giving an opinion on a homeopathic remedy for which they have no knowledge or experience. *Will he contradict my statement?*

"I have read there are potential side effects to this remedy, so there is a remote possibility it could be involved," Dr. Collins replies.

Georgie gasps and clasps her hand over her mouth, hoping no one heard her.

The family lawyer turns and takes his seat, looking pleased with himself. David jumps up and approaches the medical examiner. "Dr. Collins. In your thirty years as a medical examiner, have you ever identified a lethal effect from nux vomica?"

The medical examiner cocks his head and looks at the ceiling. "Well… no, I don't believe I have. At any rate, we couldn't determine if Mrs. Polaski took the remedy. The bottle we found was almost full, and autopsy found no trace of the remedy."

David returns to his seat to retrieve a paper that he hands to the coroner. "These are the results from my search of thirty years of inquests, confirming there are *no* reports of ill effects from nux vomica."

Georgie's relief is palpable. The medical examiner did not cast aspersions on nux vomica like she feared he would. And David's advance research paid off, leaving little doubt as to the safety of the remedy.

The inquest is over in two hours and isn't as dramatic as Georgie feared. David's line of questioning was astute, and his case preparation steered suspicion away from her therapies. Still, there is no way to predict how the coroner received all the evidence, and the final ruling rests with him.

Georgie jumps at the harsh ring of her office phone, and on answering it, hears the news she desires but also dreads. The coroner's judgment will be at four o'clock tomorrow. Waiting for the decision was almost as nerve-racking as the inquest itself, even though it was only three days. Unable to focus, she canceled most of her patient appointments and spent more time reading, meditating, or walking in the woods, none of which eased her worries. She hasn't been this anxious since Debbie's prolonged illness.

It's three-fifty-nine. Georgie sits on the edge of her seat, waiting for the start of the coroner's judgment, and feeling abandoned because David has yet to appear. Just as the coroner enters the courtroom, David rushes in, out of breath, and sits next to Georgie, whispering, "Sorry, I had another case that went longer than expected."

The coroner looks around the courtroom waiting for quiet. "This inquest investigated the circumstances of the sudden death of Rosemary Polaski to determine the likely cause of death. I will have recommendations intended to prevent such a death in the future. If warranted, I can also make recommendations for criminal prosecution."

Georgie's hand impulsively flies to her mouth. *Why did he say that?* David takes her hand in his, his gaze fixed on the coroner.

The coroner checks his notes. "I rule that the sudden, unexpected death of Rosemary Polaski resulted from interactions between medications and remedies, some prescribed and some over the counter. The deceased had consulted with two different practitioners without advising either of them. She discontinued care from her medical doctor, yet continued taking the prescribed medication without supervision. Neither doctor was aware of all the over-the-counter medications she was taking. Therefore, neither practitioner could have done anything different with her care."

Rosemary Polaski's family audibly gasps and grumbles in hushed tones. Impulsively Georgie hugs David, then pulls away, embarrassed by her display of affection. He just grins and keeps his attention on the coroner, who turns to the second page of his judgment.

"As part of my judgment, I have two recommendations. First, I recommend that the Pharmacological Association require pharmacists to check with physicians before refilling a prescription to verify the patient is still under that doctor's care. Second, when more than one doctor is involved in a patient's care, doctors should communicate to share their treatment plans. I will recommend the medical association and the naturopathic association develop communication channels between doctors and naturopaths for their common patients."

Dread replaces Georgie's initial joy. She is off the hook, but the coroner's recommendations may have opened a Pandora's box of problems for her profession. After a hasty exit from courthouse to get cell reception, Georgie calls Dwayne, longing to share her relief but also her concerns about the outcome. After five rings, the call goes to his voice mail, and she leaves a message. She forgets that David Longhurst is standing beside her.

"Why do you look so wretched?" he asks. "Most people would find this result a vindication. It could have been much worse. The daughter was definitely out to discredit you. This is a victory!"

"Yes, of course. I am cleared of blame, and I agree it makes sense to check prescriptions. But requiring naturopaths to share their treatment plan with a patient's medical doctor may not end well for naturopaths. Medical doctors will have an opening to dissuade a patient from seeing naturopaths and shut down my profession."

"Hm. Or it could open the door to better communication. Anyway, not all inquest recommendations result in any change. I suspect the coroner's recommendations may be more about grandstanding for re-election, which comes up in six months." He hesitates, seeming unsure about something. "My sources tell me the family has some political connection, and the coroner ordered the inquest to mollify them. I didn't mention this because I couldn't confirm the information and I didn't want to upset you."

Georgie stares at him in horror. "Was this whole thing a political stunt?"

David shakes his head and grimaces. "Legal actions are not devoid of politics. But whatever the motivation, it's over, and you need to enjoy this victory, because it's just that! You and I need to celebrate. Have dinner with me! My treat!"

"Well… okay. Dinner would be nice. I am hungry. I haven't felt like eating since this thing started."

"There's a great place just down the street. Shall we?" He puts out his arm for Georgie to take, and they stroll down the street like a couple on a date. It's strange yet comforting. They enter a French restaurant, small and dimly lit, and he steers her to a secluded table at the back. Georgie relaxes into her seat while David orders wine for them without asking what she likes. She takes a sip and nods her approval. Without a word, he orders their meals from a menu written in French. Georgie prefers to make her own menu decisions, but in her current emotional state, she doesn't mind that he takes charge. On edge since the investigation started, it feels good to have someone take care of her.

"I don't want to talk about the inquest anymore," she says. "Let's talk about something else. So, what do you do when you're not lawyering?"

David chuckles. "When I'm not… lawyering, I like to get out in nature—hiking or kayaking in the wilderness, sometimes rock climbing. Some people laugh at me. 'That's not very restful,' they say. But the physical challenges are the perfect break from the mental challenges of the courtroom. I used to go with my wife before we divorced."

Georgie already knows he's divorced. *Why is he mentioning it?* She doesn't respond to the mention of his marital status, rather sharing her affinity for nature. "But I'm not adventurous enough for the wilderness. Just give me a brisk walk in a nice green space!"

The meal arrives—Coq au vin, basmati rice, and Brussels sprouts. "Delicious!" Georgie says, after her first taste. Through dinner, they chat about their favorite vacation spots, wines, music, and how they got into their respective careers. Georgie is surprised they have several interests in common, including a passion for what they do. Even though lawyers make a good living, she senses David did not take up the profession for that reason. He talks about his passion for justice, just like she has a passion for healing. Georgie thoroughly enjoys herself for the first time in… she isn't sure how long. As they finish eating, a leisurely two-hour experience, she makes a private admission. *I feel so at ease with this man.*

"I insist on walking with you to your car," David says, on exiting the restaurant. "This area can be dangerous after dark." He lingers with Georgie at her car while she searches in her bag for her keys. She turns to say good night, and he leans in and kisses her full on the mouth. Taken by surprise, she pulls back, and David breaks off. She is both relieved and disappointed. *It had to stop… but… I didn't want it to stop!*

His head bowed; David runs his hand through his hair. "Ah… I'm not in the habit of kissing my clients, but with the inquest over, I'm not your lawyer anymore, and I took a chance. I hope I haven't offended you." He peers down at her, still very close.

Georgie's breath is shallow and her head swims. *Am I intoxicated by the wine or the kiss?* On an irresistible impulse, she answers him with a kiss of her own. This time, all her passion is unleashed in a full embrace, and he responds.

"Ooh… What happened?" Georgie wakes up lying on the couch in her apartment with David sitting on the couch leaning over her.

"You fainted! Are you okay?"

"I think so. How did…?"

"How did you get here? I caught you before you hit the ground and then drove you home. Those stairs to your loft are awkward, though." He flexes his arms and back.

Georgie slaps her hand over her mouth. "You mean… you had to carry me up the stairs?!"

"No big deal." He waves his hand. "You're a lightweight."

Georgie hides her face with both hands. "Oh. I'm so embarrassed! Of course, I'm grateful to you, again. You've gone above and beyond a lawyer's duty." She blushes, now recalling the moment of passion preceding her fainting spell.

"Are you sure you're okay?" David asks, brushing his hand down her arm.

Georgie senses his body heat and vibrant energy pulsing through her arm. *Too close!* "I think so, yes. I just need a good night's sleep, and with the inquest over, I'm sure I can manage that now. Please don't concern yourself anymore. I'll be fine."

"Are you sure? I can stay awhile if you like. We don't want you fainting again and hitting your head."

Danger signals flash through her mind. *Not a good idea!* "No, no, I'm fine, truly!"

David takes a long look at her, sighs, rises from the couch, and pulls out his cell phone. "Just going to call a cab. I drove you home in your car. It seemed like the sensible thing to do." He slowly taps on his phone keypad. "Now, where is that number for the cab company?"

He sure is taking his time! Is he hoping I'll invite him to stay? But I can't!

Brrrng! Georgie jumps and fumbles in her bag for her cell phone. "It's Dwayne," she says.

David backs away and, as he closes the door behind him, gives her a lingering, amorous look.

That was close! I still can't believe I kissed the man!

Still woozy and breathless, she struggles to make her voice sound normal. "Dwayne, dear, so good… to hear from you. Ah… The inquest judgment is in. The coroner absolved me of blame."

"That is great news! I was so worried about you all day. Sorry I missed your call, but I was in the middle of a dinner meeting with a client who wants to expand their business. It will mean big fees for us, which will help with

D.J.'s tuition and the lawyer's fees. So, tell me. Did you need the lawyer? Was he worth the hefty fee?"

Georgie stifles a laugh at the irony of the question. "Of course, I couldn't have managed it without him."

"Good, good. And you're okay? You've been so stressed over all this."

"Dwayne, I was! Now, I'm tremendously relieved but also exhausted. I just need to get some sleep."

Sleep does not come easy, though. She stews over why she didn't tell Dwayne about her dinner with David, the fainting spell, and how she got home. If not for the kiss, she realizes those events would just be a humorous anecdote to share with her husband. What she has done is a serious lie of omission. She prays like she has not prayed in a long time—a fervent prayer for guidance. Seldom does she receive an answer to a prayer, but this time she hears clearly: "Go home!" Unfortunately, she hears nothing about how to go home and still pursue her career.

Chapter 18

Georgie checks the call display on her cell phone and hesitates to answer it. *What will I say this time?* Since the inquest ended two weeks ago, she has been trying to re-establish her work routine. During the inquest, and even leading up to it, she had not taken on new patients, postponed some follow-up consultations, and canceled a new patient seminar. Even now her work focus is lacking, perhaps from residual stress of the inquest, but also because of David Longhurst. She harbors guilt about her behavior, but with time to process things, she is also annoyed with him for taking liberties. And he keeps calling her. First, he called to "make sure she was okay," then a few days later, "just to chat." They have no other legal matters to discuss, so there is no need to chat unless he is interested in pursuing a relationship. The worst of it is, she hasn't been able to shake her attraction to him even though she hardly knows him. *And a lawyer, no less! Not someone I would expect to like.* She has yet to sort out the source of her feelings. *Am I attracted to this man, or am I just the damsel in distress, grateful for rescue by the gallant knight?*

Today is David's third call. Despite her reservations, she answers and he invites her for drinks "to talk things over."

"I can't. There's a lot to catch up on with my patient care. I put my work on hold during the inquest."

"Well, when is a good time?"

Drat! She forgets who she is talking to. Lawyers know how to get around lame excuses. It occurs to her perhaps she should meet with him so she can gently refuse his attentions, so she agrees to meet "just for a coffee" at a busy cafe at one o'clock in the afternoon. It will be brightly lit and full of other patrons, which should be safe enough.

Georgie arrives early to get a table in the middle of the café rather than let David select a secluded table like he did at the French restaurant. When he enters the café, her senses reel, and she tries to collect herself while he places a coffee order at the counter. He sits down across from her, and her attraction to him resurfaces, making her shy and uncertain.

Georgie looks down into her coffee cup, avoiding eye contact, and gathers her resolve. "David, I am married. Given what happened… er… I don't think it's wise for us to meet socially."

"Oh! Of course, I know you're married, but you work in another city and hardly see your husband. Can you blame me for thinking your marriage isn't solid? Or perhaps even on the rocks? Your husband didn't even come to the inquest. I would if you were my wife."

Georgie opens her mouth but can't come up with a response.

"You don't seem like a happily married person to me," David says. "And there was that moment we had. You must admit it was… special." He leans in, a suggestive grin on his face.

She blushes at the memory of the moment, hoping David doesn't notice. "Um. You're right, of course. I didn't talk about my marriage. But you never asked about my relationship with Dwayne, either. You should have done that before you… kissed me." Momentarily, she is lost in his intense gaze, then gives her head a shake and breaks off eye contact. "Anyway, Dwayne wasn't at the inquest because he was drumming up new business to help pay your fees. I am committed to my marriage. I won't put it in jeopardy because of one moment of weakness."

David flashes an evocative smile. "Mm! And what a moment it was!"

The mention of their kiss triggers the same intoxication she felt in that moment. Georgie's face flushes and her breathing shallows. To push down her emotional response, she takes two deep breaths. Again, she must turn away to avoid getting lost in David's piercing blue eyes. The depth of her reaction to him surprises and scares her.

"Since we're being completely honest, I must tell you something," he says, leaning closer, his voice husky. "I haven't felt this way about someone in a long while, maybe ever. You are remarkable, and I can't get you out of my head. You say you're committed to your marriage, but your actions don't match, and I'm an excellent judge of people. It's in my job description."

His mischievous grin and bedroom eyes disarm Georgie yet again. *I can't let my emotions rule this situation.* She puts her hand over her heart. "Please understand… I am… committed, and so is Dwayne. Actions don't always tell the entire story. He may not be demonstrative, but he has always been there for the kids and me." *Am I trying to convince him or myself?*

"Fair enough. If that's what you want. Just know this. I don't think I've ever met someone with whom I connected so well. You're smart, you're passionate about your work, and you're beautiful."

Georgie blushes. "I… I… don't know what to say. You flatter me. But… I *am* committed to Dwayne. Now, I would ask you to respect my wishes and not call me again."

David nods, his smile fading. "If you say you're committed to your husband once more, I should think 'the lady doth protest too much.'" His eyebrows raise in an unspoken question, to which Georgie does not respond. He heaves a sigh. "But I will take you at your word, for now, and leave you to figure out what you want." He hesitates, perhaps to measure Georgie's resolve. "And that's my cue," he says, rising from the table and striding out the door.

Georgie lingers at the coffee shop to gather her wits, having never felt this conflicting mix of emotions—desire, guilt, and doubt—all at the same time. The extent to which David tempted her is disturbing. When she insisted on her commitment to Dwayne, it sounded hollow and, being a lawyer, David may have picked up on that. She has doubts about the strength of her and Dwayne's connection and being away Monday to Saturday is not helping. Could her attraction to David be a wake-up call? *Maybe my marriage really is in trouble.*

On Sunday after church, Georgie and Lisa meet for a walk in the woods instead of going out for lunch. Georgie has good reasons. She needs the peace of being in nature to help sort out her emotions. They walk awhile in silence, taking in the scenery, the pungent smell of wet, fallen leaves, and the chilly fall air. Georgie glances at her friend, who is looking down, deep in thought.

"Georgie. I have something to tell you. I didn't want to bring it up during the inquest, and I can't confirm anything for sure."

Georgie stops in her tracks and stares at Lisa.

"A few weeks ago, I was at a business lunch at the Grand," Lisa says, "and I saw Dwayne there with a woman. She was very stylish, and her demeanor was... how shall I say it? Friendly. I couldn't read Dwayne's face because his back was to me. And by the way, it's the second time I've seen them there together. It could be nothing, but as your friend, I think you should know."

"And you don't think it was just a business lunch? I mean, if this was a social meeting, would it be right out in the open at a popular restaurant?"

"When I first saw them a few weeks back, it looked like a business lunch. This time? Not so much."

"Oh!" is all Georgie can manage through her shock.

"But I'm sure Dwayne would never cheat." Lisa lays a hand on Georgie's arm. "He's just not like that. But I didn't want you hearing about this odd encounter from someone else."

Georgie has the house to herself all afternoon. Dwayne is out golfing for what he said, "could be the last game of the season." Georgie curls up on the couch, trying to read a book, but she can't focus. Her thoughts keep going back to Lisa's news. Could Dwayne be having an affair? If he is, does she deserve it? After all, she is the one who is away most of the time, whose eye strayed to someone else. She considered telling Dwayne about David Longhurst, but it's not like anything happened. Still, her attraction was real, and that is a betrayal. What if she confesses about David, and it turns out Dwayne's meeting with the mysterious woman was just a business lunch? To ask Dwayne about the woman is akin to making an accusation, and she has no proof of anything. Then her thoughts stray to Dwayne's near obsession with golf. Maybe his woman friend also plays golf and they're out on the course together now. She shakes her head to banish such suspicious thoughts. After all, her own behavior has hardly been loyal and honest. A gospel reading echoes through her mind: *He who is without sin cast the first stone.*

"How could things get so messed up?" She shouts to the empty house. Before she could consider her question, the phone rings.

"Georgie, it's Dr. Rice. Have I got you at a good time?"

"Hello, Dr. Rice. This is a surprise!" When she left his practice, he seemed upset by her sudden departure because he had to find a new office manager and a new naturopath. "Yes," she says. "It's an okay time."

"I have a proposition for you. Paula Weaver, the naturopath who joined us after you left, wants to move to Indianapolis. Her husband got a position in the mayor's office there. Is there any chance you want a position in your hometown?"

Georgie is momentarily at a loss for words. "Ah… well… possibly."

"I would welcome you. I've heard you are doing well at Caroll Clinic, and you would be a great asset to our female patients. You would have all Paula's patients and some of my own. I'm too busy and need to lighten my caseload."

"Hm. This is most unusual. I might consider it, but obviously, we would have to consult with Dr. Caroll. Have you broached the subject with him?"

"I will call and tell him about Dr. Weaver, so he knows what a fine practitioner she is, but I wanted to run this by you first. There's no point in starting a negotiation until we know both parties are interested."

Georgie's heart leaps in her chest. Is this an answer to her prayer? But her previous experience at Dr. Rice's clinic was not that positive. *Tread cautiously, Georgie!* "I would appreciate a few more details about your offer before you talk to Dr. Caroll. How many patients would I have? What can you tell me about Dr. Weaver? I need to know her approach is like mine to ensure my patients are not upset after all the progress they've made."

"You will have fifteen female patients of mine. I don't know how many patients Dr. Weaver has, but I can put you in touch with her. I'm sure she will be eager to meet with you today if you wish."

Georgie ends the call with Dr. Rice and phones Paula Weaver, who agrees to a meeting within the hour, but adds, "we're packing. Can you come to my house?"

It is only a ten-minute drive to Paula's home. They talk for thirty minutes about their professional interests. A recent graduate focusing on women's health, Paula impresses Georgie with her passion and enthusiasm. She is desperate for Georgie to agree to trade clinics, saying, "I'm a nervous driver. I could not manage that commute on the interstate every day."

Georgie nods her head. "I can sympathize with that, believe me."

Back at home, Georgie weighs the pros and cons of changing clinics now. On the one hand, she is comfortable at the Caroll Clinic, and she likes her colleagues. She has spent almost three years becoming known in Indianapolis through promotional talks and networking. But she has neglected her family, and Dwayne has made it clear he is not happy with her. And to her recent prayer for guidance, there was the answer, "go home." Her head tells her to stay where she is, and her heart says, return home. Surely, she can have the same success at Dr. Rice's clinic. Of course, Dr. Caroll may not go for the "trade." Or perhaps he will. The clinic had some bad press from the inquest. Just being a person of interest in an inquest is enough to cast doubt on a place of business, so it might come as a relief to Dr. Caroll to part ways with her. After two hours of going over the pros and cons, she is no closer to knowing what is best.

Dwayne arrives home from his golf game at four o'clock and does a double-take at Georgie's expression. "What's up? You look like the cat who ate the canary."

"A lot has happened since you left this morning. I may have an offer to practice here in Terrance, by trading practices with a naturopath at Dr. Rice's clinic. Highly unusual, but it could happen."

"This would make me the happiest man in Terrance!" He takes Georgie in his arms, and they embrace like they haven't done in years, without reservation or regret. She pushes aside suspicions about him and another woman. His reaction to her news speaks volumes.

The 'trade' is complete after a week of deliberation, primarily from Dr. Caroll's perspective. It turned out he was reluctant to see Georgie go, but also understood her concerns for her family. This move may be necessary for Georgie's marriage, but she will miss her colleagues, especially Dr. Caroll, who was an excellent mentor to her. She had a tearful farewell with Pam, whom she appreciated as an able practitioner, an ally, and collaborator. They vowed to keep in touch. Georgie and Paula Weaver spent two days orienting each other to their respective patient rosters, but it wasn't exactly an even trade—twenty-five patients of Paula's for Georgie's fifty-three. And Georgie was concerned about how her patients with emotional barriers to healing would respond to a new naturopath. Still, the move home had to be her priority.

Georgie enters the clinic for her first day, three years since she left the clinic, with a déjà vu feeling. Then, as now, she is the only female naturopath in the clinic. *Will this bring more opportunities or less?* Brenda, the office manager, ushers her into Dr. Rice's office.

"Welcome back, Georgie." He places his hand on a pile of thick files. "These are the fifteen patients you will take over from me. I suggest you read the files and let me know if you have questions."

Georgie raises her eyebrows. It's not much of a welcome, no queries about her specialties or the clinic hours she prefers. The difference between her new clinic manager and Dr. Caroll is striking. But she has other things to discuss. "Dr. Rice. I have a question, but on another subject. Have you ever had meetings with all your practitioners? To compare notes on cases, perhaps help each other out? At the Caroll Clinic, they hold monthly clinic meetings, and I found them very helpful. Would you consider holding regular clinic meetings?"

"Hm, I don't know. I will have to talk to Dr. Thom. We have done well here without, what did you call them? clinic meetings? Perhaps you can write a proposal—lay out what we would talk about, benefits to each practitioner, and how it will help the clinic."

"I can tell you the benefits right now. We can support each other by sharing protocols that lead to positive outcomes for our patients. Or, if we have a challenging case, we can help each other problem-solve. The Caroll Clinic is the most successful practice in Indy, and they've had monthly clinic meetings for years."

"Hm. Please write a proposal and spell out the benefits. It's not just me you need to convince. Anything else?"

Reluctant to broach another subject, Georgie forges ahead anyway. Surely this idea will get a better response. "I want to organize new patient seminars like I did at the Caroll Clinic. The seminar I developed helps new patients understand how naturopaths work and how we differ from medical doctors. Because of this seminar, we saw increased patient compliance and fewer dropouts."

Dr. Rice checks his watch and glances at his appointment book. "You sure are full of ideas. Let's talk about it after you get yourself established." He stands up and slides the patient files over to Georgie, signaling the meeting is over. She hefts the heavy stack of files in both arms, staggers back to her office, and dumps them on her desk. She slumps in her chair. *That was not an encouraging start, but perhaps I should have known.* Dr. Rice was not very helpful when she was at the clinic before, but still she is mystified how he could have a problem with her suggestions. *I should have negotiated for more before I came back.*

After going through Dr. Rice's patient referrals, she discovers it has been a while since some had a consultation, which leads her to suspect they are not active cases. As for Paula's cases, it is possible some patients do not require further intervention. Georgie's doubts are growing about Dr. Rice's promise of an established patient roster. Without active patients, she can't expect word-of-mouth referrals, which means she may need to do promotional talks. At the end of her first day, she leaves the clinic wondering if she has made a mistake. *Have I sacrificed my career for Dwayne… again?*

"This is delicious!" Dwayne enthuses over their evening meal of lasagna and salad. "I was getting bored with my cooking!" He takes a big bite of lasagna and savors it. "How was your first day?"

"Okay, I guess." She sighs. Her situation at the clinic is not what she expected, but she doesn't want to dampen the mood. And Dwayne seems too absorbed with his meal to notice her lackluster response. They lapse into silence for a few minutes. "But tell me. How was your day?"

"We may land a new client, a large company, here in town. If it works out, we will be largest accounting practice in Terrance. I would have to hire more staff." Dwayne beams with pride.

"That's great, Dwayne." She eyes her husband, who doesn't seem to notice her forced enthusiasm. They finish their dinner in silence.

After dinner, Dwayne disappears to the family room to watch a football game and soon Georgie hears him railing away at the coach and the referees—the Bears must be losing. She wonders how he finds that relaxing and retreats to her bedroom to listen to some music. On reflection, she wonders about her reluctance to share her concerns about the clinic with her husband. They used to share everything. But, in the past few years, it has felt like Dwayne didn't want to hear about her career. When she talked to him about her challenges, he often responded with criticism: "this is what you wanted," or "you should have done more research on the profession!" Now, she does not expect him to sympathize with or support her in her career. To compound the problem, they have little to say to each other beyond a few pleasantries. Now, it's like they are living in parallel, with the only intersection being their children. She tries praying. *Dear God, please give me the patience to make this move work. Help Dwayne and me rebuild our lives together.*

She dares not dwell on Lisa's report of the mysterious woman lunching with Dwayne. There is also lingering guilt about her own behavior, compounded by her lack of honesty about the incident with David Longhurst. A love song comes on the radio, and the lyrics seem to mock her own experience in which love is something she no longer understands. She turns the radio off. Is love a safe, stable relationship, or is it the feelings she had for David? Recriminations and excuses about David cycle through her mind. *It was a weak moment in a very stressful time, and I needed some affection. If I had not fainted, David would not have been in my apartment. You're justifying what is technically adultery. Honesty is not the best policy when it hurts someone you love.* Her one consolation is that the David Longhurst incident is over. She is not in Indianapolis anymore and she won't see him or hear from him again.

Georgie and Debbie sit together at the dining room table, sorting through samples of wedding invitations. The joy on her daughter's face is a tonic for Georgie—a welcome break from recent stressors. Everyone has always said Debbie is combo kid with dark hair and facial features like Dwayne, but Georgie's body shape and personality. Maybe that's why Georgie connects so well with her oldest child.

Their first task today was to complete the guest list, and it was more difficult than they expected. Debbie wanted to limit the guest list to sixty, and this led to tough decisions about cousins, aunts, and uncles from the Downie side of the family whom they rarely see. Debbie hesitated over one childhood friend she hadn't seen in a few years, and Georgie had to ask, "will she really mind if you don't invite her?" Having finished the guest list, they moved on to invitations. Georgie hopes this decision will be easier, but doesn't begrudge the time spent doing this with her daughter.

The wedding is in July and Debbie wants the invitations out by the New Year before people make their summer vacation plans. She is keeping to her plan for a simple celebration, the ceremony at New Hope church and the reception in their oversized backyard. Georgie is proud of Debbie's good sense, not following the popular trend of destination weddings in the Caribbean. Before her engagement, Debbie had made her views clear on that trend, saying, "It's not right to expect guests to pay for travel and shell out for a gift, too."

"This is the one," Debbie says, holding up a plain buff invitation.

Georgie nods her approval just as her cell phone rings. On the call display, there is an unknown number in Indianapolis. Dwayne has warned her not to answer calls from unknown numbers, likely to be telemarketing or scams, but something tells her to answer this call.

"Georgie, it's Pam. I have some awful news," she says, her voice breaking. "Mark... Dr. Caroll... he's gone... he... they found him dead in the park... where he likes to run. Oh. Georgie, it's just tragic! He was fine yesterday, then this! I just can't believe it."

Georgie feels a shock, like a jolt of electricity run through her body. "What?! Oh, Pam. How terrible! Do they know what happened?"

"Not yet. Everyone is in the dark, even Mark's widow. I guess there'll be an autopsy." Pam sounds close to tears. "Well, I... have to go. The police are here to ask me questions. It's all so... tragic!" The call ends abruptly.

"What's wrong, Mom?" Debbie rises and goes to Georgie's side.

Georgie needs a moment to find her voice, then shares the shocking news.

Debbie wraps her arms around Georgie in a long embrace. "Oh, Mom. How awful."

Georgie's stomach churns and her head swims. "It's so unexpected! Dr. Caroll took great care of himself—a good diet, regular exercise. I don't understand how this could happen... unless there was foul play."

After Debbie leaves, Georgie lingers at the table, stewing over a nagging question. *How could a seemingly healthy fifty-two-year-old just drop dead while out jogging?*

Chapter 19

Mark Caroll's memorial service is a somber affair held in a large community hall to accommodate the crowd of mourners. Georgie recognizes many of them as Dr. Caroll's patients, several members from Toastmasters, and a few local dignitaries. The eulogist, Mark's brother, barely holds it together, while several people are openly weeping, including Rachel, Marks's widow, who grips her two teenage boys for dear life. During the reception, Georgie moves through the crowd, overhearing whispers and snippets of conversation. "It makes no sense. He was so fit." "No autopsy results released yet." "Very mysterious!" Georgie finds Pam at the edge of the crowd, wringing her hands, her eyes swollen and red. Finding nothing to say, they clasp hands and stand together, surveying the room. Other mourners wander through the hall, few greeting each other or pausing at the lavish lunch buffet. On the drive home, Georgie can't shake a sense of foreboding.

"Eight holistic doctors die mysteriously," Dwayne reads the news headline during dinner. He hands the paper to Georgie, and she studies the article—an investigative report that reads like an exposé in a scandal magazine. A reporter had tracked the news from across the country, uncovering a spate of sudden deaths of holistic doctors in just a few months' time. She reads aloud with growing alarm at the shocking details. "One doctor appeared to have shot himself, one was stabbed, one bludgeoned to death in his own home, and one deemed a murder-suicide involving the doctor and her family. The others died of no apparent cause."

Her meal half-eaten, Georgie goes to the family room and turns on the television to a network news station to see the reporter being interviewed. "One might think these deaths are unrelated," the reporter says. "But as I have discovered, these holistic doctors had things in common. They all came out against the vaccination of young children. And my sources tell me the FDA was investigating two of the doctors for their innovative therapies. Is there a conspiracy against holistic doctors?" The reporter leaves this question hanging in the air. "And the police need to explain how, in some of these cases, they determined there was no foul play when the circumstances were so violent."

The names of the practitioners show on the screen; thankfully, no one Georgie knows. Not able to stomach more details, Georgie turns off the television and stares out the window as the room grows dark.

Dwayne leaves his den, having finished some work, and spots Georgie sitting in the dark. "What's with you?" he asks.

"That news report has shaken me up."

"What!? It's just one reporter's opinion, not fact. It seems way out there to me. You should know better than to get caught up in a conspiracy theory."

"Of course not. But it's still troubling so many holistic doctors died, some of them in violent ways."

Morbid fascination takes hold. Settling in her bedroom with her laptop, Georgie reads the online profiles of the doctors who died. Two were naturopaths, five were medical doctors practicing holistic medicine, and one was a chiropractor. Their websites list treatments she knows to be controversial, and some had written articles opposing vaccinations for newborns.

Despite Dwayne's opinion that this is an unfounded conspiracy theory, Georgie can't stop thinking about all the deaths happening in such a short time. Even if the timing is just a coincidence, it's still macabre. And Mark Caroll's death? There are disturbing similarities to the ones in the investigative report. His death was mysterious, and his complementary cancer therapies challenged the medical standard of care. His cancer patients had excellent outcomes, which some might view as a challenge to medical oncology treatments. Recently, he had an article about complimentary cancer care published in a prominent alternative medicine journal. Had his success put a target on his back? She dared not believe it.

She calls Pam the next evening. "How are you making out, Pam? Have you seen the news report?"

"It's shocking! I'm not sure I believe there is a conspiracy, but I caught myself checking over my shoulder when I left the clinic today."

"It must be so difficult to see patients right now," Georgie says.

"Well, I'm not very busy, and maybe that's a good thing. Several patients canceled their appointments, claiming it was out of respect for Dr. Caroll, but I'm not sure that's the reason. I think until we know what happened, our patients don't feel secure in the office, as odd as that may sound."

"So, no more news on the cause of death?"

"No. No one is telling us anything. If the police told Rachel, she's not sharing. She is in quite a state, and I just don't know what to say to her. But everyone is asking the same question. How could a healthy, fifty-two-year-old drop dead while running?" Pam lets out a loud sigh. "Of course, we know men that age can drop dead of heart attacks. They don't call it the silent killer for nothing! Still, after two weeks there should be a statement from the coroner—either it was natural causes, or there was foul play. I mean, you've been through this. How long did it take before you had autopsy results for your patient?"

Georgie shudders, not wanting to be reminded. "Oh, it was a week or so. But the patient died in her sleep—not quite the same scenario. What did the police ask you?"

"Oh, if I noticed anything different about him that day. But he was in a good mood, apparently physically fine—nothing out of the ordinary."

Georgie knows Pam lives alone and has no family nearby. "Pam, do you have anyone to talk to about this? Do you have a pastor or a close friend? Someone you trust?"

"I can call my sister, although we're not that close, or I could talk to my childhood friend." She sighs. "Thanks a lot for calling. And take care of yourself, Georgie. With everything in the news, it's frightening we might have to watch our backs."

"Pam. Call me anytime you need to talk."

After the call, Georgie meanders through the house, checking windows and doors. An involuntary shiver runs through her body, thinking about the two holistic doctors who died in their own homes. *Do I need a home security system?*

The next day, Georgie takes her own advice and calls Pastor Rick. She feels a little awkward asking for pastoral care because she hasn't been to church in quite a while. Since her move home, she has been trying to spend time with Dwayne and, with golf over for the season, Sunday morning was a good time to go out for breakfast or for a walk in the woods. She doesn't want to be one of those people who turn to the church only when in trouble. Still, Pastor Rick is gracious and welcoming when she arrives at his office. His eyes widen as Georgie brings him up to date on her troubles—the inquest, Dr. Caroll's sudden death, the rash of mysterious deaths, and fears for her career, perhaps her life. He listens without interrupting until she finishes, then leads her in a prayer for strength and for God's grace.

"I believe you are experiencing tremendous grief right now, and you need to process it," Pastor Rick says after the prayer. "A grief support group started here on Tuesday evening, and I hear the facilitator is quite good. You should try it."

Georgie takes the grief group information and, as she rises to leave, Pastor Rick says, "and Georgie, come to the worship service this Sunday. It'll do you good to be around supportive people right now."

Unsure about the grief group, Georgie agrees with her pastor's advice about attending church on Sunday. As usual, she and Lisa sit together, having the shared experience of husbands who don't go to church. For Georgie, being at the service is like finding a favorite warm sweater she had lost. The theme of the service is about the importance of a community of faith to lean on in times of trial and grief. The choir sings a song on the theme and the words go right to Georgie's heart, bringing her some solace and hope.

During the fellowship time, no one mentions the mysterious deaths of holistic health practitioners. It's a relief to talk about happier things—how good it is to be back home and Debbie's upcoming marriage. Her time at church allows her to focus on what is going well, at least for a couple of hours.

Dwayne is home in the afternoon, but he's busy working in his den, giving Georgie time alone with her thoughts. After she does some laundry, she tries to read a novel, but troubling questions keep intruding. *Is there really a conspiracy against holistic doctors? How can I proceed confidently in my practice under these circumstances?* She searches through her purse, fishes out the card for the grief support leader, and sends off an email asking to join the program. The way she is feeling, it is clear she needs a safe place to process it.

Georgie attends the grief support group on Tuesday evening, having missed the first session last week. For Georgie's benefit, Marie, the group leader, has everyone repeat their introductions and reasons for being in the group. At first, Georgie doubts she belongs in the program because most people are grieving a significant loss—the death of a close family member like a spouse, a child, or a parent. However, a few participants are like her with other kinds of grief—death of a colleague, divorce or a job loss. When it's her turn, she identifies three griefs—the death of a former mentor, the unexplained deaths of holistic doctors, and a potential threat to her career.

Next, Marie encourages everyone to name the emotions they are experiencing, and Georgie names hers as anger and fear. She is angry over the untimely deaths of Dr. Caroll and other holistic practitioners, and she is fearful for her career, especially if she practices in mind-body medicine. Her studies in mind-body connections tell her that anger and fear are harmful to her emotional and physical health. She cannot continue harboring these emotions.

The darkness of approaching winter doesn't help her mood. It's already twilight when she leaves the clinic on Wednesday, and while dashing to the car, she peers into the shadows. Once in the car, she admonishes herself for the irrational fear, but can't quell the feeling. When she arrives home, she asks Dwayne if they can install a home security system, telling him, "I need to feel safe somewhere."

The phone rings after dinner. It's Pam. "I have the results of Dr. Caroll's autopsy. He suffered a brain aneurysm, not something anyone could predict. There is no thought of foul play."

"How are you coping with everything? Did you ever talk to someone?"

"My school friend and I talked, but the best tonic is to bury myself in my work. And you know that was Mark's philosophy. He always said, 'focus on helping your patients.' Doing that is the best way to honor his memory."

"I'm impressed by how you are coping with all this. I know I shouldn't worry about what might happen, but it doesn't always work. Sometimes I can't concentrate on what my patients are saying, so I'm not very effective right now. Are you sleeping okay? I'm not."

"Sleep is sometimes off for me, too." Pam sighs. "Call me whenever you want to talk."

Georgie stares at the phone, considering another aspect of her grief—the loss of her colleague, Pam, who has been a trusted work ally.

Debbie should be here by now. The agreement was she would come today only if the weather allowed, and for now there is a clear blue sky and no snow in the forecast. Still, Georgie knows too well road conditions are not the only risks on the interstate, and to ease her worries, she calls Debbie's cell phone.

"I'll be there in half an hour," Debbie says, her voice muffled by traffic noise

Georgie sits at the kitchen island, sipping her coffee and reflecting on the past few months. Somehow, she survived Christmas, which, given recent events, was not very merry. The grief group helped her get through it, with the eight sessions straddling Christmas—four before and four after. Georgie thought the group leader made the right call in timing the sessions, no doubt aware Christmas is a difficult time of year for those who are grieving.

After almost three months at Dr. Rice's clinic, Georgie has yet to feel like a member of a team. She doesn't sense the same collegiality as the Caroll Clinic. Dr. Rice and Dr. Thom vetoed her idea for monthly clinic meetings, saying, "we're too busy with our patients, which is where your focus should be." They were also hesitant about The Naturopathic Way, her new patient seminar, citing "confidentiality concerns" for their patients.

Georgie thought her written proposal made a strong case for a new patient seminar as a clinic-wide program. She even addressed Dr. Rice's confidentiality issues by suggesting patients invite family members. If patients bring family, no one will know which one is the patient. But Dr. Rice was still cautious, agreeing Georgie could go ahead with the seminar, but only for her patients. She protested, saying a seminar for her patients will mean only a handful in attendance, but if all three practitioners send patients, there would be a larger gathering. Georgie thought it was another selling point—the more people at the seminar, the more successful the clinic would appear. Dr. Rice made a concession, saying, "perhaps I will sit in on one of your sessions to get a sense of what you are doing. Then we'll talk about making it a clinic-wide initiative."

Georgie snaps out of her musings at Debbie's arrival. It's early February, but Debbie wants all the plans in place soon because she will be too busy towards the end of the school year. As they get into Debbie's checklist, Georgie privately observes that planning for a backyard reception still requires the same number of decisions as a reception at a big venue.

Georgie starts by sharing her accomplishment—negotiating with New Hope for the loan of tables and chairs, at no cost. Debbie grins and checks tables and chairs off the list.

"Caterer?" Debbie asks.

"I have the menus for three local caterers. I suggest you and Craig choose the one you like."

"Great! We need to add something to the list—a large tent, in case it rains. I don't want my guests to worry about inclement weather."

Georgie adds to her to-do list: rent a large tent. "Good news," she says. "For the bouquets and corsages, we have flowers from our garden, and when Mrs. Dodge heard you were getting married, she offered some of her flowers, too. She is so happy for you!" They both tear up, recalling how their neighbor had helped them both through some difficult times.

"Hey, Mom! Carla, one of my attendants, does flower arranging, and she offered to make up all the bouquets, corsages, and boutonnieres. That will be her wedding gift." She checks her checklist again. "Cake?"

"Margaret Anderson, down the street, agreed to make the wedding cake. She retired from the bakery last year, but does some baking from home, and at a lower price. You can go there today and choose the cake you want."

Debbie smiles and puts a check mark on her list beside "cake."

About wedding apparel, Debbie becomes animated telling how she found a great deal on attendant dresses at an online store. For another cost savings, she convinced Craig and his groomsmen to wear suits rather than tuxes.

Georgie smirks at her daughter's pride in this frugality, perhaps a trait inherited from Dwayne. She doesn't want to bring Debbie down by reminding her that a large tent will be a pricey rental.

With today's list checked off, they pause for tea and samples of cake from Mrs. Anderson. As Debbie is oohing over the cake, Georgie asks something that's been weighing on her mind. "Debbie, are you sure you're okay with this simple affair we are planning?"

"Definitely! Big weddings are just for show—people trying to do one better than someone else. That's not what it's about at all. I am getting married to a man I adore, and I want to keep my focus on that."

Georgie can't help but be proud of her daughter's values—relationships over appearances. *Did I teach her that?*

Debbie goes to Mrs. Anderson's place to select her wedding cake, and returns a half-hour later, pleased with her choice—a three-layered white cake with lemon icing. As she prepares to leave for Indy to spend the rest of the weekend with Craig, she puts an envelope on the table, with "Mom" written on it. She hugs Georgie, saying, "Please, open it later."

Georgie fingers the envelope, intensely curious, but waits to open it when she won't be interrupted. In the evening, she retreats to her bedroom and unfolds a handwritten letter.

> Dear Mom,
>
> In those awful years when I was ill, the darkest clouds covered me and hope was something I could barely see. But you did not give up on me when doctors did. You pulled me out of the rubble that seemed impossible to escape. You are the reason I am still here today.

Georgie is in tears and grabs a tissue before she can continue reading.

> You held my hand, held it tight, and you stood by me all the way. You helped me discover a path less traveled that I could enjoy. And in you, I found my strength and the will to survive. You taught me how to overcome my circumstances, to make the most of my life. I learned from you how to turn my troubles and my bitter moments into sweet memories. You showed me the miracles that a mother's love brings. From you, I discovered the power of prayer and the power of dreams, too. I learned to trust in myself and others and love and accept myself for who I am—to be the best person I can become. Dearest Mom, I love you, and I am forever thankful for having you. I pray someday that I will be a great mom, just like you!
>
> Love, Debbie

Dabbing her eyes, Georgie shakes her head in amazement at how traumatic events sometimes have a benefit. Debbie suffered trials at a young age and came through as a balanced individual with a strong sense of what matters. She put in a call to Debbie and simply says, "Thank you! I love you too!"

Debbie's letter and its sentiments give Georgie hope that perhaps her current trials will help her be stronger, too. She heaves a sigh, reminded of the contrast to her other two children. Daphne was home two weeks ago for some much-needed dental work, using her parents' dental plan, of course. She had the gall to say, "I just don't resonate with life in America anymore. I have great friends in Paris and I love my job. Nothing at home can compare with working at the Louvre!" She also made a disappointing announcement. "And please tell Deb how sorry I am that I can't come to the wedding. I can't take time off during the height of tourist season." Georgie laments Daphne's apparent drift away from her family. Still, her fluency in three other languages has taken her somewhere, to a position as a tour guide at the Louvre. Georgie finally has hope for Daphne's career, even though it is across the pond.

As for D.J., both Georgie and Dwayne have concerns, but for different reasons. Dwayne's unstated but obvious focus is the 2.3 GPA needed for football eligibility, and right now, D.J.'s grades are not there. He missed last season because his GPA was only 1.9. Georgie is conflicted about it—pleased D.J. is not risking his life playing football, but upset about his grades. More than once, she considered a drastic move, to stop pushing him to improve his grades, so football would not be a choice. Georgie called her mother for a sympathetic ear, and when D.J. was home for the weekend recently, her father called D.J. to come over "for a chat." When D.J. came home, he fended off questions about his conversation with his grandfather. Curiosity got the better of Georgie and she called her father. She recalls his words clearly.

"I told him in no uncertain terms that if he suffers another head injury while playing football, he will risk permanent brain damage," her father said. "You and Dwayne have to talk him out of this crazy notion of playing again!"

For once, Georgie and her father agreed, but when she spoke to Dwayne, he shrugged and said, "if D.J. thinks he can do it, I say let him try."

Dwayne left it up to Georgie to reason with D.J. about the importance of good grades, not just so he can play football, but for his long-term future.

D.J. did not take her advice well. "Mom! You don't believe I can make it in football!"

"That's not it at all. I'm afraid you won't survive football!"

"You and Gramps worry too much. I've had no headaches for almost a year. I know what I'm doing!" D.J. stomped up the stairs, saying over his shoulder. "It's like you don't want me to be successful."

As Georgie prepares for bed, she despairs over that recent interaction with D.J., so like her disagreements with her father. *Dear God, please help me speak to my son in a way that won't create a rift between us.* The prayer brings little solace. A rift may be unavoidable because Dwayne won't back up her concerns about football. It's a familiar feeling, like years ago when he left her with all the tough decisions about Debbie's health care. There are uneven stitches woven through their twenty-four years of parenting—when she zigs, he zags. But he isn't likely to change now. If that is how it is, she resolves to have the emotional strength to be the nagging, unpopular parent.

Chapter 20

Georgie arrives at New Hope Church for a meeting with her pastor and a lay leader to pitch an idea she had before returning to Terrance. Because of the inquest and Dr. Caroll's death, she hadn't the motivation to act on her idea until now—a weekly meditation group, like the one at Community Church. She meditates every day but yearns for the group experience. Something about being in a group makes meditation more satisfying. She considered looking for an existing group but prefers Christian content, and she wants to introduce the practice to members in her church.

Pastor Rick and Sarah Barber, the church board chairperson, listen to her proposal for a series of guided group meditations. Sarah voices concerns about the lack of volunteers in the church to organize the group and turns to the pastor, seeking his reaction.

"There is value in meditation," Pastor Rick says. "I feel we could entertain the idea if there is a Christian approach. Who would lead the meditation?"

"I would find a trained meditation leader," Georgie replies.

"Good! I would like to know who you find. And, as Sarah says, our volunteers are all tapped out. If you agree to organize and promote the series, I am in favor of offering it."

When Georgie arrives home, she gets right to work to find a suitable meditation leader. Checking online, she discovers another church in the city already offers meditation and they list the name of their leader, Destiny, from Mindful Meditation Center. Georgie calls Destiny, who invites her to sit in on a session the next evening.

Georgie plans to observe the meditation group rather than immerse herself in the experience. She notes Destiny's meditation is simple, based on deep breathing, and the mantra word "Maranatha," Aramaic for "your Lord is come." Despite Georgie's intention to observe, the meditation pulls her into a relaxed state, and when she opens her eyes, she senses calm and peace among the group, matching her own. It wasn't just the meditation words. Destiny's demeanor and velvet voice made it effective. To get a sense of the woman, Georgie engages her in conversation.

"When I come from Jamaica," Destiny says in a faint island accent, "everythin' move too fast, you know? Meditation slow everythin' down for me." She shares more of her life story, revealing she is also a person of faith.

Georgie discerns Destiny will be an acceptable meditation leader for New Hope and asks about her availability.

"I could start next month after this session ends," Destiny says. "I only have a few evenings open and I have to charge a small fee. Will the church be okay with that?"

"I'm sure we can handle that." Georgie resolves to pay the fee herself if New Hope Church won't cover it or if they don't want to charge participants. It will be worth it to be in a meditation group again, while also introducing meditation to others.

One week before the first meditation session at New Hope, Georgie has seven people preregistered, a result of her efforts in promotion—distributing flyers and making announcements at church. She ends the call from the seventh participant, when Dr. Rice appears at her office door.

"A minute, Dr. Downie?" He says, still standing in the doorway. "After sitting in on your Naturopathic Way seminar, I have decided to recommend it to my patients and their family members. The way you explain the differences between naturopathic and conventional medicine is valuable information for our patients, and because you don't call it a new patient seminar, I can refer any of my interested patients." Dr. Rice smiles. "I'm going to recommend Dr. Thom send his patients, too."

Still on a high, a half-hour later, Georgie has another call.

"Georgie, I really miss your Naturopathic Way seminar," Pam says. "I raved about them to Paula, and she's wants it for her patients, too. Would you consider coming here once a month to give the seminar to our new patients? I think having an outside presenter will strengthen the message for patients, and I would pay for your time and gas. It's well worth it to help my patients stick to their protocols."

Georgie doesn't hesitate to say yes, thankful for a chance to reconnect with Pam. When she left Caroll Clinic, she thought it spelled the end of their collaboration that had been so productive. She never expected the Naturopathic Way seminar to restore their connection. They laugh together about the timing of Pam's call the very day Dr. Rice and Dr. Thom embraced the seminar.

"I took your advice about keeping busy," Georgie says. "It's been therapeutic to focus on helping my patients, but I also organized a meditation group at my church. That has been a much-needed tonic, too."

"How is it going with your practice? Are you delving more into mind-body work?"

"I've been taking more spiritual counseling courses, but I'm not ready to promote mind-body work in my practice yet. I need to get acquainted with all my patients and get used to working at this clinic. It's totally different from Caroll Clinic." *And not always in a good way!*

Georgie's comment leads them to reminisce about Mark Caroll and what a supportive colleague and mentor he was. They agree the best way to honor his memory is to keep doing their best for their patients.

Georgie arrives home from the last of six meditation sessions at New Hope Church, pleased with Destiny's leadership. Georgie enjoyed the group meditation experience, although sometimes she felt the weight of an organizer's responsibility. Her attention often strayed to a concern for how other participants were engaged in the meditation because, if they did not like the experience, that might mean the end of meditation at the church. At Pastor Rick's urging, she devised a feedback form for participants to complete at the last session. He felt a favorable response would be needed for the church board to agree to another meditation series.

Settled at her dining room table, Georgie eyes the pile of feedback forms. Before reading them, she completes her own feedback form, praising Destiny's leadership and noting her preferred elements, the meditation for Letting Go and the one for Anxiety and Stress, based on Philippians 4:6-7.

Do not be anxious about anything, but in every situation, by prayer and petition, with thanksgiving, present your requests to God.

Bracing herself, she reads the comments from other participants. "Uplifting," says one. Another says: "I feel a calm I've longed for but never found." A third writes: "I would like another series like this." There are more with similar sentiments. Tears form in her eyes as she nods her head. *Yes! I experienced those things too!* Based on these comments, surely the church board would approve another meditation series.

It occurs to her she has been sleeping more soundly and more focused at work. The worry about being attacked has faded, too, likely because no other mysterious deaths have been reported. She reflects on the saying, "time heals all wounds." Her discovery is that healing doesn't just take time—it also takes effort.

This week was momentous for another reason. Georgie completed another distance course in spiritual counseling, with four more to go for her certification. She was in the middle of a course on divine guidance when Dr. Caroll died, and, unable to focus, she put her studies on hold for a while. Taking the courses reminds her of Dr. Caroll, who once advised her to finish the certification before adding mind-body work to her practice. In some ways, she agreed with that advice, but without naming it, she has incorporated some aspects of mind-body healing into her patient consultations. Still, it's like she is just skimming the surface of what she could do to help patients with emotional barriers to healing.

Recently, a solution has formed in her mind, inspired by her own positive experiences in groups—meditation, prayer, and grief support. It occurred to her that a group experience might be an effective approach to offer mind-body medicine. A group setting may be less threatening than one-to-one counseling, which some patients resist. Being in a group provides a sense of belonging, that others share the same concerns. Groups also encourage accountability—no one wants to admit to others they did not do their homework.

Dwayne is at a conference for the weekend, giving Georgie uninterrupted time to explore her idea for a group program on healing mind-body issues. To glean ideas, she pores through her self-help books and spiritual counseling course materials. Her experience with patients also provides clues about the most common emotional barriers to healing. It soon becomes clear there are several such barriers, requiring a series of seminars, each addressing a different issue. The task seems daunting: How to fill several seminars with engaging material? How to make it attractive to participants? When she gets frustrated by the challenges of creating a program, she goes for a walk or stops to meditate.

By the time Dwayne arrives home from his conference late Sunday afternoon, Georgie has identified four distinct principles for mind-body healing. The foundational principle is, "take responsibility for one's own health and healing." Her patients who take an active role in their healing always have better outcomes. She has noticed those with mind-body health issues are more likely to abdicate responsibility for their health care to others.

"Surround oneself with supportive people," her second principle, speaks to the importance of cultivating affirming human connections. Recognizing which relationships support healing is a challenge for many people, but more so with those she wants to help with her seminars.

The third principle is "forgiving others and oneself." Perhaps the most critical to healing, this principle is likely the most challenging to put into practice. Who can say they have mastered forgiveness in all situations? She fears this principle will be the most difficult to address, to ensure people in the seminar will benefit.

"You are not alone," her fourth principle, stresses how connection with God supports us spiritually and emotionally. Her own breakthrough in coping with challenges came after she sought guidance through meditation and prayer and stopped trying to fix problems by herself. Because faith perspectives vary, she has concerns about how to craft this topic into a seminar. She dislikes generic references to God, such as Source or Universal Consciousness, but it may be necessary to ensure participants with different faith perspectives can still benefit.

As she prepares for bed Sunday night, she has a satisfying sense of accomplishment, but also a suspicion there are other principles.

Georgie is preparing to spend another Saturday working on her seminar series, thankful her work with patients in the past week provided some inspiration. One patient admitted to being riddled with guilt about her past mistakes that Georgie assessed was not conducive to the patient's recovery. That encounter reminded her of how mistakes have haunted her and how guilt has sometimes weighed on her spirit. This led her to identify a fifth principle:

"learn from mistakes, let go of guilt." Another patient seemed fearful of everything, even about making health-promoting changes. Georgie could understand how this might happen. Her fear and anxiety over the mysterious deaths of holistic doctors had temporarily sapped her motivation and energy. For inspiration, she read John 4:18. *There is no fear in love. Perfect love casts out fear.* From A Course in Miracles, she recalled the premise that there are only two emotions: love and fear. Scanning the workbooks, she found two relevant lessons: *Today belongs to love. Let me not fear,* and, *All fear is past and only love is here.* Her sixth principle would be "focus on love, not fear."

Further inspiration came from an unexpected source. On Friday evening, Georgie watched the movie Pay It Forward. Several characters struggled with trauma and addictions, but they gained personal healing after the protagonist inspired them to help others without thought of reward. The powerful message in the film reminded Georgie of her commitment to serve others and how fulfilling it has been. She has become aware how focusing on the needs of others can relieve worry for one's own struggles. The phrase from the prayer of St. Francis came to mind: *it is in giving that we receive.* Her seventh principle will be "serve others."

Most of Saturday Georgie devotes to crafting the key points for each seminar topic, still unsure if there is another principle. In the evening, exhausted from her day-long creative efforts, she relaxes by watching a romantic comedy on TV. Dwayne watches with her for a while then retreats to his den, likely to stream an action/adventure movie. Georgie chuckles. There's a reason they call romantic comedies chick flicks.

Sunday morning, Georgie takes a break by going to church. Pastor Rick's message poses the question: "Does God want us to be happy?" He speaks to the theological question about whether the call to be Christ's disciples requires suffering. During the rest of the message, Georgie is distracted, considering the role happiness plays in one's emotional and physical health. One of her spiritual counseling courses focused on affirmations—positive statements about oneself or one's situation, whatever the current reality. At their core, do affirmations represent a decision to be happy? Georgie rushes home from church and adds her eighth principle, "decide to be happy." Now with eight principles, it feels like a comprehensive package. She is not sure why, but eight seems like the ideal number for a series.

Working through Sunday afternoon and evening, she comes up with a rough draft of each seminar. Before putting more effort into the details, she needs an outside opinion on the overall concept and emails the outline to Pam. Just before bedtime, Pam emails a reply, "You're onto something with this. Keep working on it."

During a third Saturday dedicated to fleshing out the seminars, Georgie has a breakthrough by incorporating adult education approaches—using life experiences as learning tools and encouraging self-direction. After the lecture portion of the seminar—explaining the principle and presenting case examples—she plans to engage participants in self-assessment, group discussion, and end with guided meditation. Georgie already approached Destiny, who agreed to lead the meditation portion. To encourage participants' self-direction, she must also devise exercises for them to do between sessions.

The question of the frequency of sessions is easy for Georgie to answer. Even though actual change can take longer than eight weeks, monthly sessions would drag out the process and be less impactful. She expects self-help groups like AA are effective because they hold weekly meetings.

On Monday evening, Georgie goes to Lisa's house to show her the detailed seminar outlines. She could email the outlines but prefers to see Lisa's reaction. Waiting for Lisa to read through the outlines, Georgie tries to gauge her friend's response.

Lisa looks up from reading and smiles. "Wow! This is amazing and well thought out," she says. "What are you going to call it? You need a unique and catchy title."

Georgie has yet to give the series a name, but right in the moment, a title pops into her head. Perhaps it was percolating in the back of her mind for weeks. "The title is Emotional Effectiveness."

On Tuesday morning, her session outlines in hand, she approaches Dr. Rice about offering her seminar series at the clinic. Based on her previous experiences, she isn't expecting a ringing endorsement. She finishes her proposal and waits with bated breath.

Dr. Rice peers over his glasses, his face stony. "How do you know this will help people?"

"There is solid research behind the principles. I have spiritual counseling training and the clinical experience to back them up."

He studies her for a few moments. "Still, I need to know it will actually help patients before you can offer it at the clinic."

Georgie stares at him, incredulous at the impossibility of his request. "How can I know the seminars will help patients if I can't offer them to patients?"

He shrugs. "You're clever. I'm sure you will figure it out."

Georgie retreats to her office, fuming over Dr. Rice's response, feeling like a caged bird. Every time she tries to stretch her wings, he closes the cage door.

Through the week, her irritation with Dr. Rice builds and she finds it difficult to be civil to him. Despite meditation and prayer, Georgie cannot discern a way forward with her program. It is almost like the grief she felt after Dr. Caroll's death when toxic emotions were dominating her life. By Sunday, she is so bothered by the situation, she must drag herself to church. At coffee and fellowship, Pastor Rick seeks her out to ask how she is doing in her practice.

Can he sense I am struggling?

"Are you familiar with a catch-22? I developed seminars on mind-body healing for my patients, but I can't hold the seminars at my clinic until I can prove it will help patients."

The pastor furrows his brow, then his face brightens. "What about offering your series here at the church first?" He pauses, looks away, then back at Georgie. "If you are testing out the program, maybe you would consider offering it for free."

Georgie raises her eyebrows at the unexpected idea. It's not ideal because the participants may not be like her patients. Still, what other options are there? Then it comes to her; it makes perfect sense. Offering the program as a trial at no cost would allow her to assess participant response without the pressure of delivering the intended benefits. *Why didn't I think of that?* She jumps at her pastor's offer and says a private prayer of thanks for her church community.

The forecast of forty percent chance of rain tomorrow, Debbie's wedding day, is creating tension in the Downie household. Georgie prays the weather forecast is wrong, even though the guests will have cover under the large tent now set up in the backyard. She took the week off for last-minute preparations—checking with the caterers, ensuring delivery of tables, chairs, the tent, and cake. Much of this must be done the day before the wedding. Debbie is there to help, but Georgie doesn't want to say what she was thinking. If a small reception in the backyard is keeping it simple, she would not want to organize a big, fancy wedding.

Georgie ends her call to Mrs. Anderson, confirming the cake will be ready to pick up on Saturday morning. Dwayne is standing right beside her, frowning, hands on his hips.

"You planned this affair," he says, "and expect me to do all this work in the yard. I don't have time."

Dwayne's intensity catches Georgie off guard. *Where is this coming from?* "This 'affair' is our daughter's wedding!" A quick turn of her head confirms Debbie is out of earshot on the back deck, helping Carla make up the bouquets. "Please, Dwayne, let's not stress over this. It will all be fine. Why don't you get D.J. to help?" She goes to the back door and surveys the yard. "I'm not sure why you're concerned. The yard looks great."

Dwayne looks over his shoulder and shakes his head, clearly not satisfied.

Is my husband becoming a perfectionist?

Saturday dawns a beautiful day, the forecast changed to sunny with cloudy periods. Early in the morning, Dwayne and D.J. put up the decorations in the backyard, and once they hang the bunting and bows, the quality of the grass and hedges doesn't seem as important.

Debbie is radiant in a simple white gown, her dark brown hair coiled in an updo, encased by a wreath of baby's breath. Craig arrives on time, albeit looking a little nervous, fidgeting with his tie. Georgie cries unabashedly as her oldest daughter and her new husband walk triumphantly out of the church. Watching the happy couple pose for their wedding photos, she prays they are a good match for each other. She knows that, over time, people can change or develop different interests. So many marriages fail these days with the most common explanation: "we just grew apart."

Despite Dwayne's pre-wedding angst about the yard, many guests comment on the beauty of the setting for the reception. One of Dwayne's colleagues from work asks, perhaps in jest, if he could rent the yard for his daughter's wedding. After hearing this, Dwayne appears more relaxed and able to enjoy the wedding feast. Georgie enjoys herself too but laments the absence of Daphne, who tried to make up for it by sending a funny video montage to Debbie. The video is an enormous hit with the guests, but Georgie sees it as a poor substitute for Daphne's presence as the maid of honor. It is the only damper on what is otherwise a joyous day.

The next morning, Dwayne plans to drive D.J. to college football training camp. The doctor cleared D.J. to play, but only if he wears a neck collar and a special helmet with extra padding. Georgie expressed her doubts those measures would provide protection from further injury, but both D.J. and Dwayne scoffed at her concerns. As they pack up the car for the two-hour drive to Bloomington, father and son talk football—prospects for D.J. to make first-string tackle, and the team's chances for the season. Georgie is not going with them, partly in protest, but also because post-wedding cleaning and tidying can't wait. And she is due back to the clinic tomorrow. She waves and forces a smile as they drive away, slumps her shoulders and retreats to the house. Worry for her son may become her constant companion. *I can't go through D.J. having another head injury!*

Chapter 21

After months of research, writing, and fine-tuning, the Emotional Effectiveness program is starting this evening at New Hope Church. From the first sketchy notes to the completed product, Georgie was on an emotional roller coaster between confidence and doubt about her creation. Every day, it seemed, she either tweaked something, abandoned an idea, or did further research. No matter how many times she went over the materials, she would find something to improve. She joked with Lisa, saying, "I'm just a compulsive editor!" Twice, she shared her plans with Pam, who gave some helpful suggestions. Beyond preparing the materials, the challenge was attracting participants because Dr. Rice forbade Georgie from inviting her patients. If they heard about it elsewhere else, he said that was fine. He remained concerned about the clinic's reputation with an untested program.

Early on, Georgie knew she needed help with marketing and, back in August, asked Lisa for help. To guide the creation of posters, fliers, and social media ads, Lisa asked for specific details—seminar elements, how people will benefit, perhaps some catchy phrases. Georgie identified the major benefit as "emotional balancing to support physical health no matter your situation." The catchy phrases she left for Lisa to craft.

After Georgie shared all the seminar elements, Lisa commented that the interactive activities suggested workshops more than seminars. "I consider a seminar to be mostly a lecture, while a workshop has interaction and discussion. What you call this program will matter. Believe it not, some people prefer lectures rather than sharing their personal issues with others."

Georgie agreed and changed the program descriptor from seminar to workshop.

Lisa also insisted the promotion include Georgie's credentials as a naturopath and a spiritual counselor, even though she has not completed all the counseling courses. Georgie was a little uncomfortable with this, but Lisa was firm in her stance. "Strut your stuff, girl!"

Lisa's promotion worked. The day before the workshop was to start, Georgie had nine participants registered—an acceptable, manageable number for a trial run of the program. Georgie called Lisa to thank her for the marketing help, but also to share her feelings of apprehension. In testing her self-assessment tools, she answered the questions herself, and didn't always like her answers, in particular the ones about forgiveness. "You know, I'm not sure I've fully forgiven my father, and being upset with him always leads to a headache. Then there's the wine. After a blowup with him, I often drink too much."

Lisa made a surprising suggestion that Georgie share her struggles with extending forgiveness to her father. Georgie was reluctant, fearing people would think less of her, but Lisa convinced her it would make her more relatable.

At five minutes past seven, eight participants, all women, sit in a circle regarding Georgie with expectation. She smiles at them, hiding her disappointment that number nine is a no-show. To avoid starting on a negative note, she doesn't mention the no-show.

Georgie proceeds with the introduction to the first principle, the lecture portion. From the nods on their faces, the participants seem to accept the wisdom of taking responsibility for one's health and healing. But Georgie wonders if this response is a function of who is in attendance. These women may be more emotionally aware than her patients and, based on how readily they accept the wisdom of the principle, it seems likely. Destiny arrives near the end of the session and leads a meditation called, "I am enough." Georgie takes the relaxed faces of participants following meditation to mean that Destiny provided a meaningful experience.

As participants depart, Georgie notices a message on her cell phone—she had it on mute during the session. The woman who was a no-show left a message apologizing for her absence and asking if she could still take part. Georgie considers this for a few minutes, having no plan in place for handling absences. Since this is a trial run, she allows the request if the woman can familiarize herself with the first session materials. For future reference, it will be helpful to know whether a latecomer can engage with the program.

The eighth session of the workshop series concludes. Georgie ushers the last woman out and flops into a chair in the meeting room, holding the written evaluations. She is eager to read them, but apprehensive about how participants reacted to the workshops. There were a few challenges during open discussions, and she was not sure how well she handled them.

During the second session, "surround yourself with supportive people," one woman posed a tough question: "If my husband isn't supportive, does that mean I should leave him?" Georgie tried to walk a fine line with her response, explaining the principle was about identifying people one *could* rely on, even more important when in a troubled relationship. She offered to speak to the woman after the session, but she seemed okay by then. Was it the self-assessment of one's existing supports that made a difference? Perhaps Destiny's meditation on gratitude helped calm the woman's concerns.

As Georgie expected, the session on forgiveness was challenging for her and the participants. She took Lisa's advice and shared her struggles to forgive her father and the mind-body connection to her headaches. One participant seemed indignant, asking, "What about real trauma? How can I forgive my father for emotionally abusing me as a child?" Others in the group looked to Georgie for an answer and lessons from in A Course in Miracles provided her with a response. "Forgiving someone does not mean you have to forget what they did or condone it. You don't have to restore a close relationship, either. Forgiving is about having compassion for another's failings—perhaps their personal anguish or trauma caused them to lash out at you. Forgiving someone is more about letting go of judgment rather than forgetting the grievance. And judgment can make us suffer as much as the actions of a perpetrator. It is our judgments that are toxic to us." The participant who admitted to past abuse questioned how she could let go of *all* judgment. Georgie reassured the group this principle is likely the most difficult to embrace and to give it time.

At that session, Destiny's meditation evoked vivid imagery on how to extend forgiveness by imagining being in a golden bubble of acceptance, then expanding it to those who have hurt us. Participants made a collective sigh when the meditation ended.

To prepare for the forgiveness session, Georgie had spent some time assessing the strained relationship with her father. Did the workshop principle mean she needed to understand her father's failings or pain? She had meditated on it for several days, seeking to understand the source of his verbal attacks and discerned he had taken his strong convictions and beliefs to an extreme. He believed he was right, that there was only one way to practice medicine. Then it had dawned on her. If these are her father's flaws, does she have the same flaws? She has an equally strong conviction about alternative medicine. She had prayed fervently and even wrote out a prayer that she kept by her bedside. *Dear God, I know that Your mercy flows to me in spite of my failings. Help me let go of my anger for my father and place in my heart the same unconditional love for him You give to me. Help me see my father through Your eyes.* Yet, resentments towards her father linger. She would have to keep repeating the prayer until the message got through.

Tonight, in the last session, "you are not alone," participants seemed soothed by the principle that God is there for them. There were no tough questions, but Georgie suspected because of the workshop's location, all her participants were people of faith. People without a faith perspective might not accept the principle as readily. When the meditation on oneness ended, the participants sat for a few minutes, smiling at each other, then before leaving, two women spontaneously hugged Georgie.

Georgie leaves the church without looking at the evaluations. Once at home, she sits at the dining room table with an herbal tea, staring at the stack of paper, fearful of what she will find. Eventually, curiosity wins out over fear. Six people reported a breakthrough in understanding the source of their anxieties. All participants had physical ailments, which they said improved somewhat. Momentarily disappointed, Georgie decides it is not reasonable to resolve physical health issues after only eight weeks. Perhaps she will devise a follow up evaluation a few months after the workshops to assess long-term impacts. During the series, Georgie also learned only five of the nine participants were in the care of a health practitioner. She sighs and shakes her head—this is the downside of testing the program on people other than patients. Their response to this workshop may not predict how patients benefit from it. Reading further, she sees some suggestions for improvement, about organization and timing, things she will need to work on before offering the series again.

The next morning, Georgie goes to Dr. Rice with the participants' feedback, which, she is prepared to claim, is sufficient evidence her workshops will benefit her patients. She can't believe his response. The positive energy she feels from the workshop series drains away. *Why did I come to this clinic?*

In the evening, Pam calls sounding down, too.

"What's going on?" Georgie asks.

"Lots! Rachel is keeping ownership of the clinic and will maintain Mark's name on it, like a legacy. I'm good with that. But Rachel doesn't know enough about naturopathic practice to be clinic director. Roger refused to do it, so Rachel asked me. But it's a big learning curve for me because I've never managed a business before." She sighs. "But I don't want to go on about my issues. I called to find out how your workshop series went?"

"Well, I guess. The evaluations were good overall. The problem is Dr. Rice still won't allow me to offer it to clinic patients. He says I need to offer it again, but this time for a fee, to ensure people still report benefits when they pay for the workshops."

"What? Your own patients aren't involved? Georgie, I've seen you leading seminars. You are good at connecting with people, and from what I read of your workshop materials, I believe you can make a difference."

"Thanks for the vote of confidence, Pam."

"Hey, I just had a great idea! If you want to come here to hold your next workshop series, I would welcome you with open arms. You can keep the workshop fees if you like."

"Thank you, Pam. That's a generous offer! Could you find ten to twelve participants?"

"I expect so. Some of your former patients will be eager to see you again, and I suspect a few of my patients are candidates for your program. Hey, are you coming to the National Naturopathic Conference here next month? We could talk about this more then."

Georgie is excited to be attending her first naturopathic conference. The event has always been too far away, but this year it's in Indianapolis. Because of the unpredictable weather of November, she opted to stay at the hotel for the weekend rather than driving back and forth. Memories of her accident on the route to Indy still make her a nervous driver, and a hotel stay seems like a vacation, which she welcomes. She stands in the crowded hotel lobby and spots Pam entering the front door.

"Pam!" Georgie calls to her former colleague and crosses the lobby to greet her. "It's terrific to see you." As they hug, Georgie realizes she hasn't seen Pam since Dr. Caroll's memorial a year ago. She doesn't want to say anything, but Pam looks older, perhaps from the stress of Dr. Caroll's death. "Let's grab a bite before the first session," Georgie says. "I didn't get dinner before leaving Terrance."

Georgie orders a chicken quesadilla and a salad, but Pam has already eaten and just orders a tea.

"I have fifteen people preregistered for the workshop series if you hold it on Saturday afternoons," Pam says, after they place their orders. "They seem eager to get started, so I think you should launch in January. It's the time of year people like to make life changes."

"That's great that you have so many participants, but I'm not sure about January. I was thinking of March, so winter weather wouldn't interfere with attendance, and I'm not keen on driving the interstate during the winter, either."

"All the participants live right in the city, so the weather won't bother them that much. If you can't get here, we can always cancel that session and extend the series by another week."

Reluctantly, Georgie agrees to the January start date. When she finishes her meal and they rise from their chairs, Georgie impulsively hugs Pam, saying, "this means so much to me!"

Together, they join the hundreds of other delegates for the keynote address in the main conference hall. Pam has been to conferences before and says, "It's important to attend the keynote because it sets the tone for the whole conference."

An hour later, they leave the conference hall. "Well, the keynote was okay," Georgie says. "The speaker knows his stuff, but his presentation style is tedious—too many ums and ahs. I guess Toastmasters turned me into a compulsive speech evaluator." She chuckles and Pam smirks.

Georgie notices the hotel lounge is still open. "Do you want to join me for a drink?"

"Not for me. I'm driving, and I should go home and get my beauty sleep." Pam waves and heads to the parking garage.

Georgie pauses at the lounge door and almost doesn't go in. Since her revelation about using wine to handle stress, she always hesitates before indulging. This time, she is not under any stress, so it should be okay to have one glass of wine. After all, she enjoys the taste.

She relaxes in a cozy booth and orders a glass of Shiraz, her favorite. With her first sip, she looks over the rim of the glass and freezes. There, not ten feet away, is David Longhurst just getting up to leave. She keeps still with her head down. *Maybe he won't notice me.*

David turns and spots her. Flashing his engaging smile, he strolls over to her table. "Georgie, what a surprise! It's been a while." He gazes directly into Georgie's eyes. Her heart flutters and her face flushes. She looks down into her wineglass to avert her face and hide her reaction. *What am I? A schoolgirl? Why does he do this to me?*

"Hey, David. Yes, what a surprise," she says, hoping her lack of enthusiasm will discourage him. But he sits down uninvited. Annoyed that he joined her without asking, it also occurs to her strange that he is here. The conference delegates booked the whole hotel for the weekend.

"I'm here for the naturopathic conference for the weekend. What brings you here?" she asks.

"I was meeting with a client of mine, a naturopath from Chicago. Funny thing! After your inquest, I started getting calls from other naturopaths about their legal issues. You made a name for me in alternative health legal defense. Quite a niche!" He chuckles. "Of course, I wondered if you might be here. And here you are!" A boyish exuberance crosses his face, and he spreads his arms as if ready to embrace her.

Georgie smiles in spite of herself, sensing the same intoxicating effect as the last time she saw him. She gives her head a shake. "Yes, here I am!" She gulps down the last of her wine. *I need to end this before he tempts me further.* "Well, I have an early morning. I'd better be off." She fishes in her bag for a ten-dollar bill, places it on the table, and pushes her chair away from the table.

He stands up too, downing his drink. "Sure, I understand. You're not on vacation. And it's getting late for me too." He eyes her intently. "Hey, I'd love to hear how you're doing with your practice. How about I treat you to lunch tomorrow? I owe you something for all the legal work I'm getting."

Can I trust myself with this man? Georgie turns away and busies herself with her jacket and bag, stalling while she comes up with an excuse.

"I promise I won't bite," he says, as if reading her thoughts.

She snickers. "Well, of course not, but I won't have much time for lunch. The conference schedule is tight."

His smile fades, then brightens again. "Hey, I might be here around lunchtime, anyway. I'm meeting with my naturopath client again at some point this weekend."

"Sure." Hoping her tepid response will discourage him, she strides to the elevator without looking back. *That was close!* Tomorrow she'll have Pam with her at lunch to keep her from the temptation that is David Longhurst.

The weekend of intense learning is over, and Georgie is driving home, tired but relieved David Longhurst did not find her again. She had a text from him, though. "Wonderful to see you again!" Not knowing what to say, she didn't text a reply. *This man does not give up easily!*

She arrives home and enters the family room to find Dwayne watching a football game. He raises his hand in greeting without breaking his concentration on the game. She sits down beside him.

"Hey! Did you have a good weekend?" she asks.

"Yep." His eyes remain glued to the TV.

Georgie shares her news about the workshop series at the Caroll Clinic and how good it will be to run the program with actual patients.

"What?! You're going to be traveling to Indy again?" He turns the TV volume down and turns to face her squarely. "You were supposed to be done with working there!" He runs his hands over his face then clasps them together. "Georgie, we need to talk. This conversation will not be easy. Before you came back to live here full time, you might recall I wasn't sure we were going to make it."

Georgie nods warily. "Yes, I remember you said that if I didn't come home. But I came home!" *Where is he going with this?*

"Yes, you came home! But it's been a year now, and there isn't much change. You're out almost every evening giving talks, and you work all weekend on that workshop series of yours. Why can't you just see patients on weekdays and allow us to have a life together?"

Georgie stiffens at yet another criticism of her career. "Dwayne, this is how it is to be a health professional. You, of all people, should understand what it takes to build a business. To grow my practice, I need to work outside of patient consultations. And my workshop series will be a big part of my practice and generate income."

"I expected you to say this." He rises from the couch, walks over to the window, his back towards her. "Georgie, we've grown apart. It doesn't help that I never see you, but really, we don't have any common interests." He turns to face her. "Think about it. Without the kids to talk about, what do we have?"

Georgie swallows hard on the lump forming in her throat. She has harbored similar concerns about their relationship but maintained hope things would improve.

"I think we need a trial separation," he says, his arms crossed. "I will take a room near the office, and you can stay in the house for now."

"Oh!" She splays a hand over the stabbing sensation in her heart. "Ah… It sounds like you have this all figured out. Is there no room for discussion?"

He shakes his head.

"If that's the way you feel, then I can't stop you from leaving." Her mouth goes dry, knowing she must ask a burning question. "Dwayne, I have to know. Is there…," her breath catches in her throat, "… someone else?"

He looks down at his feet. "No, not exactly, but there could be."

"And what is that supposed to mean? Either there is, or there isn't!"

He shrugs his shoulders. "I have a… friend. We've had dinner together a few times, but nothing more than that."

With all the dignity Georgie can muster, she rises from her chair. "Well, I guess that's it then." She turns on her heel and marches up the stairs to her bedroom. Feeling faint, she lies down on the bed, and she hears the front door close. A glance at the closet reveals Dwayne has cleared out most of his clothes. *He planned this before even telling me!*

With a trembling hand, she wipes away tears and searches her feelings. She has failed at the most important relationship of her life and faces an uncertain future, but mostly she feels betrayed. Dwayne claimed to support her career but repeatedly criticized her for spending time on it. Twenty-five years together! Now it seems to be over because of her career. Her rational brain engages, forcing her to admit there were other issues. Dwayne had the infuriating habit of making all his decisions based on money. They often disagreed on their approach to parenting, and he left her with all the tough decisions about the kids. He would not go to church, nor did he have an interest in spiritual growth. *Has our marriage been crumbling for years without me noticing it?*

She winces at the pain needling across her forehead, closes her eyes and starts her favorite meditation for calm. But worries about her future interrupt her mantra, so she turns to prayer: *Dear God, the temptation to quit this marriage is strong. I don't see how to work things out with Dwayne. But Lord, you have laid it on my heart not to quit, but to keep fighting for this marriage. Please bring healing to our hearts that we may survive this trial and come out of it together. Amen.*

Prayer usually helps, but the words seem hollow and the sentiments merely dreaming. Dwayne's actions suggest he has already given up on their relationship and, given her own doubts, she cannot see how she will fight for her marriage.

Chapter 22

The house is almost empty, just Georgie and the dog now. As she prepares for her walk, bundled up against the December wind, she pats the dog's head. "Poor old boy." Shadow is getting on in years and lags when he used to pull ahead on the leash. This time he peers outside, sniffs the air, then slumps down on the doormat. "Too cold for you?" She shrugs and steps out the door by herself, the chilly air stinging her cheeks, turning onto her favorite walking trail crisp with a skiff of snow. While walking, she makes mental notes about today's appointments and tomorrow's meditation group at New Hope. The church asked her to organize a meditation series during Advent and Destiny agreed to lead it again, with Georgie continuing to cover the fees. It's her way of giving back to her church community, and she also benefits from being in a group meditation, now more than ever. It also gets her out of the house, once a haven but now just a reminder of her shaky marriage.

Crunching through virgin snow feels like a metaphor for her unexpected transition to life as a separated woman. Relationships with her family could change too, judging by their mixed reactions to her news. D.J.'s primary concern seemed to be about where to stay when he comes home from school. The house is his home, but he gravitates more to his father. Georgie broke the news to Daphne during a video chat. Her middle child was shocked but preferred to put a hopeful spin on it, saying, "Mom, you two can work it out!" Debbie may have taken it the hardest, and calls every few days, sympathetic, but unsure what to say. Claire frowned at the news and shook her head, but said little. Perhaps she isn't surprised, or it's just that she has her hands full caring for George, who relapsed and is now permanently wheelchair bound. Melanie heard the news from their mother and called to commiserate. She's never been in a committed relationship and had little wisdom to offer on how to manage this drastic life change. Linnie hasn't called, but that was no surprise.

Christmas at the Downie residence is likely to be strained. Dwayne announced he would come home for Christmas "for the kids," but Georgie expects his presence will just make things awkward. It doesn't feel honest to pretend things are okay when they are not. Forcing an artificial joy into the proceedings will cause additional strain, reminding her again why many people feel stressed at Christmas.

Preparing for her upcoming workshop series at the Caroll Clinic has been therapeutic—better than fretting about her personal life. Many of the fifteen people registered are her former patients, some of whom had resisted mind-body counseling. It was a little curious, but it confirmed her sense that a group program is more appealing than one-on-one counseling.

"They seem quite willing to fork over the five hundred dollars," Pam said, when they spoke last. "No one batted an eye! Maybe you're not charging enough!"

Georgie voiced her concern that some people who need the workshop may not afford it and asked Pam to let her know if anyone balked at the fee. With a group of fifteen, Georgie could afford to offer a few people a discount.

Pam had a different take on it. "The fee works out to about sixty dollars per session—far less than they would pay for a one-to-one consultation. Most people can easily spend sixty dollars for one evening out, but you will make a tremendous difference in their lives. You are offering a great value."

Georgie agreed to stick with the five-hundred-dollar fee, though doubts remain about the claims of benefit she must make to participants.

As she returns from her walk, a smile spreads across her face. *What would I do without Pam?* Her unwavering faith and encouragement provided a much-needed confidence boost. Lisa, her other source of moral support, also gave a stamp of approval on the value of the workshops. Since the separation, Lisa has also been extra attentive, calling almost every day and planning outings to the movies, lunches, and for walks. Georgie congratulates herself on mastering her second workshop principle, "surround yourself with supportive people."

Thankful for the clear sky and dry roads, Georgie drives home late Saturday afternoon after the first session of the Emotional Effectiveness workshop series at Caroll Clinic. The workshop participants are all clinic patients with significant health issues. Some are her former patients, which means they could skip the getting-to-know-you phase. Her first impression is that these participants are more motivated to embrace the workshop principles than the church group. Is it because they have more health concerns? Or because she's had a supportive relationship with some of them? She hopes their motivation will translate into the intended benefits of the workshops.

The first workshop series at her church last September was a test of the program. For this series, with its accompanying fee, Georgie is making claims that participants will become emotionally balanced and better able to manage physical health concerns. She says a calming mantra to push away her fear of failure. With an apparently failed marriage, her confidence has recently taken a hit. Running this workshop series is also the biggest risk she has taken since she became a naturopath.

From the first session today, Georgie learned something valuable about the number of people she can handle. Fifteen participants required more moderating than nine—the number in her first series. It was challenging to finish the program on time without cutting off discussion prematurely. Perhaps in a future series, she would cap the number at ten people. For this series, she will ask participants to extend the sessions by a half-hour, hoping this won't make her appear disorganized.

The fifth session of the workshop series ends, and while packing up her materials, Georgie muses about some challenges during the session. Some participants questioned how they could just decide to be happy. One woman argued, "there is no way anyone could be happy if they were in *my* shoes." It was a tense moment, but Georgie believes she convinced the woman to keep an open mind and focus on doing the homework—daily affirmations, journal things to be grateful for, and take time for a fun activity every day. Reflecting on her own advice, she makes a private admission that lately, she has struggled with deciding to be happy. *I need to do the homework too!*

On four of the five Saturdays, the weather cooperated, but last week it started snowing in the afternoon, and she stayed overnight Saturday at Pam's. She smiles, remembering how much fun they had, eating popcorn, and watching a silly chick flick. The downside was having to call on Dwayne to take care of Shadow. Their conversation was stilted, the irritation in his voice clear as he grudgingly agreed to stay at the house overnight. That interaction was a reminder of how difficult deciding to be happy can be.

Georgie leaves by the back entrance to the clinic, locks the door, turns, and stops in her tracks. Leaning against a car in the parking lot is David Longhurst. He gives her a broad smile and a wave. She has no choice but to approach him because he parked his car next to hers.

"David! What a surprise! How did you know I'd be here?" She dumps her bag in the trunk.

"Oh, I have my ways."

Hands on her hips, Georgie looks at him sideways. "Really? One thing I liked about you is that you are upfront. Where did that guy go?"

"That guy?" His face is in a mock pout. "He found this wonderful woman, but she won't give him the time of day."

Georgie cocks her head and points to herself as if to say, "who me?"

He nods, still pouting.

Georgie laughs. "So, how did you know I was here? Or is it a secret?"

"Okay, okay. I found out from a client of mine. He told me his wife is going to a workshop every Saturday with Dr. Downie. Imagine my surprise that you are back in town. Anyway, I'm here because I owe you a meal. When we met at your conference, I promised to treat you to lunch, but we never connected."

Georgie shoves her hands in her pockets and leans on her car, facing him. *Why am I fighting this? My marriage could be over.* "You know what? Why not? I'm as hungry as a horse."

He throws his head back, laughing. "Can I drive you to the restaurant? It's hard to find, and there isn't much parking nearby."

"Hm. Okay." *I'm not sure this is a good idea!* She checks the time on her cell phone. "I need to get home by seven o'clock to let my dog out."

"Can't your husband do that?"

Unprepared for the question, Georgie hesitates. *Do I want him to know I am separated?* "Ah, Dwayne's not at home today." Technically, it's not a lie.

After a twenty-minute drive, they arrive at a small diner. Joe's Place says the sign. As they enter, Georgie almost laughs at the interior, the epitome of the descriptor, "hole in the wall." The fifties style diner has a black and white tiled floor, red leatherette-covered booths on one side, a bar with stools on the other, and in the back corner, an old jukebox playing an oldie. Three patrons sit on barstools, and a family occupies one booth. There is a distinct aroma of deep-fried food and a faint odor of cigarettes from when restaurants allowed smoking. Georgie arches her eyebrows and her jaw drops.

"I know, the place looks like a dive," David says, "but the food is excellent."

At least he's not trying to impress me!

Georgie has a green salad and a chicken wrap with the diner's special sauce—ready in only ten minutes. "Excellent, as promised!" she says.

While eating, they chat about their work—he regales her with recent antics in court, and she explains how she came up with her workshop series. He seems interested in her creation, asking insightful questions, and listening to what she has to say. She enjoys herself, but part of her is also sizing him up. *Is he a player, or is he seriously interested?* In just over an hour, he drives her back to her car.

"Dinner next Saturday?" He asks, as if this is already a regular thing.

Georgie marvels at his confidence. Or it is cockiness? She can't tell. "I'll think about it, David. Usually, I drive here with my meditation leader. So, dinner is not possible most weeks unless you're okay with her joining us."

David's face falls, but he pledges to text her next Saturday, "just in case." As she sits in her car, waving goodbye, she shakes her head, amazed how difficult it is to resist this man's charms. All the way home, she contemplates her conflicted feelings about David. *He could be a player—only interested when someone is hard to get. But still! He's easy to talk to, and he makes me laugh.*

Georgie pauses outside Dr. Rice's door and takes two deep breaths to steel herself for the conversation she must have with her clinic director. *Can I really do this?* She sits on the edge of the chair opposite his desk. He leans back in his chair with his arms folded.

"Dr. Rice, I ran my workshop series for a fee to patients at the Caroll Clinic and the response was better than the free series at the church." She holds up the participant evaluations. "I believe the people in this workshop benefited more because they were more in need of help." She gathers her resolve. "I regret having to say this, but here is my position. I need to hold these workshops at this clinic, or I will find another clinic where I can practice my specialty."

Dr. Rice breathes in sharply and leans forward. "Ah… no need to make an ultimatum. I was ninety percent sure you could offer the workshop here after you ran one series for a fee. I just wanted you to be sure it would be beneficial to patients. This was to protect your reputation as well as the clinic's. You must understand that."

"I understand being careful, but here's the thing. Because you blocked me from holding my workshop here, it will not be exclusive to this clinic. Caroll Clinic has already asked me to hold another workshop series starting in April. There are already registrations. Participants in the first series spread the word, unsolicited, I might add."

Dr. Rice rolls his eyes and heaves a sigh. "Okay, you can use our meeting room for the workshop series. Just clear the time with Brenda."

Georgie wants to celebrate, but she also is sad for Dr. Rice because he allows fear to govern his decisions. Was he affected by the rash of mysterious deaths of holistic doctors? Or did something happen in Chicago?

Rising to leave, Georgie glances at the walls and recalls something she wanted since first walking into the office. "I would like to repaint the office, perhaps a soft green. These gray walls are not conducive to my workshop objectives or my patients." Dr. Rice waves his hand in resignation and they haggle for a few minutes, agreeing to split the cost fifty-fifty. *Did he agree to re-paint because I threatened to leave the clinic?* It's not the way she wants to work with her clinic director.

April has been a hectic month. Georgie is halfway through two workshop series running concurrently at two locations—Tuesday evenings at Rice's clinic and Saturday afternoons at the Caroll Clinic. "Back by popular demand" is how Pam worded the promotion she put out to the broader community. Georgie learned her lesson about numbers and capped the Caroll Clinic group at ten people, with four on a waiting list for a future series. The Rice Clinic group has nine participants. At first, she doubted her ability to manage two series, but starting them in the same week helped. By focusing on one session each week, she has immersed herself in the workshop materials and managed the workload.

From the series in September and January, she learned to answer tough questions and direct discussion so sessions could end on time. For the Indy group, she had to find another meditation leader. Destiny couldn't commit to a Saturday anymore because of family responsibilities. Fortunately, Sally, the meditation leader Georgie met at Community Church, was available.

Keeping busy had one benefit. She hasn't had time to dwell on her separation, which shows no signs of resolution. She and Dwayne have barely spoken since their Christmas at the house. Meanwhile, the three dinners with David in April and May were a pleasant distraction from her personal turmoil. However, she declined his invitation to a musical theater production because it felt more like a date than sharing a meal together. She is still not sure about his intentions, but he impressed her with one thing he did—recommend she apply for a copyright for the Emotional Effectiveness program. His rationale was convincing: "When the program is a success, someone could come along and steal the idea. You would have no legal recourse to stop them." At first, she wondered if he said this to flatter her, but after researching copyrights, she had to admit his advice made sense. And his suggestion showed an interest in her career, a stark contrast to Dwayne.

Georgie is in her office revising her notes for the seventh session at Caroll Clinic. Two participants in Tuesday's session at Rice Clinic were concerned that strict adherence to a focus on love, not fear, could leave them open to abuse. She wants to be prepared should similar challenges arise at the Caroll Clinic group on Saturday. The phone rings, interrupting her train of thought, and she hesitates before taking the call.

"This is Dr. Pomeroy," says a deep male voice. "I'd like some information about your Emotional Effectiveness program."

"Of course. But do I know you, Dr. Pomeroy?"

"Well, no, you don't. I know your father, though. I took on a few of his patients after he had his stroke, and I've always been a big fan of your father. But I will get to the reason for my call. One of my patients took part in your program last fall at a local church. She told me it opened her eyes to why she's always sick. I have to say her lack of progress had frustrated me, too. We could never find the right combination of anti-depressants for her, but since going to your program, she is doing much better."

"That is so good to hear. I'm pleased for your patient. Um. I gather you're a medical doctor, but you know I'm a naturopath, right?"

"Yes, yes. I know."

Georgie almost drops the phone, sputters for a moment, then gives him an outline and rationale for the workshops, adding, "the principles I teach are for emotional healing. I offer no remedies for physical health problems. I'm not looking for new patients for my one-to-one consulting practice because I'm busy enough."

"Those would have been my primary concerns. Based on what I've heard, I would like to refer two patients to your next workshop series."

Her next series will not be until September, but he seems fine with that. The call ends, and she stares at the phone, in wonder at this unexpected turn of events—a referral from a medical doctor. Something else is wondrous. Her practice *is* busy enough that she doesn't need more patients—a reality that snuck up on her. It's been a while since she needed promotional talks or worried about filling her schedule. Dwayne had been right about one thing: it takes five years for a business to become successful. In June, she will be in practice for five years.

Georgie is keen to hear Lisa's reaction to the call from the doctor and goes over to her house in the evening. Sipping their herbal teas in the kitchen, Georgie shares her news.

Lisa exclaims, "Wow! A medical doctor making referrals to a naturopath! I didn't think I'd live to see the day."

"The irony is that my father's reputation may have helped on this one. Wait until I tell him that!"

"Georgie, I don't want to bring you down, but there's something you should know. I saw Dwayne at the Grand again, with the same woman. This time, they held hands across the table. It was definitely not a business meeting."

Georgie's throat closes momentarily, but she looks at her friend with a faint smile and finds her voice. "I'm upset but, truthfully, also relieved. Dwayne is making his choice and knowing this will help me move on with my life, too. It's been six months since we separated, and it might sound terrible, but I don't miss him all that much. He may have been right that we grew apart. I used to think that a lame excuse for a marriage to fail, but now I know how it can happen."

"And what about your lawyer friend?" Lisa bats her eyes with a suggestive smile. "What's going on there?"

Georgie smirks. "Oh, he's interesting and fun to be with, but I have no plans to carry on with him, if that's what you're wondering." She wags her finger at her friend. "I'm enjoying being on my own without men making my life complicated. The past few years with Dwayne have been much too complicated."

By coincidence, after Georgie returns home, Dwayne calls, saying he wants to come over Sunday to talk but won't say what it is about. Georgie suspects this about getting a divorce. Neither of them has attempted to reconcile, and there is Lisa's report about the other woman. Georgie tries not to stew about it, waiting for Sunday to arrive.

Dwayne arrives Sunday afternoon at three-thirty, clad in his golf attire and an hour later than he promised. *Heaven forbid he should cut his golf game short!* Georgie stifles the urge to say something about his timing, infringing on her Sunday afternoon visit with her parents. They sit facing each other at either end of the dining room table.

"Georgina, I want a legal separation." His voice is flat, his face stony. "I suggest you get a lawyer."

Georgie stares wide-eyed at her husband, all but a stranger, who skipped any pleasantries, not even a "how are you?" His abrupt request and demeanor suggest he has no affection left for her. But since her conversation with Lisa, she accepts that her feelings for Dwayne have also faded. *But why isn't he asking for a divorce?*

"Dwayne. Can you tell me why you want a legal separation?"

"We need to sell the house and split the profit. With the kids gone, you don't need the space, and I have no desire to live here. From what we would get from the sale, you could get an apartment or a condo."

Georgie stifles a snort. "Ah. So, you're thinking of me now? Somehow I doubt that."

Dwayne scowls and rolls his eyes.

Georgie wonders if the other woman has a part in his plan, but she lacks the emotional energy to get into it. Still, she suspects there is something more to his motivation. "Is there some benefit to a legal separation besides padding lawyers' pockets? Can't we just agree to sell the house and split the profit fifty-fifty?"

"This is not just about the house. Without a legal separation, we are liable for each other's debts or business losses. My company is solid, but you've been the subject of an inquest, and you're running these experimental workshops. Someone could sue you. I don't want to be liable for your risky ventures."

Georgie shakes her head. "Well, that makes sense now. It's always about money with you."

He glares at her and crosses his arms.

"I'm too busy right now to process this, and I'm not keen on the expense of a lawyer," she says.

"Well, I don't want this to drag on." He rises from his chair and leaves abruptly, as if he did not expect her to agree readily.

Georgie sits at the table, trying to make sense of Dwayne's motivations. Is this about money or his mysterious friend? To find out, she would have to hire a lawyer.

Shaken, she still makes her regular Sunday visit to her parents. Usually, she steers the conversation away from her profession because it upsets her father—his health is fragile. Today is different. First, she brings him up to date about her workshop and the four series she already led before getting to her big news. "You won't believe this, Dad. I had a call from a medical doctor who wants to refer patients to the workshops. You know him—Dr. Pomeroy."

George Novak's eyes widen, and he leans forward in his wheelchair. "Georgie, I'm having trouble understanding how this happened. Dr. Pomeroy is an experienced physician, and I wouldn't say he's pro-naturopath. He knows your profession, right?"

"Of course!"

Her father leans back in his chair. "Tell me more about your workshops."

Georgie outlines the eight principles for emotional balancing and how she organized the workshops.

George Novak looks over his glasses, his eyes squinted. "I can't pretend to know about addressing emotional issues or how this creation of yours helps people. If you are getting results, then good for you, but…"

Georgie rolls her eyes. There is always a "but!"

"Georgina, I know how protective doctors are about our patients. If any of these workshop referrals become one of your naturopathic patients, I predict some backlash coming your way."

Georgie nods her head, considering a response that won't lead to an argument. "Dad, I'm sure you're right. I shouldn't accept Dr. Pomeroy's workshop referrals as my naturopathic patients. In fact, it might be a sound policy for any participant referred by another health professional. Mine is a stand-alone program as a complement to any doctor's therapy. I'm sure I can set guidelines so practitioners will be comfortable making referrals."

Her father looks at her sideways. "That might save you. But don't get your hopes up."

Disappointed but not surprised at her father's guarded reaction, Georgie rises to leave. "Well, Dad, I think building bridges between professions is worthwhile. I remain hopeful for more collaboration."

She is loath to admit it, but her father made a good point. One doctor making referrals to her program will not change the current animosity between doctors and naturopaths. The schism between the professions won't be easy to bridge. It will take a broad-based strategy to reduce the current level of mistrust and misunderstanding. She has no idea what that strategy might be.

Chapter 23

Georgie bids goodbye to the last participant, sees her out the door of the Caroll Clinic, and trudges back upstairs to the conference room to take a mental break before returning to Terrance. With the eighth session finished here and at the Rice Clinic on Tuesday, Georgie can now take stock of how the workshops went. Leading two sessions in the same time frame was a lot to manage, but not for the reason she expected. The challenge wasn't in delivering the workshops; it was connecting with twice the number of participants. Each group had a unique atmosphere because of the personalities involved. In the Caroll Clinic group, the challenges started in the first session. One participant, not a patient of the Clinic, seemed intent on denying the principle's validity. "Doesn't my doctor have responsibility for my health?" she asked. Later, she posed another troublesome question. "What if, through no fault of your own, I am exposed to a deadly virus? How is that my responsibility?" Georgie hoped she redirected that question by stressing the importance of being active participants in our health care, through activities we can control, like diet and lifestyle. She wasn't sure it had made an impression. That same participant questioned concepts in other sessions, which were an annoyance, but also kept Georgie on her toes.

In the session on learning from mistakes, there was tension among the Rice Clinic participants about how to admit to one's mistakes without incurring guilt—an emotion that can harm health. They agreed there was a fine line to walk—accepting responsibility for one's mistakes without being overly self-critical. One participant made the astute point that learning from mistakes involved forgiving oneself, showing how the workshop principles are inter-related.

The principles in the final three sessions were challenging for some participants to accept. One participant in the Caroll Clinic group had ancestors who had died in the holocaust. She was indignant at the imperative to offer forgiveness in all situations, demanding to know how she could be expected to forgive the Nazis. Georgie had a question like this in one of her previous series and was ready with a perspective on forgiveness, using the prayer by an unknown prisoner in the Ravensbruck concentration camp:

O Lord, remember not only the men and women of goodwill but also those of ill will. But do not remember the suffering they have inflicted on us; remember the fruits we brought forth thanks to this suffering: our comradeship, our loyalty, our humility, our courage, the generosity, the greatness of heart which has grown out of this. And when they come to judgment, let all the fruits that we have borne be their forgiveness.

"Focus on love, not fear" triggered discussion and questions about the value of healthy fears. In both groups, there was vigorous debate about which fears were healthy and which ones were irrational. Everyone agreed with the participant who said, "as women, we should have a healthy fear of walking alone at night in a big city." Georgie emphasized the point of the principle is that love should be the predominant emotion, a primary focus, not that we should fear nothing.

In the last session, "realize you are not alone," both groups had vibrant discussions primarily because some participants were atheists. Georgie used alternative terms for God—universal consciousness and spiritual energy—but the atheist participants even questioned these concepts. The discussion lapsed into a metaphysical area—the nature of the universe and human's place in it—that threatened to distract from the intended benefit of the session. To redirect the conversation, Georgie assured them it was not her goal to evangelize, rather to raise awareness that healing is possible through the emotional energies of love, joy, and peace that are easier to achieve when one has faith in a higher power than ourselves.

Georgie lingers in the conference room to read the workshop evaluations. After reading the last one, she breathes a sigh of relief. Most participants report benefits. One evaluation says, "somewhat helpful," perhaps the woman who questioned everything. The saying "you can't please everyone" pops into Georgie's mind. Two participants comment that meditation did little for them, confirming the need to explore other mind-body therapies to appeal to different preferences. On her drive home, she stews over how to make such a change. Where to start?

The next day, Georgie wakes up with her worst headache in years and cannot get out of bed. It's Sunday, but she can't face going to church. She lies in bed all day, trying to meditate and pray her way out of the pain, but by evening, there is still a persistent throbbing behind her eyes. *I thought I was past these headaches. What is going on?* She has a bowl of leftover soup, lets the dog out, and goes back to bed.

On Monday morning, her headache is severe enough to warrant canceling her patient appointments for the day. By noon she surfaces and spends the afternoon trying to piece together what could have triggered this episode. She already determined her headaches are stress related and searches for potential stressors in her recent activities—running two workshop series concurrently and maintaining a full schedule of patient appointments, some of which had complications. A patient with rheumatoid arthritis had a health crisis requiring extra hours of problem-solving. Another patient with Lyme disease was not progressing as well as Georgie expected. And perhaps she is more bothered about her marriage breakdown that she cares to admit.

Something comes to mind from one of her courses in spiritual counseling—practitioner self-care. *Do I need more self-care?* She allows herself twenty minutes of meditation and a walk in the woods every day, but perhaps that is not enough. *When was the last time I had a break from work?* Beyond an occasional weekend away, it was before naturopathic college. *Have I become a workaholic?* She makes a cup of chamomile tea, plants herself on a stool at the kitchen island, and considers this question, but stops when she realizes this is focusing on the problem. Better to pose a solution-focused question. *How can I organize more self-care?*

Through the evening, an idea forms in her mind, but it's something that will require help to flesh out. She texts her favorite collaborators, Pam and Lisa, and invites them over on Saturday with the promise of an exciting adventure. The act of taking this step helps. Within an hour of calling her friends, her headache eases.

At ten o'clock Saturday morning, Lisa and Pam are both sitting on Georgie's backyard deck, enjoying the warmth of the late May sun. They sip their coffee and eye Georgie with curiosity.

"Okay, Georgie! Spill! What's this 'adventure' all about?" Lisa gestures air quotes. "Why all the mystery?"

"Yeah! You are borrowing on my good faith, asking me to drive here without telling me what this is about," Pam says in a playful reproach.

Georgie grins at her two friends. "Trust me. This is exciting!" As she explains her idea, their faces light up, and they both become animated, asking questions, and making suggestions, "what about this?" and "I think this would work well." After six hours of brainstorming, planning, and a pizza delivery, they agree the event will be a great success if the organizing is any measure.

Driving down the quiet country road, the morning sun filters through the trees, casting long shadows like paths into the unknown. *What will this weekend bring?* Georgie turns in at the rustic sign inscribed, "Healing Acres." It is four weeks since she met with Lisa and Pam to put this weekend together—a self-care retreat for health practitioners. Georgie suspected she was not alone, that other practitioners give of themselves and don't do enough to restore themselves physically and spiritually.

Both Lisa and Pam threw themselves into organizing the weekend retreat. Lisa insisted on taking the lead to organize the location and the menu, saying, "Georgie, you need this retreat more than me, and I want to do this for you." Pam took the lead in organizing the retreat activities, with planning coming together almost organically. Pam's idea was brilliant: each practitioner would offer one self-care activity or therapy to share with the others. As each practitioner would also be a participant, no one would receive a fee, making the weekend more affordable.

They agreed to a group of eight women and they each invited at least one other practitioner. Georgie invited her meditation leader, Destiny, who then asked her yoga teacher, Aanya. Lisa invited Rhonda, a naturopath and long-time customer. Pam invited Paula, the naturopath who traded clinics with Georgie. To round out the group, Georgie asked Sandra, an acquaintance from Toastmasters and a clinical psychologist.

As she drives into the parking area, Georgie's eyes drink in the peaceful setting of the century-old home nestled in a forest clearing. Gretchen, the retired nurse who turned her ancestral home into a small retreat center, is standing outside, waiting to greet everyone. Healing Acres Retreat came on a recommendation from Destiny, who was there for an event in the past and raved about the accommodation, the setting, and Gretchen's cooking.

All the women arrive on time for the scheduled nine o'clock start. Lisa has a smoothie ready for everyone, knowing some women drove a distance and will need sustenance to take them to lunchtime. They all settle into various couches and cushions in the spacious glassed-in porch with a view of the woods behind the house.

"Welcome to this self-care retreat," Georgie says. "Over the next day and a half, I hope we all can benefit from the self-care activities we will share with each other." She puts her hand over her heart and looks around at the seven women. "What you take from this weekend is in your hands and your hearts."

Each woman introduces herself and shares her reasons for coming to the retreat. It does not surprise Georgie to hear a few admitting they are here because of overwork and exhaustion. Still, she senses their upbeat energy.

Pam passes out a retreat itinerary to each woman saying, "these activities are voluntary. If you prefer taking private time to rest or reflect, please do that." She picks up a stack of hardcover books and hands one to each woman. "This is a gratitude journal for you to record reflections during the weekend or in the future." The women grasp their journals and leaf through the pages, admiring the colorful graphics and inspirational sayings.

Lisa stands up to complete the orientation. "Gretchen will direct you to your rooms—four of us are in bedrooms in the house, and four are in cabins." She gestures to a row of cabins at the edge of the woods. "Take some time to settle in. Our first activity will be at ten o'clock, a group meditation with Destiny."

Destiny gestures outside. "It's going to be a great day to be outdoors, seventy-four degrees, they say. We'll meet on the lawn between the house and the cabins. I have mats so the grass doesn't stain your clothes."

Georgie settles into her cabin, grateful it affords her a view of the woods. While waiting for the first activity, she sits by the window drinking in the scenery, feeling herself relax.

At ten o'clock, everyone gathers on the lawn and sits in a circle on their mats. Rhonda and Sandra look apprehensive. "I'm new to meditation," says Sandra, "but I'll try it." Rhonda nods. "It's new to me too."

Destiny's meditation about igniting healing energies seems apt for the weekend. During the thirty-minute session, Georgie senses her experience is heightened by the fragrant pines and birdsong echoing from the woods. It occurs to her she should meditate outdoors more in the future. As the session ends, Georgie opens her eyes and notices the reluctant participants, Rhonda and Sandra, are both grinning.

A scavenger hunt in the woods takes them to lunchtime. Georgie organized it, thinking a simple walk in the woods would not provide enough direction. "Find three things that inspire or intrigue you and save them for another activity on Sunday," she says to the women. "Gretchen tells me there are two different paths you can follow and they both loop back here. If you stay on the paths, you won't get lost." As Georgie wanders along a path by herself, she hears laughter nearby. Some women obviously walked in a group. *Not everyone enjoys a solo walk in the woods like I do.*

Lunch is a delicious quinoa and bean salad on a plate of greens with a raspberry vinaigrette. Freshly picked berries round out the meal. Over lunch, Rhonda offers the group an activity—to eat mindfully. On the table, she spreads out two decks of affirmation cards adorned with colorful artwork and inscribed with unique statements about various issues—health, success, creativity, self-esteem, or release of fears.

"Go through the cards and pick one or two affirmations that speak to your life right now," Rhonda says. "Instead of talking through lunch, I encourage you to focus on eating this fine meal and reflecting on your affirmations."

"Can't we talk?" Paula asks. "When can we get to know each other?" Her comment confirms Georgie's impression of Paula as an extrovert.

Rhonda looks at Georgie and then responds to Paula, "Just give it a chance."

Georgie is reminded of how challenging it is to meet everyone's preferences for self-care. "There will be opportunities for conversation and sharing at dinner and this evening," she says to Paula.

Paula shrugs her shoulders and joins in with the others, who sort through the cards to make their selections. Georgie chooses a card with the affirmation: *"Divine wisdom is mine. This day I receive guidance to serve my higher self and lead me to my life's purpose."* Her reflection centers on the importance of daily meditation and prayer to keep her focused on her purpose of helping others heal.

After lunch, there is an hour of free time for rest, reflection, or journaling. Georgie settles under a tree in the woods, revelling in the scent of moss and earth, and the rustling of wind in the leaves. She opens her journal, a sturdy hardcover book with illustrations and daily writing prompts. *Pam has gone to some expense!* She jots down thoughts about her affirmation card, musing about how she can be more attentive to divine guidance.

At three o'clock, there are two options—yoga with Aanya or energy balancing with Paula. Georgie is curious about the energy balancing and joins Paula, along with Lisa and Pam. The others opt for yoga. Before becoming a naturopath, Paula trained in energy medicine—testing energy patterns and engaging bodily energies to promote well-being. She spends twenty minutes with each person, assessing their energy patterns and teaching movements to rebalance or release blocked energies. Georgie learns a movement called "connecting spirit and mind" meant to open oneself to new possibilities. Paula offers different energy balancing tips for Lisa and Pam.

After the sessions ends, Aanya offers another round of yoga for those who had opted for energy balancing. Paula, Lisa, and Pam take advantage of the opportunity while the others retreat to their rooms or take another walk in the woods. Georgie is content to sit outside her cabin near the forest, reflecting and writing in her journal. She pens a response to the writing prompt, "Name five things you do well." Some things she lists are surprising, like public speaking, a talent she would not have claimed a few years ago. As she gazes up at a large oak tree waving in the breeze, she is reminded of the expression, "you can't see the forest for the trees." Being busy has kept her focused on everyday concerns. *Am I missing the big picture?*

For dinner, Gretchen offers the choice of a vegan or animal protein meal. Georgie opts for the salmon steak in lemon sauce with basmati rice and asparagus spears. The vegan meal is a tofu vegetable stir-fry. Simple, yet delicious, is the verdict among the group.

Rhonda introduces a dinner activity intended to support optimal digestion. "You can talk with each other all you want," she smiles and nods at Paula. "But I want you to stop every few minutes and take two cleansing breaths. Deep breathing is highly beneficial to digestion." Everyone joins in the exercise, but every time Paula breathes deeply, she giggles. Others join in, and soon everyone is laughing, and Sandra finally asks, "why are we laughing?" Everyone looks at each other and shrugs, bringing on more snickers. Through her own laughter, Rhonda says, "I never know how this exercise will go. This was the best fun yet! And laughing makes you deep breathe, too!" It occurs to Georgie that she spends most of her time trying to be a responsible adult. How freeing it is to act like a giddy schoolgirl.

The meal is topped off with a dessert of rhubarb crumble to critical acclaim and requests for the recipe, to which Gretchen shakes her head, saying: "It's a trade secret."

For the evening activity, the women gather in the enclosed porch for a time of conversation and sharing. Sandra leads the group in a get-to-know-you activity using three questions: What is the most courageous thing you have ever done? What is your favorite animal and why? And, where is a happy place for you? As everyone takes turns responding to the first question, they discover several in the group are risk-takers involved in pastimes like skydiving and rock climbing. Rhonda talks about the courage it takes to become a health practitioner, making them all risk takers. Everyone nods their head. To the second question, most women admit to being dog lovers because of their loyalty. Rhonda says she is a horse person, while Lisa has always preferred cats for their independence. Much laughter ensues after Paula shares some jokes about the differences between dog people and cat people. They finish the evening talking about their happy places, mostly nature-related—the mountains, lakes, the ocean, and the woods. Just talking about everyone's happy places makes Georgie feel like she has been there. Sandra closes the session reading a passage from a book about living with intention.

Georgie's impression is that the women are enjoying themselves, but she longs to hear what Lisa and Pam think. After the evening session, she takes them aside. "How do you think it's going?"

"Great!" they say in unison. Lisa wags her finger at Georgie. "Don't you worry about how others are faring. They're all adults who can take responsibility for what they get out of this. The question is: Are you enjoying yourself?"

Georgie laughs at her long-time friend and nods her head. "Definitely!"

In the morning, Georgie wakes up refreshed, more than she has felt in a long time. Is it the clean country air? Or the laughter of the previous evening? Or the chance to reflect? Though the sky is gray, she is optimistic about the rest of the retreat. Before going to breakfast, she practices the "connecting spirit and mind" movement, finding it energizing and a good morning stretch, too. The smell of freshly brewed coffee wafts through the air, beckoning her to the dining room.

During a breakfast of homemade yogurt, granola, and fresh fruit, they decide to move the morning meditation inside because of the threat of rain. Gretchen quickly pushes furniture aside in the enclosed porch, where everyone joins Destiny's meditation to increase positive energy. As Georgie opens her eyes, she senses this meditation was the perfect set-up for the next activity, an optional time of devotions.

Georgie invites everyone to stay for a devotional time, and four women remain seated. Aanya stands up but asks, "Is it okay if I join? I'm not a Christian." Georgie smiles and motions Aanya to a place beside her. Rhonda and Sandra go for a walk in the rain, saying communing with nature is worship, too. Georgie uses a practice called praying with scripture that she learned in the prayer group at Community Church. They read Romans 12:6-9 three times and take turns sharing personal reflections, inducing an active discussion about the imperative to cultivate and use one's gifts for others' benefit.

At ten o'clock, they all gather on the porch for what Georgie hopes is the highlight of the weekend—the creation of dream boards. Gretchen pushes four tables together, so everyone is seated facing each other. Lisa takes the lead on this activity with help from Pam and Georgie. Prior to the weekend, they all scrounged materials—old magazines, bright paper, markers, scissors, and Bristol board—that they now spread across the tables. Rhonda offers some of her affirmation cards "to use as inspiration." At breakfast, Lisa reminded everyone to bring the items they collected during their woods walk yesterday.

"This activity is about depicting a dream or priority of yours creatively, through pictures, phrases, or keywords," Lisa says. "You can use any materials on the table, and your scavenged items, to make your dream board." Some women appear lost; perhaps this is a novel activity for them. Lisa extends her hands palms up. "There are no rules for completing a dream board, no right or wrong way to do it, but I have some direction for you." She hands out a paper to each woman. "These are three prompting questions for your dream board. I suggest you focus on answering one."

The women silently read the questions: What does your best life look like? How can you make the world a better place? What is your big adventure goal (something that scares you that no one knows about)?

Gradually, everyone warms up to the activity, cutting, pasting, and drawing on their creations. Georgie marvels at how the women become fully involved in activities they likely haven't done since childhood. The occasional question punctuates the reflective exercise: "Has anyone seen the red marker?" "Has anyone found a picture of a beach?" For her dream board, Georgie chooses the focus, "how to make the world a better place." She finds images of forests, hopeful faces, prayer hands, the words "understanding" and "caring," and adds an acorn from her scavenger hunt, as a symbol of new beginnings. From an affirmation card, she prints the phrase "walk where there is no path."

At lunchtime, Lisa must use her powers of persuasion to tear the women away from the activity by promising they can finish their boards after lunch.

Pam whispers to Georgie, "Clearly, this activity is a hit."

For lunch, Gretchen serves black bean burgers or chicken burgers in lettuce wraps, raw vegetables, guacamole dip, and hot scones with homemade jam. While eating, the women are talking and sharing stories like old friends. Lisa and Paula have hit it off and are laughing together about something. Georgie sits beside Rhonda, a naturopath from another clinic in Indy, and discovers they share concerns about the strain between their profession and medical doctors. Rhonda is also interested in mind-body medicine, something Georgie guessed from the Rhonda's use of affirmation cards.

After lunch, they gather at their dream boards for a final thirty minutes of creating when Lisa announces the last activity—sharing their dream boards. As they go around the table, it seems easier for the more outgoing women, Paula, Lisa, Sandra, and Destiny, to talk about the meaning and imagery on their dream boards. Rhonda, Aanya, and Pam show their dream boards, but give little commentary. Rhonda says only that the activity was fascinating and gave her a lot to think about. Georgie has the impression that Aanya is shy, and she already knows Pam is not fond of sharing a lot of personal information. After everyone shares, the women sit quietly and regard each other.

"I wish the weekend didn't have to end. I so enjoyed this," Destiny says.

Rhonda and Aanya nod in agreement.

Paula's face brightens. "Can we do it again?"

Georgie raises her eyebrows at Lisa and Pam, who grin and nod their heads.

"I'm certainly up for it, and it appears like my sister organizers are in favor," Georgie says. "For the next retreat, we may need ideas for different activities. Please send us your suggestions."

The retreat ends at three-thirty, and as the women prepare to leave, there are hugs all around.

"I'd love to keep in touch," Paula says. "Can I have everyone's email?"

Georgie volunteers to share emails with everyone in the group.

"I really enjoyed meeting all of you," Aanya says, her hands in a prayer pose. "Namaste."

Georgie loads her belongings in her car, then turns to Lisa and Pam. They linger, sharing their favorite moments and their sense of accomplishment. Georgie regards her friends fondly and gathers them in a group hug. "Thanks for making this happen!"

On the way home, she glances at her dream board in the back seat. That activity stimulated an unexpected idea, a big idea, on how she could make the world a better place. She did not share specifics with the group, just that her dream was about making her profession more effective. It could take some time for the idea to germinate.

Chapter 24

Georgie finishes her meditation, inspiration for positive energy, grateful to Destiny for emailing the guided meditation to everyone who attended the retreat. It's Saturday morning, a week after the retreat, and Georgie opens her email to read through the feedback from all the participants. Her goal for the retreat was for practitioners to experience different self-care activities for stress relief, and that benefit comes out in their comments. There are some interesting suggestions for activities at future retreats—massage, Reiki, Pilates, drawing, felting, a guided nature walk, an inspirational movie on Saturday evening, and playing a cooperative game.

Recalling her own retreat experience, Georgie recognizes what she gained from it. She is experimenting with energy balancing, starting each morning with the grounding exercise Paula taught her. Rhonda's mindful eating is another health-promoting activity she is implementing. She is also considering including some of these self-care activities in her workshop series as alternatives or additions to meditation, to appeal to the other senses. Just now it occurs to her she could ask Paula to do a session on energy balancing, and Aanya to introduce participants to yoga. The prospect of collaborating with the other practitioners is energizing. She had a sense from their dream boards they have unfulfilled dreams for their health care practices. *There must be ways we can support each other.*

Georgie's dream, her big idea, as she calls it, has been percolating in her mind since the retreat, but it was born out of traumatic events—the inquest and the mysterious deaths of holistic doctors. The coroner at the inquest recommended medical and naturopathic associations direct their members to collaborate more on patient care. David Longhurst warned her nothing would come of it, and so far, he was right, but she wasn't sure the coroner's idea was the best approach, anyway. It seldom works to force change on established institutions. The mysterious deaths of holistic doctors linger as a potential warning that straying from one standard for medical care could lead to censure or persecution.

In Georgie's view, there is an urgent need to build understanding between medical and naturopathic doctors. Years of mistrust and competition have produced no winners, only losers—patients who suffer from fragmented, ineffectual health care and holistic practitioners, like Dr. Rice, who fear trying anything new. The dream board activity helped her see past the potential negatives and focus on the possibilities for positive outcomes. Still, acting on the idea could be challenging because of entrenched societal attitudes about how doctors should work with patients. It's not just the medical community that needs a shift in perspective.

No one knows about her idea yet. Today, she plans to run it by Lisa and Pam at their retreat debriefing meeting. This time, they will meet at Pam's place in Indy, and on the drive there, she chats with Lisa about her idea.

"I think you can do anything you set your mind to," is Lisa's simple response.

Georgie hoped Lisa would give more specific feedback, but she realizes Pam is likely to have more insights because she is in the same profession.

Arriving at Pam's, the welcome aroma of espresso and fresh-made scones greet them. "No! I can't take credit. I know a great bakery," Pam says, holding up her hand.

After they de-brief the retreat and discuss ideas for the next event in the spring, Georgie shares her plan with Pam.

"Well! It's bold!" Pam says, wide-eyed. "I expect some medical doctors won't take part, and some may oppose it, even work against you. You're a braver person than me."

"Of course, that is possible," Georgie replies, "but I think it's better than tiptoeing around the medical system like we have been doing."

Dr. Rice grimaces and shifts in his chair as Georgie enters his office for a meeting she requested. She almost feels sorry for him. *Is he expecting another idea he won't like?*

"Dr. Rice, I plan to communicate with medical doctors about my involvement with their patients and propose that we share details of our treatment plans. I believe I can convince doctors such sharing will help avoid negative interactions between pharmaceuticals and natural remedies. Instead of focusing on our differences, this would put our focus where it should be—on our patients' well-being."

Dr. Rice stands up behind his desk, hands on his hips. "You're going to do what?"

"Dr. Rice. Phillip. We—medical doctors and naturopaths—need to work more in collaboration. It was the coroner's recommendation at the inquest. I'm just taking a pre-emptive step to get it started. Somebody needs to act, and I think I'm the right woman for the job."

The clinic director slumps back into his chair, takes off his glasses, and runs his hands down over his face. "I'm not sure what you hope to achieve. We already advise our patients to tell their doctors they are consulting with us. This precaution has worked well, and the naturopathic profession is surviving."

Georgie stares at him, her mouth agape. "But is surviving enough? Shouldn't we be focused on thriving? On having the freedom to practice? That will not happen while we have that quackery website making baseless accusations to smear our reputations. The worst threat might come from medical doctors who warn their patients against our care. It amounts to veiled hostility for which we have no defense because we can't see it coming."

"Well…" Dr. Rice rifles through papers on his desk as if something will give him a clever comeback. "I agree. The situation is not… ideal. But, Georgie, contacting medical doctors may heighten their hostility. It just takes one doctor to launch a campaign against you, and by extension, the whole profession comes under fire. I've seen it happen when I was in Chicago. What you are doing could undermine the trust we naturopaths have achieved. I urge you to reconsider."

Georgie will have to ask him about what happened in Chicago, but not today. She raises her voice in defiance. "And that trust is precarious because the medical establishment is just waiting for a slipup from us. I was in their crosshairs, and I don't want to go through that again." She can feel her temper rising. Dr. Rice looks similarly upset. She takes a deep breath and softens her tone. "Dr. Rice, I understand what you are saying. There may be risks to my idea, but I firmly believe it will be worse to do nothing. We must work toward integrating health care for the sake of our patients. I believe the first step towards integration is the creation of a communication channel between medical doctors and naturopaths."

"It's still pie-in-the-sky." Dr. Rice shakes his head. "You may have good intentions, but that doesn't mean it will improve our situation."

Georgie stands up, chin thrust forward with hands on her hips. "One of my patients in Indy died, and I attribute her death to the disconnect between medical and naturopathic doctors. Her medical doctor wasn't aware of my involvement or my remedies, and the patient somehow felt she had to choose between us. She was also self-medicating, which is the primary reason I did not get into legal trouble. But why was she self-medicating? Was it because of mistrust between medical doctors and our profession? Doctors need to work more cooperatively, and it needs to start somewhere. It's my practice, and this is what I plan to do."

Dr. Rice groans and throws up his hands in surrender. "Don't come crying to me when you lose all your patients."

Georgie begins the next day by asking her patients to sign a consent form so she can contact their medical doctor to request reciprocal sharing of their medications, therapies, and interventions. In her letter to medical doctors, she names the program Cooperative Care.

Dr. Rice arrives at Georgie's office door unannounced, concern on his face. "Brenda told me you've had several appointment cancelations. Has this anything to do with your cooperative care experiment?"

Georgie stares at him, annoyed he is checking up on her, like a boss. It has been three months since she started communicating with medical doctors. She cannot confirm the reasons for the cancelations but must concede it could be related to cooperative care. Only three medical doctors responded directly to her request to share their treatment plans. As for the rest, she can't tell if they oppose her plan or were too busy to respond. It is possible some doctors are advising their patients to discontinue naturopathic care, hence the appointment cancelations. Georgie considers all this, and it dawns on her there could be an upside to the situation.

"Yes, the cancellations could be related to Cooperative Care," she replies. "But there is another way to view this. I may have saved myself some aggravation. I've been practicing long enough to know my reputation suffers by trying to help people who bail when their doctors object to naturopathy. Those patients typically give up too soon on my therapies, and then blame me for their lack of progress. Who knows? Maybe they go back to their doctors crying about how I couldn't help them. On the upside, the patients who have continued in my care seem impressed by my cooperative approach. They are more receptive to what I recommend."

"Hm." Dr. Rice frowns and shakes his head. "Well, I hope you know what you are doing. I would hate to see you lose more patients."

Georgie is once again reminded of her poor fit with Phillip Rice. He resists any new idea and typically responds out of fear. A wry smile crosses her face. He would benefit from attending her workshop session, "focus on love, not fear."

As Dr. Rice departs, Brenda calls from the front desk. "Georgie, there's a Dr. Pomeroy on the phone for you. Can you take the call?"

It has been one week since her September-October workshop series ended, in which Dr. Pomeroy's two patients were participants. *Is he calling about them? Were they unhappy with the program?* Georgie was considering how to tell Dr. Pomeroy his patients may need to improve their diet. Based on the snacks she saw them eating, she guessed their diets were poor, which could impact their mental health. She spoke to each woman in private, stressing the importance of a wholefood diet, but was unsure they knew what that meant. She couldn't pursue it further. To mention diet again could affect their participation in the workshop, and she could not confirm their diets were unhealthy.

Georgie must write a report to Dr. Pomeroy but has yet to decide on the exact message. Because of the experience with his patients, she is planning a change for future workshops—a diet screening tool for participants before accepting them into the program. Those with a health-promoting diet would benefit most from the workshop series, and with people on waiting lists, she could afford to choose her workshop participants.

Georgie picks up the phone. *No point in putting this off.*

"Dr. Downie. I'm intrigued by this cooperative care idea of yours," he says. "I'd like to hear more about it."

Georgie breathes a sigh of relief—this is not about her workshop series. Recently, she had a new patient who was also a patient of his, and she sent him the letter about cooperative care. She gives him a five-minute explanation of her motivation and goals.

"I think you should make a presentation about this at the local medical association luncheon," he says. "The speaker for next week's meeting canceled and I'm in charge of finding a replacement."

"Excuse me! What did you say?"

"I think your idea is interesting, but the medical doctors need to hear directly from you, not in a letter, which they may never read. I read your letter because we already have a connection through your workshop."

"You make a good point, Dr. Pomeroy. But are you sure they will listen to me… a naturopath?"

"You never know until you try."

Georgie likes Dr. Pomeroy. For a medical doctor, he is forward-thinking, even a rebel. She weighs the risks of this offer. In a room full of doctors, some will surely challenge her and discourage others from participating in cooperative care. However, as Dr. Pomeroy suggests, this is a chance to give doctors a face to her idea. *It can't be worse than an inquest.*

Standing in the spacious dining room at the country club golf course, Georgie scans the sea of faces, all doctors and predominantly male. She grips the podium with both hands to keep them from shaking. Her mouth is dry. *Water! Drink some water.* During her talk, she notices several raised eyebrows and sideways glances, but then spots one smiling face: Dr. Pomeroy. She gets through her fifteen-minute presentation by focusing on him. As the emcee thanks her and calls for questions, she braces herself for negative responses.

"Why haven't I heard about this inquest and its recommendations?" A young doctor asks.

"That you should take up with your medical association, who would have received the coroner's report. I would encourage you to read it. The coroner recommended doctors and naturopaths communicate about their therapies and protocols. I am merely following through on those recommendations."

"What's in it for you?" asks another doctor, with his arms crossed, casually sitting back in his chair.

"Better care for patients; doing everything I can to prevent unfortunate interactions between medications and remedies, like the one my patient had."

A third doctor stands up. "There's not enough scientific evidence for the effectiveness of naturopathy." He looks around the room, holding out both arms. "Everyone here knows this, but you don't have the nerve to say it. Why should doctors cooperate with people practicing health care that is unproven and perhaps even harmful?"

Georgie is almost grateful she had to defend her profession with her father for years. It should help her respond to this challenge. "On one point, I agree with you. There are no scientific studies on naturopathy. I would welcome that kind of research, but no one wants to fund studies on the effectiveness of naturopathy. However, we in the naturopathic profession have lots of clinical evidence that we help our patients, should anyone care to ask." Georgie hesitates before raising a critical point. "Naturopathy comes from ancient traditions about the healing power of nature. Much of our focus is on diet and lifestyle change that are primary prevention for serious illness and helpful in easing suffering for those with a chronic illness. Naturopaths are not in competition with your medical practices. We complement your treatments."

Georgie scans the room and still sees scowls on several faces, which means she hasn't made a strong case yet. "A growing number of people are consulting with naturopaths, often in conjunction with medical treatments. Would this be trending upward if we weren't helping people? Whether you like it or not, inter-practitioner communication and cooperation are more important than ever if we all care about the same thing—the well-being of our patients."

The doctor who is standing opens his mouth and closes it again, perhaps realizing if he argues, it will appear he doesn't care about his patients. He looks around the room and when no one else speaks, he takes his seat. With no other questions, the emcee thanks Georgie for her time and she makes a hasty exit, wondering if she made any impression on the room full of doctors. Sometimes a lack of questions means a lack of interest.

The next day, she is still mulling over what she said at the doctor's luncheon. *Did I support my idea? Did I give enough information? Too much?* Her office phone rings.

"I think you should take this call," says Brenda.

This sounds ominous.

"Good morning. This is Hiroshi Suzuki, a freelance reporter. I was at the medical association meeting yesterday, and you left before I could speak to you. Your presentation about cooperative care was intriguing, and I believe a magazine would publish a story about it. Would you agree to an interview?"

Georgie hesitates. *Is this a joke?* "Who did you say you are?"

The caller repeats his name and his request.

Georgie has heard reporters can twist stories to suit their own agenda. "I need to know the angle of your story and that I can sign off on the content before it's published."

"Of course, I would give you a draft of the article before publication. As to the angle, I would pitch the story to a new publication focused on supporting the businesses of health practitioners. The magazine is interested in innovations in health practice, and your idea for cooperative care is just that. If we do the interview today or tomorrow, we might get it in the December issue."

Georgie likes what she is hearing but asks if she could also talk about her other innovation, the Emotional Effectiveness workshops.

"That sounds just as intriguing," says the reporter and sets a time for the interview for the following day.

Georgie stares out her office window, marveling at this unexpected development. An article in a magazine could launch cooperative care into national awareness. And a realization strikes her. This chance to promote her ideas came about because she took significant risks—first to implement cooperative care and then make a presentation to medical doctors. Most gratifying is that she acted despite her fears, not something she would have done in the past. It reminds her of her workshop principle—focus on love, not fear. *Could teaching the principle help me put it into practice?* On a whim, she types in "teach" and "learn" in the search engine, and finds the adage: *As you teach, you learn.* She leans back in her chair, smiling to herself.

Chapter 25

Georgie reads the magazine article featuring her Cooperative Care plan for the third time, gratified at the mention of the Emotional Effectiveness workshops as an indicator of her "innovative approach to naturopathic care." Pleased with the tone of the article, she wonders if this coverage will bring her ideas more acceptance among medical doctors. The magazine is not that well known, and it turns out the readership is primarily alternative health practitioners. Perhaps the most she can hope for is inspiring other naturopaths to follow her lead in Cooperative Care. That at least would give her some company in her quest.

Georgie grabs the magazine and rushes out the door to a dinner Lisa organized to celebrate Georgie's "imminent fame." On arrival at the Henrietta's, she walks into, "surprise!" yelled in unison by her retreat sisters, as they are calling themselves now—Lisa, Pam, Paula, Rhonda, Sandra, Destiny, and Aanya. In her September workshop series, she brought Paula, Rhonda, and Aanya into different sessions to offer their mind-body techniques. The response was favorable. Many participants said they appreciated an introduction to these different approaches to balancing mind and body. Paying other practitioners for their time meant less profit for Georgie, but she felt good about supporting other women in their careers.

Georgie looks around the table at the seven women with whom she now shares a unique kinship. In response to their congratulations on the magazine article, she thanks them for all their support. Through dinner, the conversation turns to brainstorming activities for the next self-care retreat in the spring before circling back to Georgie's recent success. She smiles at them, grateful to be part of this group of women—all committed to health and healing. By the end of the dinner, there is agreement among the group. Georgie needs to apply for a copyright for the Emotional Effectiveness workshop.

At home from her celebration dinner, she sits with an herbal tea and considers how to proceed with the copyright. Should she approach David Longhurst? He once suggested she copyright her workshop and offered his help with the application. She doesn't want to call him, but he is the only lawyer she knows, and there is her other legal issue. Surely, he can advise her on that, too. She has dragged her feet on Dwayne's request for a legal separation, telling him she will get to it when she isn't so busy. It is now a year since their split, with no sign of reconciliation. It's time.

She already decided not to hire a Terrance-based lawyer to handle the separation agreement. Dwayne knows all the lawyers in town, either through work or from golf, so she is leery of having one of them represent her interests. The only lawyer she knows is David, but he doesn't work in family law. He could not represent her, nor would she want that, but no doubt he knows a good family lawyer in Indianapolis. The sticking point is that she never told David about her separation. Given her recent actions, even though she was afraid, she feels brave enough to call him. She starts with the simple request—the copyright application.

"Hey, congrats on the article!" David says right away.

"How did you hear about that?"

"Remember, I'm doing legal work for a few high-profile naturopaths. Because of your inquest, they all know your name and one of them emailed me the article. Someday, I'm going to brag about how I knew Dr. Downie when..." He chuckles. "But seriously, copyright application is a piece of cake. I can start the process tomorrow. No charge!"

"Thanks, David. Ah, there is something else—another legal issue. And it means I must confess something to you." She gathers her courage. "Dwayne and I separated almost a year ago." She plows on, not wanting to make it a big deal that she kept this from him. "Now he wants a legal separation. Could you recommend a lawyer to represent me?"

Silence.

"Are you still there?"

"Yup. Just taking this in. Hm. I wondered last January when you agreed to dinner, and since then, you've been… friendlier. It was strange, given your past behavior. What…? You didn't trust me enough to tell me?"

"I didn't want you to get the wrong impression. It was safer for me if you thought I was still with my husband."

"That's ironic! I thought less of you because it seemed you were cheating on your husband."

"Hm. I guess it must have looked that way."

David gives an audible sigh. "Okay, tell me, was this separation his idea or yours?"

Georgie is amazed how quickly David can switch gears from personal to professional. "It was his idea, and I've found out he is seeing someone else. Not sure about proof of adultery, but that's why I need a lawyer. He wants to sell the house and divide the assets, and I need to make sure what we do is… fair."

"Yes, with assets to divide, you need good representation. I can recommend a couple of good lawyers." He sighs, again. "Ah, yes. I guess I'm supposed to say I'm sorry your marriage failed, but I'm not. You must know I would like to see more of you. And you know what else? I was right, after all. Your husband doesn't appreciate you."

I need to tell him! She is thankful this is a phone conversation. It should be easier to say what she needs to say without David's eyes boring into her soul, making her heart flutter and muddling her thinking.

"David, I enjoy your company, and I do like you, but I'm just not interested in getting involved… with anyone, actually. I need to be on my own right now. It feels like I've spent my life going along with what the men in my life wanted, and now I need to focus on my own goals. I hope you'll understand."

Another long pause. "Well, that is disappointing. I could say I'll wait for you, but there's no guarantee. I have other women clamoring at me for a… relationship."

Georgie chuckles in relief. "I'm not surprised. You are a catch, David! While we're being honest, I've suspected you're a bit of a player. You kept asking me on dates because I kept you at arm's length. You saw me as a challenge. Am I close?"

"Agh! That's a dagger in the heart. What, now you're a psychotherapist? But truly, I do like you a lot." He pauses, perhaps waiting for Georgie to soften her stance. "Well, I guess there's nothing more to say for now. I will email you the names of a couple of family law attorneys along with the copyright papers."

"Thanks, David." Georgie can't help herself and softens a little. "In other circumstances, I might have been interested in a closer relationship."

"That helps my pride a little. Take care of yourself. Don't be a stranger!"

Georgie ends the call and breathes a sigh of relief. *This honesty stuff feels good! Maybe honesty is another principle for my workshops!*

Georgie is driving to her parents' house for the family Christmas dinner. She glances at D.J. slumped down in the passenger seat, his eyes glued to his cell phone. He said little since Georgie picked him up from Dwayne's place where he spent Christmas eve. Perhaps he feels guilty about it and is not sure what to say. When he is home from college, he spends most of his time at Dwayne's, but Georgie sympathizes with his situation. It must be difficult having two "homes" and having to decide where to stay. She understands too that Dwayne and D.J. have more in common, specifically their passion for sports.

Georgie pulls into the driveway behind Debbie and Craig's car. They were driving in today from Indianapolis. Debbie got a teaching position there in the fall, so neither she nor Craig must commute. Georgie is especially happy for them because of her own experiences with commuting and the strain it had on her marriage. She has also enjoyed being able to visit Debbie more often. When she held a new patient seminar at Caroll Clinic in October, she stayed overnight with Debbie and Craig.

Upon entering, Georgie's senses revel in the blended aromas of roast turkey, cinnamon, and pine from the Christmas tree. There to greet her is Debbie, who gives her a lingering hug. Her mother gives a one arm hug and, with the other hand, takes the squash casserole Georgie's offering to the feast, off to the kitchen. And a surprise! Melanie appears from the kitchen to offer a big bear hug. She hasn't been to a Novak Christmas in years. Linnie calls out "Merry Christmas" from the living room where she, Brad, Michelle and Ted are sitting with Georgie's father.

Missing from the gathering is Daphne. She hasn't been home in two years, and it seems she is now a Parisienne with little interest in seeing her family. It's also the second family Christmas without Dwayne's presence. Georgie hopes there won't be a repeat of last year with several snide comments from Linnie and her mother about her failed marriage. "What did you do wrong?" and "You will have to make amends to Dwayne somehow."

As usual, the Christmas dinner table is overflowing with sumptuous food—turkey, stuffing, five different vegetables, mashed potatoes, fresh rolls, and two kinds of pie for dessert. After finishing the meal, everyone lingers sipping wine, too stuffed to move.

Melanie stands up and clinks her wine glass for everyone's attention. "Who here knows about our exciting family news?"

George and Claire look at each other. Linnie scans the room to find out who knows what is going on. Debbie's Cheshire Cat smile is evidence she knows.

"We have a national celebrity in our midst," Melanie says, holding up a copy of the magazine with Georgie's face on the cover. "Our Georgie is the subject of a special report in this health magazine. What? No one else knew?"

Debbie's smile spreads across her face as she raises her hand.

"Mom, why didn't you tell me? That's so cool!" D.J. says.

"That's so wonderful!" says Claire, coming around the table to hug Georgie.

Linnie is speechless, her mouth hanging open. Brad mumbles, "congratulations."

George Novak motions to Melanie for the magazine. He puts it on his lap and one hands his wheelchair away from the table, gesturing to Georgie. "Come. My office."

Georgie has no choice but to follow and, as she departs, hears Linnie ask Melanie, "What is this all about? Do you have another copy of the magazine?"

Her father maneuvers his wheelchair behind his clinic desk, unused since he had to stop practicing medicine. Georgie sits in the chair where his patients used to sit, the power dynamics not in her favor. She fidgets in her chair, waiting while her father opens the magazine and slowly reads the article, with interjected "hms" and "ahs." He closes the magazine and looks up.

"Georgina, it seems you are becoming the champion of integrative health care, or cooperative care, as you call it and...," he pauses, looking down at his hands folded in his lap, "well... I'm proud of you. I haven't agreed with your career choice, but it's obvious you have your patients' best interests at heart."

"I appreciate you saying this, Dad." Georgie's relief is palpable. She fully expected never to be in her father's good graces again.

He leans back in his chair and purses his lips. "It's hard for me to admit, but you might have ideas on how to improve health care. What is most impressive is your determination; you believe in what you are doing. I've seen people effect change, and it's always because they don't give up."

"Thanks, Dad." Her father's sudden change of tune is startling, and it reminds her of something. "But you taught me that. You always said, 'it takes determination and hard work to realize your dreams.'"

"Right, I did, didn't I? And all these years, I thought you totally rejected my advice." He smirks, then turns serious again. "There is something I need to tell you. It's been weighing on my mind—something you don't know about when you had meningitis as a child. Do you remember it took a long time for you to recover?"

Georgie nods, curious at this abrupt change of topic. "Yes, I do. I was tired of being in bed, yet too tired to get out of bed, if that makes any sense. I remember wondering if I would ever get out of that bed."

"Yes, that was the size of it. Anyway, you had a long recovery by most standards. I was extremely worried about you, fearing you might have long-term health effects. For a while, you had trouble hearing and your concentration was muddled. We were afraid you might have permanent hearing loss and perhaps cognitive impairment, both potential aftereffects of meningitis. The specialist had little to recommend except bed rest and time."

"I recall you were really concerned. I overheard you and Mom whispering outside my door about something that sounded serious. And, one time, Linnie waltzed into my room and told me I almost died. That shook me up!"

"I am sorry you were so scared. Your mother and I were, too. What you don't know is what I did to help you. A colleague told me of a... doctor who had helped his patient recover from meningitis and a speedy recovery at that. And, well... I took you to see that doctor." He looks down at his hands. "That doctor was a naturopath."

"What?!" Ire rises in her throat.

"The naturopath put you on some herbs and vitamins and within two weeks, you were fine and back at school."

"Dad, how could you?! How could you lie to me, and for all these years?"

He shrugs his shoulders. "I wasn't sure the naturopath helped you. You might have been recovering, anyway. But it is also possible he made a difference, and so now I am asking your forgiveness for not admitting this to you, especially when you became a naturopath."

Georgie stares at him, incredulous, not sure how to respond, considering the years of emotional pain when her father wouldn't speak to her, even shunned her.

"Georgie, I was prideful and closed-minded. I still have trouble believing in naturopathic practice—pushing supplements and promising to prevent illness—but now I understand there is something to it. It's the biggest regret of my life that I didn't respect your right to practice in the health field of your choice."

At this heartfelt confession, Georgie feels like a weight is lifting from her shoulders that she didn't realize was there. "Well, Dad, you don't know how long I've wanted to hear you say this." She pauses, weighing her response—her own admission. "I need to ask your forgiveness, too. I went all negative on medical doctors, thinking naturopathy was superior. You had every right to be offended. But now I understand it's not about choosing one discipline. It's about finding what works best for each patient. When D.J. had his head injury, the surgeon likely saved him from permanent brain damage. I couldn't do anything to help him. But I can help people with troublesome health issues—adrenal fatigue, IBS, anxiety—when medical doctors often fail. That's why I want to champion cooperative care, to make use of the best of both practices."

"It is a worthwhile goal, Georgie. I don't expect I'll live to see actual changes, but I hope you will. And for what it's worth, I forgive you, even though my actions were more grievous." Her father smiles and raises his good arm, inviting her for a hug. She puts both arms around her father.

"I love you, Dad." Tears stream down her face as they embrace.

"I love you too, Georgie," he says, his voice breaking.

They take a few minutes to compose themselves, then rejoin the family for the gift exchange and family games. Georgie's mind isn't on gifts or games, though. As she watches her family enjoy their Christmas gathering, she goes over all that's happened in the past eight years—the trials and the triumphs. She endured legal troubles, family health issues, and threats to her career. Over that time, she defied central figures in her life—her father, her husband, clinic managers, and even a would-be suitor. Not only did she stand up to disapproval of her goals and dreams, but she challenged the status quo in health care. The key to it all was trusting in her dreams for more effective health care.

Her father might be right. Her efforts might not bring about change to the health care system. But not trying would be worse. If Cooperative Care doesn't take off, perhaps it will lead to another initiative that would integrate health care. It was all about taking the first step. What was that saying? *You pass failure on your way to success.*

Georgie smiles at Debbie, who just shared how long it took her Grade 2 students to grasp a math concept. It reminds Georgie how frustrating it was when she was learning how to be effective in her profession. *What have I learned from five years as a naturopath?* Certainly, she discovered how to help people heal, but she also experienced healing for herself, both physically and emotionally. A willingness to learn also led her to find a supportive group of women who believe, as she does, in holistic health and professional cooperation. Smiling to herself, she suspects she has lots more to learn, but that is an exciting prospect, too.

A profound sense of gratitude settles into her being. Her faith in the call God placed in her heart has seen her through many ordeals. Fear and regret no longer weigh her down, replaced now by love for her calling, and optimism for what lies ahead. And the key, she realizes, is forgiveness.

She says a silent prayer. *Dear God, thank you for showing me how to forgive. How to abandon judgment of the frailties of others and even my own failings. Forgiveness allowed me to offer to others the gifts which You have given me. Forgiveness shines away my doubts and lights my way. My mind is at rest. My heart is filled with peace.*

Author Notes and Acknowledgements

While this novel is a work of fiction, the story reveals present-day issues with health care in North America, where Western medicine and holistic health care are pitted against each other. Through the story of a fictional naturopath, my aim was to shine a light on the benefits of holistic health practice and the challenges its practitioners face because of misunderstandings of mainstream medicine and society.

Story lines and themes come from my personal experiences, clinical practice in holistic nutrition, and involvement as a leader and a participant in groups for personal and spiritual growth.

The storyline about the sick child reflects actual events while caring for my daughter, Jill, who suffered from a mysterious illness from age twelve to sixteen. She regained her health because of holistic health practitioners, and has since grown into a healthy, courageous woman. In this story, I attempted to portray the anguish of parents with sick children, their doubts about health care decisions, and the long-term outcomes of surviving such trials. The letter from the protagonist's daughter, I derived from a letter my daughter wrote to me in 2013, twelve years after she recovered.

I extend my sincere appreciation to my naturopath, Dr. Michael Reid, for helping me survive ovarian cancer eleven years after diagnosis, and for providing me valuable insights into the practice of naturopathy, specifically complimentary cancer care. I did my best to portray the benefits of naturopathic practice, but also the challenges for practitioners in a society oriented to allopathic medicine.

Ailments addressed by this story's fictional naturopaths are composites of actual patient cases from my eighteen years in practice as a holistic nutritionist, a discipline aligned with naturopathy. I drew on my experience in a health practice in which successful outcomes rely on patients' self-direction and motivation to make diet and lifestyle changes.

Inspiration for the storyline about a spate of mysterious deaths among holistic doctors came from an opinion piece on doctorspatch.com in December 2016. The article explored allegations of a conspiracy against holistic doctors which, to my knowledge, has never been proven nor disproven.

The protagonist's perspective on the emotional and spiritual aspects of health reflects my education in holistic nutrition at the Canadian School of Natural Nutrition, my Christian faith, and five years of studying A Course in Miracles. The eight principles for emotional effectiveness that the protagonist devised I created for my first book, "You Can Be Well: The Holistic Nutrition Guide to a Healthy, Balanced Life."

In the story, the protagonist discovered the benefits of group work for support and healing. For this, I drew on my social work education, my work in community development, and leading spiritual growth groups at my church.

My years as a member of Toastmasters provided me with insights into effective speaking and promotional talks.

Thank you to Cindy Peterson for all that she taught me about meditation and mindfulness, and to Mala Singh for her instruction in energy balancing.

I am exceedingly grateful to my advance readers: Cherylynn Desjardins, Dorothy Brown Henderson, Paula Mercer, and Chris Weaver. Your insights and honesty in evaluating my work were critical in bringing this project to fruition.

To Cherylynn Desjardins, my online writing buddy, I am grateful for her encouragement, and our musings about writing, career, family, and our dog babies.

Finally, to my husband, Derek, I could not have completed this book without his unwavering support and encouragement. Writing can be a lonely exercise, but Derek was there to keep me company throughout.